DECK THE HOUNDS

ALSO BY DAVID ROSENFELT

ANDY CARPENTER NOVELS

Rescued

Collared

The Twelve Dogs of Christmas

Outfoxed

Who Let the Dog Out?

Hounded

Unleashed

Leader of the Pack

One Dog Night   THRILLERS

Dog Tags   *Fade to Black*

New Tricks   *Blackout*

Play Dead   *Without Warning*

Dead Center   *Airtight*

Sudden Death   *Heart of a Killer*

Bury the Lead   *On Borrowed Time*

First Degree   *Down to the Wire*

Open and Shut   *Don't Tell a Soul*

NONFICTION

Lessons from Tara: Life Advice from the World's Most Brilliant Dog

Dogtripping: 25 Rescues, 11 Volunteers, and 3 RVs on Our Canine
    Cross-Country Adventure

DECK
THE HOUNDS

David Rosenfelt

MINOTAUR BOOKS
NEW YORK

DECK THE HOUNDS. Copyright © 2018 by Tara Productions, Inc. All rights reserved. Printed in the United States of America. For information, address St. Martin's Press, 175 Fifth Avenue, New York, N.Y. 10010.

www.minotaurbooks.com

The Library of Congress Cataloging-in-Publication Data is available upon request.

ISBN 978-1-250-19848-8 (hardcover)
ISBN 978-1-250-19849-5 (ebook)

Our books may be purchased in bulk for promotional, educational, or business use. Please contact your local bookseller or the Macmillan Corporate and Premium Sales Department at 1-800-221-7945, extension 5442, or by email at MacmillanSpecialMarkets@macmillan.com.

First Edition: October 2018

10 9 8 7 6 5 4 3 2 1

DECK THE HOUNDS

I've come up with a solution to the homeless problem.

I'm not talking about the overall homeless problem in America, which is obviously tragic, and which saps the life and dignity from those swept up in it. I'm aware of how lucky I am, and I attempt with intermittent success not to take it for granted.

I've dealt with the macro homeless issue by donating to charities set up to deal with it. It's impersonal, I know, but it makes me feel better, and I hope it's doing some good.

The solution I'm referring to relates to the "Andy Carpenter encounters a homeless person on the street" dilemma. What I've come up with isn't perfect, and it isn't right for everyone. In fact, it's earned me some scorn from people when they watch it in action.

Every time I run into a homeless person looking for money, I give him or her twenty dollars. I know the argument that they might not put it to good use, that they might use it to buy alcohol, or drugs, and that by giving them money I might only be exacerbating their problems. I understand that point of view and I respect it.

But these people are on the street, and they are cold, and I don't need the money, and they do. So I give it to them. And if I'm doing a bad thing, then I accept the blame. It just feels like walking by and not helping is a worse thing.

But I occasionally run into a situation that, for me at least, is even more heartbreaking. And that is when the homeless person has a dog with him or her.

That is a killer, and that is what is happening now. I have just left my office on Van Houten Street in Paterson, New Jersey. Happily, I wasn't there to do any work and I didn't actually go into the office. I was simply there to drop off my rent check to Sofia Hernandez, who owns the fruit stand on the first floor. The reason I drop off the checks rather than mail them is that if I mail them I can't pick up any delicious oranges.

In the one-block walk from the office to my car, I encounter a person on the street in front of a pawn shop. He is bundled up in a blanket, with probably all his possessions next to him in a plastic bag in a shopping cart. The poor guy is huddled against the unseasonably freezing cold air, and huddled with him is his dog. He or she seems to be a golden mix, only about forty pounds and cute as hell.

Tomorrow being Thanksgiving makes this situation even more upsetting. It's my favorite holiday of the year, a day of gorging on great food and football. The fact that I will be in my recliner chair, stuffing my face and rooting for the Giants in the comfort of my nice warm living room, makes the fact that this guy will be spending it on the cold cement even more terrible and unfair.

I don't know why the existence of the dog makes the situation so much more tragic to me; I suspect it reflects a flaw in my character. But I can't help it.

Over time I have refined my response to this exact situation, and I execute it now. I give the man twenty dollars, and a PetSmart gift card for fifty dollars. I always carry a bunch of them in my wallet for this specific purpose. I keep the oranges for myself.

When I give the money and card to him, his response is, "Thank you for your generosity. I can assure you it is much appreciated and will be put to very good use." He turns to the dog. "Isn't that right, Zoey?" Zoey, for her part, has no comment to make on the matter.

What he has said is a bit jarring, and probably highlights another one of my character defects. I guess I expected him to grunt a quick thank you, but instead he spoke crisply and concisely, with a tone that I would more expect to hear at the Harvard Club than on the cement in front of a pawn shop. Which is not to say that I would be allowed into the Harvard Club; I'm sure their sophisticated bouncer would keep me from getting in the door.

So I just mutter a quick "you're welcome" and go on my way.

I am Andy Carpenter, doer of good deeds.

Our Thanksgiving dinner is our last meal before Christmas.

That's because my wife, Laurie, has a rather unconventional view of the Christmas holiday. She loves it so much that she has decreed that it will last from the end of the Thanksgiving meal until the end of January.

Repeatedly showing her the calendar has no effect. She thinks there are five seasons . . . winter, spring, summer, fall, and Christmas. I'm a fan of Christmas myself, but there is something a tad weird about waking up to a recording of "Jingle Bells" as we approach February.

But the dinner is fantastic, so I am not focusing on the length of the Christmas season right now. Laurie has made turkey, candied yams, mashed potatoes, and has introduced an absolute winner, a corn crème brûlée. She's also made some healthy vegetable stuff, but since I wouldn't eat it if you strapped me down and tried to force-feed me, I don't ask what it is.

Afterward, during dessert, our son, Ricky, mentions something about Facebook. He's not allowed on, since he's under the thirteen-year age limit, but he set up accounts for Laurie and me a few weeks ago. He's the only one among us that has any tech ability, so we relied on his expertise.

Unfortunately, in all that time I've accumulated a total of one Facebook friend, Laurie. So I rarely log in, since there's nothing for me to do there.

It's like coming home after being away for a week and finding no messages on my answering machine. Or like going to my high school prom with my sister, which I did not do simply because I am an only child.

It's social media, but it makes me feel antisocial. Ricky said that the problem is that no one realizes I signed up, so what I have to do is "friend" people, which means asking them if they would be my friend.

I don't think so.

Who begs for friends? What if they say no? Or what if they don't even answer, leaving me to wonder if they never saw the request, or saw it and decided to ignore it? Maybe they would want to reject it, but thought I would feel bad, so they instead would leave me in Facebook purgatory.

Laurie is an entirely different case. I secretly looked at her profile the other day, and she has seventy-six friends. Seventy-six! I don't think I know seventy-six people, even if you include those I nod to while I'm walking Tara and Sebastian.

Laurie asks me, "You enjoying being on Facebook?"

"Not really," I say. "My social calendar is pretty full. If I stayed on Facebook all day, I'd never get anything done."

"Dad only has one friend," Ricky says. "You."

"Thanks, Rick."

Laurie shakes her head. "That's so sad. You want me to ask some people to be your friend?"

The only bright side to all this is that I'm not on Twitter. "Must you humiliate me? Can we talk about something else?" I ask.

Laurie nods. "Sure. When do you want to get the Christmas tree?"

"Why do you want a Christmas tree?" I ask. Laurie knows that even though I'm fine with the idea of having a tree, the act of decorating it with the ten million lights and ornaments she always wants is torture.

"Tell him, Ricky," she says.

He smiles. "Because it's Christmas."

I could mention that it is actually Thanksgiving, but I'd get nowhere. And since this conversation is not going well, I stand up and say, "Let's watch television."

I turn on the local news, since we are having dinner in that window between football games. I turn it on even though I know Laurie does not like the idea of it being on during family meals.

"Thanksgiving should be a time for human interaction," she says. "For talking."

"They talk on television," I say, and in fact the news anchors are talking when they come on. "See?" Then, "Hey, that's Ralph."

They're showing a photo of Ralph Brandenberger, the guy who runs the Passaic County Animal Shelter. I turn up the sound, and although we've missed the first half of the report, it appears that a homeless man with a dog was attacked last night. He fended off his assailant, and his dog apparently bit the guy as well.

Just before the segment ends, they cut to the homeless man talking to a reporter. He is saying, "I want my dog. Why won't they let me have my dog?"

"I know that guy," I say. "I saw him yesterday on the street near my office. I gave him money. And I gave him one of the PetSmart cards."

"It was ten degrees yesterday," Laurie says.

"What are you saying? I should have given him my coat?"

"He lives with his dog on the street?" Ricky asks, not fully understanding. "On the sidewalk?"

"Yes," I say.

Laurie is quiet for a few moments, an intense look on her face. When she gets that look, it rarely ends well for me. "Let's help him," she says.

"Yeah, let's help him!" Ricky agrees, strongly endorsing the idea. I'm having trouble remembering an idea of Laurie's that Ricky has not strongly endorsed.

"How?"

"We won't know that until we start," Laurie says. "But let's try and get him what he needs. His dog back, for one thing. You should be able to do that. And then a place to stay, out of the cold."

"You mean a house?" I ask. "A hotel room?"

"The apartment above the garage . . . maybe. We'll see. But let's get involved. Let's do something for this man."

"Yeah," Ricky says. "Come on, Dad."

"I'm not sure this is a good idea." If I want to put the brakes on this, I'm going to have to come up with much stronger statements than wimpy ones like that.

Laurie says, "That's okay. I'm sure."

Ricky nods. "Me too."

"Other than the fact that you're a terrific human being, why do you want to get involved in this?" I ask Laurie.

"Tell him, Ricky."

Ricky smiles. "Because it's Christmas."

I'm feeling terrible about this, Andy."

I'm at the Passaic County Animal Shelter, talking to Ralph Brandenberger. Ralph's a good guy and is especially caring about the animals. He does the best he can while being constantly overcrowded and underfunded.

"You talking about the dog from last night?" I say.

He nods. "Yeah, but there are rules, you know? And I might bend them sometimes, but this was on television."

"Which rules are we talking about?"

"Well, for one thing, the dog bit the guy; she drew blood. And it's on tape, for God's sake. So I have to hold her for ten days."

I hadn't seen this on television—it must have been the part of the story that we missed—but Ralph tells me that somebody pulled up in a car, got out, and tried to mug the homeless man. Apparently, the assailant confused homeless with helpless, and this guy is far from helpless. He fought off the attacker, and the dog, Zoey, bit him as well.

A person that was either on the street or in an apartment above one of the stores must have heard or seen the commotion and called the police.

A video of the entire thing was captured by a security camera covering the front of the pawn shop. So Animal Control, in the person of Ralph, knows that the dog bit the guy. They have to hold her for ten days to make sure she doesn't have rabies, even though the victim took off.

"What's the protocol after that?"

"I'm checking into it, but I don't think I can just give her back to the guy. He doesn't have an address, which is required, and even if he did, the fees for retrieving a dog amount to almost three hundred bucks. There's no way this guy can pay that."

"Can you give the dog to me?"

"Sure. You're a rescue group, so you'd be authorized to take her, as long as you held her for the ten days. Would you do that? It would be a big help and it would sure make me feel better."

My friend Willie Miller and I run a rescue group called the Tara Foundation, which is what Ralph is referring to. Since we are a registered rescue operation, he is allowed to give us the dog.

"No problem, and I'll pay the fee."

"There's one other thing, about the dog . . ."

"What is it?"

"Our vet checked her out. She's pregnant."

"That's okay. We'll take care of her and find homes for the puppies. Do you have any idea where the owner is?"

"Are you kidding? I thought you knew."

"Knew what?"

"He's here; he's outside the dog's run. He's been here since we took in the dog."

The runs in the shelter are half indoors, half outdoors, with a door separating them that stays open during the hours that the shelter is open. This way the dog can be inside or out, and the door can keep the dog inside in inclement weather.

Ralph points to the window, and I look through it. The homeless man is lying against the cage on the outside portion of the run, and the dog is up against the cage. It is among the saddest things I've ever witnessed.

"Why don't you let him inside; they could hang out together in the adoption area? It's cold out there." There is a room where prospective adopters can meet the dogs they are interested in. It would seem to me that they'd be a lot warmer and more comfortable in there.

"I offered, but he didn't want to," Ralph says. "The guy's a little weird."

"What's his name?"

"You know, I never thought to ask," Ralph says. "I'm embarrassed to say that."

"Don't worry about it, Ralph. I'm going to talk to him, and I'll be taking the dog. How much do I owe you?"

Ralph figures out the amount and I write him a check. Then I go outside to talk to the man, who is still lying next to the cage, reaching his hand through to gently pet the dog. It's not that difficult, because the dog seems equally anxious to make the connection and is lying right up against the cage near him.

"Hello, remember me?" I ask.

He looks up, thinks for a moment, and says, "Twenty dollars and a PetSmart card of a still undetermined value."

"Fifty bucks."

He nods. "Very generous. Thank you again."

"You're in a difficult situation. I saw what happened to you on TV, and I'd like to help."

"I just want my dog."

"I believe I can make that happen."

That prospect obviously interests him, because he stands up. When he does I am surprised by his size; he's got to be six foot three. I had never seen him erect before. He's thin, probably a result of not getting enough food and nourishment.

"How?" he says, clearly wary of my offer.

"What's your dog's name?"

"Zoey."

"Zoey bit someone, so she can't be released for ten days, to make sure she doesn't have rabies. Then she can't go to you, because the rule is that you have to have a residence."

"And you can circumvent these rules?"

I keep being surprised by how intelligently he talks, and I keep being annoyed with myself for being surprised. Homeless does not equate with stupid.

"In a manner of speaking," I say. "They can give her to me, because I run an accredited rescue group. And after ten days I can give her to you, because you'll have a residence."

"No, I won't."

"My name is Andy Carpenter," I say. "What's yours?"

He looks at me suspiciously and hesitates, as if his name is his only possession, and he's afraid I'll steal it.

Finally, "Don Carrigan."

"Come on, Don, let's get Zoey and get out of here. I'll tell you about it on the way."

It's feeling sort of uncomfortable in the car.

Carrigan is in the passenger seat with Zoey in his lap, but he's not saying much, and I'm sure he's trying to figure out what the hell is going on. I know I'm trying to figure out the same thing, and I'm the one that's doing it. Zoey, for her part, seems fine with the whole situation, looking out the window and treating this as an adventure.

"How long have you had Zoey?" I finally ask.

"About six weeks."

"She was stray?"

He nods. "And so was I. We have much in common."

"Dogs are comforting," I say.

"That they are. Might I ask where we are going?"

"To my house. We have an apartment that will be yours to use."

"To what do I owe this kindness?"

"It's Christmas," I say.

"Already?"

I shrug. "Don't ask."

I guess that's sufficient because he doesn't respond and goes back to silently petting Zoey.

After another five minutes of silence, I ask, "Where are you from?"

"Is it a condition of this generosity that I provide biographical details?"

I shake my head. "No, this is pretty much unconditional."

He smiles slightly, the first hint of one I have seen. "Because it's Christmas."

I return the smile. "Exactly."

We pull into the driveway of our house on Forty-Second Street in Paterson, and I see Laurie looking at us through the window. We have a detached garage, and the apartment is above it. "Home sweet home," I say.

I open the door to the car and the burst of cold air comes barreling through. The wind has picked up, which makes it seem a hell of a lot colder. I think that might be why weather people always talk about wind-chill factor.

We start walking toward the garage, with Carrigan for some reason carrying Zoey. The door to our house opens, and Laurie, Ricky, and Tara, our golden retriever, come out and walk toward us. Sebastian, our basset hound, clearly felt that this was not worth getting out of bed for. Sebastian wouldn't get out of bed if I drove home with LeBron James, Beyoncé, and the pope.

"Hi," Laurie says. "I'm Laurie, this is Ricky, and that's Tara. Welcome."

"Thank you," Carrigan says. "This is Zoey." He puts Zoey on the ground and she and Tara do the requisite sniffing of each other's private areas. "I appreciate your hospitality."

"Our pleasure," she says. "Come on in."

We all head up to the apartment. Carrigan seems to hesitate

at the doorway, as if not sure he wants to step across that threshold.

He finally does so, and on the way up the stairs, I ask, "Is Zoey housetrained?"

Carrigan shrugs. "I have no idea. I've never seen her in a house."

The apartment itself is modest, but reasonably comfortable. There is a bedroom, bathroom, kitchen, and living room. None of them are what I would call spacious, but they don't feel cramped.

There are televisions in both the bedroom and living room. I show Carrigan where the remote controls are, since I consider them the most important appliances in this or any other house. He seems familiar with how to operate them, which sort of surprises me.

"Come in here," Laurie says, and as I turn to follow her voice to the kitchen, I notice that Carrigan is opening a window. He seems on edge, nervous in a way I hadn't noticed before. I don't ask him about it, because it's really not any of my business.

"It's fifteen degrees out there," I say. "The thermostat is over there, and—"

He interrupts, almost with an urgency in his voice. "It's better this way. Is that all right?"

"Sure."

With that, we walk into the kitchen. Laurie has the refrigerator open and says, "I didn't know what kind of food you liked, so I just got a lot of different things."

We look in the refrigerator and it is packed with stuff, as are the cabinets that she opens. There is also a healthy supply of dog food. Carrigan and Zoey can eat well for quite a while, which I suspect was Laurie's goal.

"If there's anything you or Zoey particularly like that we don't have, please tell me," Laurie says.

"There's ice cream in the freezer," Ricky adds.

"This is rather overwhelming," Carrigan says, and then adds, "As well as inexplicable."

"Laurie is the master of the inexplicable," I say. "I can't even explain how inexplicable she is."

She proceeds to show him where everything else is: the towels, the toilet paper, the smoke detector, the shampoo, the vacuum cleaner, and on and on. Tours of the Louvre have been conducted with less attention to detail.

"You want that open?" she asks Carrigan, referring to the window. At this point it is cold enough to hang meat in here.

"Yes."

She nods. "Okay. Do you have a driver's license?"

"Expired."

"Then if you need to go anywhere, Andy or I will drive you. If you need anything else, please let us know."

"At the risk of stating the obvious, you did not have to do all of this," Carrigan says.

She smiles. "It's Christmas."

"Don't ask," I say.

have to admit that I'm feeling pretty good about what we're doing.

As is so often the case, Laurie is right; we're helping someone who needs it, and it's not a hardship for us at all. It's also a very good message to send to Ricky, although he was already a main proponent of it.

I haven't been to Charlie's, a sports bar that represents my one and only hangout, in a week, so I decide to go tonight. The Giants are playing on *Thursday Night Football*, so the place will be packed, but I have a regular table with Vince Sanders, the editor of our local newspaper, and Pete Stanton, a captain in the Homicide Division of the Paterson Police Department.

I ask Laurie if she's at all worried about being alone with Carrigan, even though he's not actually in the house. She gives me that "you're an idiot" look. Laurie is a former cop and current private investigator, and she can handle herself in a dangerous situation a hell of a lot better than I could. Of course, that's not a high bar to exceed.

"Maybe we should google him," I say. "We might be able to learn something about his background."

"His background doesn't matter. We're doing this because of his present situation. If we start to investigate him, even online, it feels like we're intruding and violating his privacy."

"Okay."

I get to Charlie's just before the opening kickoff, so Vince and Pete barely nod in my direction. They used to pretend to be glad to see me, knowing I'd pick up the check. Now they just charge their food to my tab whether I'm there or not, so they can cut down on the insincere sociability.

At halftime Vince says, "You're going to be in the newspaper tomorrow."

"Why?"

"For taking that homeless guy home. You're nuts, by the way."

Pete nods. "Totally nuts."

"We're being nice and charitable; I'm aware those are genes you two are deficient in."

"He could be a serial killer," Pete says, as he gets up to go to the bathroom.

"Thanks for the upbeat assessment, Pete." Then I turn to Vince. "Why is it going to be in the paper?"

"It's a human interest story; it appeals to humans. Don't ask me why."

"You would be the last person I would ask about anything having to do with humanity. Where did you hear about it?"

"Ralph Brandenberger, the guy who runs the shelter. You want to give me a quote for the story?"

"No. We're not doing this for publicity."

"Touching," he says, looking around. "There's not a dry eye in the place. How about telling me his name? Brandenberger didn't know it, and so far we're just calling him 'homeless guy.'"

I'm torn on this. On the one hand, I really would prefer that the story be private, and I'm certain Laurie would as well. But on the other hand, there's obviously no way for me to stop it, and referring to Carrigan as "homeless guy" seems to strip him of some dignity.

"His name is Don Carrigan," I say.

"Sounds familiar. What else can you tell me?"

"Nothing."

"No background? Former career? Reason he's homeless?"

"No, no, and no."

"You're a big help," he says.

Vince takes out his cell phone and calls the paper to instruct them to use Carrigan's name in the story. Pete comes back as the second half kickoff is about to take place, so all further conversation about Carrigan, or anything else besides the Giants' inability to cover wide receivers, is shelved.

After the game ends with a fairly rare Giants victory, I go home and tell Laurie about the upcoming story about Carrigan. I ask if she thinks I did the right thing in giving his name, and she says, "I think it's okay. But you need to show him the story tomorrow."

"I will. There was no way I could talk Vince out of running it. He thinks it's a human interest story; I guess he has humans working for him to tell him what interests them."

She smiles. "Vince is a good friend; he'd be there for you if you needed him."

"Yeah. Meanwhile he and Pete are on a lifetime free burger and beer scholarship." The truth is that I'm absurdly wealthy from an inheritance and lucrative cases, so I'm happy paying for them. But I'm even happier complaining and rubbing their noses in it. That's what friends do.

"I'm trying not to be nosy," Laurie says, "but I couldn't help seeing Don sitting in the garage with Zoey before."

"With the door open?" I ask, and she nods. "Maybe he's just used to cold air, or not used to heat."

She shakes her head sadly. "I can't imagine what the poor guy has gone through."

"Speaking of that, have you decided how long we're going to make him not go through it?"

"Let's take it one day at a time," she says.

"As opposed to two days at a time? Or no days at a time?"

"Andy, trust me on this."

As I'm heading out for my morning walk with Tara and Sebastian, I see Carrigan sitting in the open garage.

"We're going to the park," I say. "Feel like taking a walk?"

He thinks for a moment and nods. "Yes. Thanks for thinking of me."

As we start out, I see that the newspaper is on the front lawn, wrapped in plastic. I haven't gotten a chance to look at it yet; I had forgotten about the story.

"When we get back, I want to show you something," I say.

Carrigan doesn't respond; he doesn't really seem like the curious type.

So I continue, "There's a story about you in the paper. About what happened the other night, Zoey's situation, your staying here . . . I didn't tell them about any of it."

"That's okay."

"But I did give them your name. I hope that's not a problem."

He shrugs. "No one will care, so why should I?"

We walk for about a half hour; it's cold but sunny and quite beautiful out. We don't say much; if not for me we wouldn't say anything. I ask him if he likes football, and he says, "Used to." Then I ask him if he grew up around here, and he says, "No."

Fascinating stuff.

We get home, and I have breakfast with Laurie and Ricky. Then I walk Ricky to school, which is about ten minutes from our house. He goes to School Number Twenty, the same one I attended about six million years ago.

When I get home, I notice that there's a commotion of sorts going on near my house, and as I approach I see that it is actually at my house. A little closer, and I've narrowed it down more specifically, as there are four police cars in my driveway.

It's the garage.

Nonsensically, the first thing I think of is carbon monoxide poisoning. The reasons it is nonsensical include the fact that the garage door has been open, and there is no car in the garage. Those two factors reduce the carbon monoxide risk quite considerably.

Laurie is standing at the end of the driveway, as officers are blocking the route to the garage. "What the hell is going on?" I say.

"I don't know. I saw Pete go in there with a bunch of other officers. They had their guns drawn."

"Did you talk to him?"

"No, he didn't stop in for coffee first."

So we stand here for at least ten minutes, waiting for something, anything, to happen. Finally Pete and the other officers come down with Carrigan; his hands are handcuffed behind him.

They walk near us to a waiting car, and I yell out to Pete, asking what is happening. "We just arrested your tenant for murder," Pete says.

Carrigan looks over to me as well, and simply says, "This is not right."

"Don't say anything to anyone," I say. "Not one word. I'm an attorney, and I'll meet you down at the jail."

"What about Zoey?" he asks, elevating himself considerably in my mind by showing concern for his dog.

"She'll be fine," I say. "I promise, we'll take care of her."

Within five minutes they've all left, and the only sign that they've been there at all are the neighbors still milling about, trying to get up the courage to ask us what happened.

"I think googling him might have been a good idea after all," I say.

She nods. "You get Zoey from the apartment, and I'll meet you at the computer."

According to Google, Don Carrigan is wanted for murder.

Based on today's events, I've got a feeling Google is right about this one.

The victim was Steven McMaster, a wealthy business executive who was murdered in his home nine months ago in Short Hills, New Jersey.

He came home from a business dinner and was likely accosted just before entering the house. The murderer then probably forced him to open the door and they both went inside. This would explain the lack of a burglar alarm activation, although the system was elaborate.

The criminal then murdered McMaster, brutally, by breaking his neck. There were no neighbors within shouting distance in the area, as the houses are apparently on large pieces of property. So no one saw or heard anything out of the ordinary.

The house was ransacked, including a safe, which McMaster was likely forced to open. In fact, he was killed in front of that safe, so the theory was that the killer decided that once the safe was open, there was no longer any reason to delay the murder.

DNA evidence at the scene tied Donald Carrigan to the crime. Carrigan is referred to as a former Green Beret and veteran of the Iraq invasion. The police issued a warrant for his arrest, but subsequent stories refer to his still being at large.

The media coverage, at least as Google tells it, gradually died down as no arrest was made.

Google doesn't have very much to say about Carrigan's background. We find a few different Don Carrigans. One is a head of a pharmaceutical association in Denver; another is an apparently ace TV journalist in Portland, Maine.

The one we think it is, based on the Green Beret mention, is originally from Pittsburgh. He is a graduate of Ohio State, and became a teaching assistant there before joining the army. He does not seem to have ever been married.

Google does not have any images of him, but it certainly seems like we have the right one. How he went from what we know to being a murderer, or an accused murderer, does not readily leap from the computer screen.

"So what now?" I ask.

"Now we go talk to him."

"Aren't we carrying this Christmas thing a little too far?"

"I said talk, Andy. I didn't say represent. I want to hear his side of it."

I nod. "Okay. Let's go and get this over with."

I've met with many people at the jail after they've been arrested. Obviously, they are almost always my clients, or I wouldn't be there in the first place. And this is the first time that I can remember Laurie going with me; she no doubt wants to hear Carrigan's story for herself.

It takes about an hour for us to be brought into a room to wait for Carrigan, and then another ten minutes for a guard to show up with him. As jail waiting times go, this is positively warp speed, and I'm glad for that.

Carrigan is handcuffed but otherwise looking none the worse for wear. He doesn't have the look of panic that I often see, and I can only speculate that is because he does not have that much to lose. But he does seem jittery, much like he was in the apartment. Of course, he and I don't go back that far, so I don't know if this is his normal demeanor.

"Are they treating you okay?" Laurie asks.

He nods. "I have no frame of reference, but I would say reasonably well."

"Did they tell you why you are here?" I ask.

Another nod. "I am accused of committing a murder. They haven't informed me of the identity of the victim, and I haven't asked because I've been following your directive not to speak."

"Good. The man's name is Steven McMaster. He was accosted and murdered at his home in Short Hills, and his killer then burglarized the house."

"This has nothing to do with me. I've never heard of the man, I've never met the man, and I certainly never killed the man."

"There was apparently DNA evidence tying you to the scene," I say.

Carrigan looks confused. "Where did you say the murder took place?"

"Short Hills."

"Nothing could tie me to the scene, because I have never been there."

Laurie asks, "Do you have any idea why they are accusing you?"

"None whatsoever."

"Do you have a criminal record?"

He nods and says, "Vagrancy. Some arrests for assault, but no charges filed."

"Okay," I say. "We'll see what we can find out."

"You're acting as my attorney?"

"Do you have anyone else?"

"No. Nor do I have any money to pay your fee, regardless of what that fee might be."

"Let's not worry about that right now. If I don't take the case, I'll make sure you are well defended by the public defender. I know the people over there pretty well."

"Is this more Christmas charity?"

"So far," I say. "In the meantime, continue not talking to anyone."

"How is Zoey?"

"She is fine; you don't have to worry about her," Laurie says. "Tara and Sebastian will like having another friend around the house. Is there anything else we can do for you?"

He hesitates. "I'm not sure . . . I hate being confined . . . I'm claustrophobic. I don't know what can be done, but I get anxious."

"We'll see what we can do," Laurie says.

Before we leave, we stop in to the jail infirmary. It's an advantage of defending so many accused criminals that I know pretty much everyone in the place. The head nurse is a terrific lady named Daphne Collins, who has a perpetual smile and an infectious laugh, neither of which makes any sense in these surroundings.

We tell her what's going on, and she promises to have the doctor check Carrigan out right away. This is not a problem that is particularly rare, and she said the usual protocol is to prescribe a mild sedative.

"It will take the edge off," she says.

"Thanks, Daphne. Edge removal sounds like a really good idea."

This is a unique situation for me.

I don't mean because I have provided unsolicited food and shelter to a man wanted for murder, though that is a first also. And I don't mean because I am reluctant to take him on as a client; I never want any clients. I have been trying to retire for years; I just can't seem to pull it off.

The reason it is so unusual is that I am literally the reason he is in prison. I started it by taking him off the streets and bringing him home. Technically he had a choice in the matter, though it was the only way he had any chance of getting his dog back.

But if that wasn't enough, I was solely responsible for putting his name in the paper, which had the effect of placing a law enforcement target on his back. I told them who he was and where he was. Now that may turn out to be a service to society in getting a murderer off the street, or it may not.

I sort of need to know for sure.

Laurie's quiet on the way home. I'm not going to start the inevitable conversation; my goal would be to put it off until sometime in the next century. But I am curious what she's thinking.

She seems to have had an unnatural obsession with helping Carrigan, though I'm not sure if that attitude is still operative. Laurie and I basically live on opposite sides of the law enforcement tracks. As a defense lawyer, I'm always suspicious of the government, and willing to believe that defendants can be wrongly accused.

As a former cop, she subscribes to the "they wouldn't have made the arrest without a damn good reason" approach. She successfully stifles her bias in this regard, or at least hides it, because she now works as an investigator for a defense attorney, namely me.

It will be interesting to see if she views Carrigan in the same way.

We get home and head into the kitchen. She starts by wiping off the table, even though it looked pretty well wiped to me. Then she sets down two cups, one for each of us, and brews coffee, which she pours.

All of this takes about five minutes, during which I am just sitting at the table, watching. It is as if she is the grounds-keeper at Yankee Stadium, getting the playing field ready for the game.

Actually, I'm not just sitting here; I'm also trying to figure out what her point of view will be. If she's in fact gearing up for "the talk," then she must want me to defend Carrigan. Because she would know that if she was opposed to it, I would just say "Me too," and we'd move on.

She finally sits down and asks, "So what are you thinking?"

By asking what I'm thinking, she's clearly trying to get the unimportant stuff out of the way first. "I have no idea whether he's guilty or innocent," I say. "But he's entitled to a good defense. I can tell Billy to put one of his top people on it."

Billy is Billy Cameron, the head of the Public Defender's office. He has some terrific lawyers working for him, very capable of handling this case, wherever it might go.

"So you don't want to take the case?" she asks.

"That's too limiting. I don't want to take any case. I'm retired."

"You've been retired for ten years, but you still keep taking cases."

"Those were practice retirements; this is the real thing."

She nods. "Okay; you're entitled to do whatever you want."

This is already not going well. "You believe in him?"

She nods. "For some reason I do. I realize that I have no evidence to support my intuition, but I trust it. So I'm taking the case."

"Excuse me?" I ask, which is really just a way of buying time. I know what she means, but I don't know why I'm bothering to buy time. There isn't enough time in the world for this to end well.

"I'm taking the case. I'm an investigator, Andy, so I'm going to investigate. And whatever I come up with, good or bad, I will turn over to whichever lawyer Billy assigns to the case."

"You think he's wrongly accused?"

She shakes her head. "I have no idea. My instinct is to like and trust him, but I obviously could be wrong. But here's what I'm right about: he's a veteran who was living on the street, and who claims he is innocent. That's enough for me to find out the truth, one way or the other. He's earned that, and I'm going to give it to him."

"So you want me to do this?" I ask. I don't mention that I

find it interesting that Carrigan did not seem worried when I told him his name would be in the newspaper story. If he knew he was wanted for murder, that should have panicked him. To bring that up would be to weaken my position; right now if my position was any weaker it would lie down and scream, "I've fallen and I can't get up!"

"It doesn't matter what I want," she says. "You're a big boy; you'll make your own decisions." Laurie is a conversational maestro.

"If I don't do it, will there be any sexual repercussions?"

She smiles; she knows she has me. It's the look of a winner; Ali smiled the same way when Foreman hit the canvas. "It's hard to say, but doing this on my own would be really tiring," she says. "I might want to go right to sleep . . . EVERY. SINGLE. NIGHT."

"You think you've won, don't you?" I ask.

She smiles again, another annoying winner's smile. "Let's just say I am quietly confident."

The first thing I do is contact the court and register as Carrigan's lawyer.

This takes a little longer than usual because the court of jurisdiction is not in my home base, Passaic County. The murder took place in Short Hills, which is in Essex County. That's probably one reason why the Carrigan name didn't ring a bell when I first heard it.

If I wind up ultimately representing Carrigan and if we go to trial . . . two enormous ifs . . . then we'll file for a change of venue to move the case to Passaic County. We'd have a decent chance of prevailing, since the victim was a well-known, well-respected citizen in his home community. And it's not like we're petitioning to move it to California; Jersey courts usually are willing to accommodate one another.

But I'm a long way from that; I still feel like I'm going to have to be dragged kicking and screaming into a major role in this case. Of course, Laurie is very capable of doing the dragging, and kicking and screaming has never worked for me before.

At this point I would ordinarily call a meeting of our whole team. It's early, so I wouldn't be giving assignments and getting into the meat of it; it would be mostly to let people know we've got a client, and to tell them to be ready.

But I'm not ready to make that full commitment, so I don't call the meeting. I do place calls to two of the team members, to give them small assignments that we need to take care of in order to get the ball rolling.

My first call is to the other lawyer in my basically dormant firm, Hike Lynch. I make it the first call in order to get it over with, since talking to Hike is not exactly a day brightener. Hike is not just a glass half empty guy; he thinks the glass can never hope to be filled again.

"Hey, Hike. It's Andy." I never ask Hike how he is; it would be an unnecessary conversational gambit, since he's going to tell me anyway.

"I've got food poisoning. I haven't spent ten minutes off the toilet since Wednesday."

"Sorry to hear that. In the future you might want to avoid poisoned food." I don't like to show Hike any sympathy; he just uses it to ratchet up his tales of anguish.

"Thanks, Andy, that's helpful. I think I threw up a lung."

"So you've only got one left?"

I think he comes to the conclusion that he's not going to get too far with this, so he asks, "Are you calling because we've got a client?"

"I wouldn't go that far. We're in the exploratory phase right now."

"Who is it?"

"A guy named Don Carrigan. He's—"

Hike interrupts. "I read about him. I've gotten a lot of reading done, because I haven't gotten off the toilet in—"

"I got the picture, Hike. If you can interrupt your reading

and lung-throwing, I need you to contact the Essex County prosecutor's office so we can start getting the discovery documents."

While Hike is completely miserable, he is also a terrific attorney who never fails to accomplish whatever I ask of him. This will be no exception.

I finally get myself off the call and then place a second call to Sam Willis. In real life Sam is my accountant, with an office just down the hall from mine. But in attorney life Sam is a key, if unusual, investigator for me. Sam is a computer genius, capable of hacking into anything and everything, seemingly at will.

So I will it, and Sam hacks it . . . sometimes legally, sometimes not. I've come to terms with that, and the coming to terms was not actually that difficult.

Sam is also wildly enthusiastic about working on my cases; he fancies himself as Eliot Ness with a keyboard. This time I tell him that I want him to dig up as much as he can about two people: Don Carrigan and Steven McMaster, now known in New Jersey legal circles as the murderer and the murderee.

"I'm on it," Sam says, and then adds, "Good to be back in the action."

"If you do a good job on this, I'll let you shoot somebody," I say.

"You always say that and then you never do," he says.

There's nothing left to do now besides wait for the discovery documents and whatever Sam turns up. Law enforcement didn't pick Carrigan's name out of a hat; they have a reason to think he committed this crime. That doesn't make them right, of course.

That is still to be determined.

Zoey is handling the upheaval in her life rather well.

She's gone from an unknown existence which left her abandoned on the street, to a new owner who called the frozen pavement their home, to an apartment above our garage, to a life of comfort with two new siblings, Tara and Sebastian.

It takes me three weeks even to adjust to things like Daylight Savings Time, but Zoey seems a bit more adaptable. Right now she is lying on a large dog bed, butt to butt with Sebastian, though his butt is considerably bigger than hers. They are each energetically working on chewies that Laurie has obviously provided, and the task is consuming their total focus.

Tara lies on her own bed, also enjoying a chewie, though she eats hers with considerably more dignity. Tara is a very elegant young lady.

I let them finish before I take them for their morning walk, even though it's going to leave me pressed for time. I walk them with three leashes, and I'm starting to look like one of those professional dog walkers. But they're easy to handle;

Tara really doesn't need a leash at all, Zoey is fairly gentle, and Sebastian moves at a glacial pace.

With that finished, I head to the courthouse for the arraignment. I've never actually been to this courthouse, since I've never tried a case in Essex County. But Carrigan had been transferred here from Passaic County since I saw him last.

I let my GPS handle the logistics, and Shirley, my GPS's disembodied voice lady, performs perfectly. I've become completely dependent on her; I think I would drive off a cliff if she told me to.

Hike is going to meet me here, as is Laurie after she gets Ricky off to school. I told Laurie that I was sure Hike would be willing to pick her up and drive her, and she told me she was sure she would rather go by herself. I understand the sentiment; being stuck in a car with Hike would be the other reason I might want to drive off a cliff.

I have arranged to meet with Carrigan in an anteroom before the arraignment, mostly to discuss with him what will be happening. It's basically straightforward: The state of New Jersey will say that he is a murderer, and he'll say that he isn't. Then a trial date will be set, and they'll take him away.

Carrigan looks none the worse for wear when I see him, which I suppose makes sense. I would think that compared to sleeping on frozen pavement, the Essex County Jail might seem like the Ritz-Carlton.

"How's the claustrophobia?" I ask.

"Lurking under the surface, but the meds are helping. The nurse in Passaic County took care of it, and made sure the medics here knew about it. She speaks pretty highly of you; is there anyone you don't know?"

"I only have one Facebook friend," I say.

"That's one more than me."

I take him through the procedures of the arraignment, and he mostly nods, asking only a couple of pertinent questions. Carrigan is a quick study; I have to come to understand it and am no longer surprised when he demonstrates it.

When I get to the part about his being called on to make a plea, he says, "What if I plead guilty?"

I'm taken aback by it. "Then you'll be punished as a murderer, and you'll be represented through the process by a public defender."

"Because you only want to defend me if I'm innocent?"

I nod. "Correct. And innocent is what you told Laurie and me that you were."

"I'm innocent of this crime."

"But not others?"

"Let's say I've done things I'm not proud of," he says, softly.

"In Iraq?"

He doesn't answer. I'll take that as a yes. "So pleading guilty to a murder you didn't commit will even the score?"

"No. But what are we holding on to here? What if we go through this and win? I'm not exactly loving life, you know? Nor am I a productive member of society."

"Let's take things one step at a time, or don't put the cart before the horse, or we'll cross that bridge when we come to it; just pick any cliché you want. But for right now, I can't be a party to you rendering a plea contrary to the facts. So you need to make the call before we head into the courtroom."

A long pause, and then he nods. "Okay. The truth. But one thing I have to insist on: we have the trial as soon as possible, even if that goes against my interests. I cannot deal with this confinement for an extended period, even with the medication."

"Fair enough," I say.

We enter the courtroom and sit at the defense table. Hike is waiting there, and I introduce him to Carrigan. Hike handles himself very well; he doesn't even tell Carrigan that we're going to lose and he'll be executed, which is probably what he's thinking.

Laurie is in the gallery just behind us, looking serious and determined. I've seen that look before; I'm glad I'm on her side.

The opposing counsel walks over to shake hands; he's at least six two and has one of those faces that people other than me consider good-looking. You know, the chiseled features and the little indentation in the chin . . . I hate chiseled features and indented chins.

He's smiling the confident smile of a person who thinks he's going to win. "I'm Raymond Tasker," he says. "Better known as the enemy."

"Good to meet you, enemy. I'm Andy Carpenter."

"You going to plead it out, Andy?"

"How about if I keep you in suspense?"

He shrugs. "Suit yourself."

"Thanks. I will."

I don't like this guy. I know it's just a first impression, but those are the kind of impressions I'm most comfortable with. Looking too deeply into a person is tiring and not usually worth the trouble. And in this case, especially since he's the self-identified enemy, I'm going to stick with not liking him.

Judge Seymour Harris comes into the courtroom and we're underway. And twenty minutes later, we're no longer underway. The charges have been announced and Carrigan has said in a firm voice that he is "not guilty." I must admit it had me in suspense; I wasn't sure he wouldn't change his mind.

Judge Harris asks if there are any other matters to be discussed, and we move for a change of venue. He takes it in stride and asks that each side submit written briefs on the matter, and he sets a tentative trial date, bowing to our demand for a speedy trial. If the change of venue is granted, I will make the same demand in Passaic County.

I raise the issue of bail, but for a case like this there is no chance it will be granted, and Judge Harris shoots it down immediately. Then he slams his gavel down, and the battle has been officially joined.

There are a number of situations from which there is no escape . . . where death is certain.

Were Ernie Vinson the reflective type, he might ponder them. Maybe some form of extremely deadly disease? Jumping from an airplane without a parachute? Sunbathing at ground zero of a nuclear explosion?

But he was not the reflective type at all. In fact, Ernie took it as a badge of honor that he did very little thinking of any kind; he just followed his instincts.

Those instincts had gotten him pretty damn far, and much further than any of the losers he had grown up with. He had money, more than he ever imagined having, and he had earned every penny of it.

But he had recently cut a corner, then exacerbated the problem, and then lied about it. That left him, at least metaphorically, with a deadly disease and about to bail at 35,000 feet with no parachute into ground zero of an upcoming nuclear explosion.

Ernie learned of his fate on the local TV news, which in itself was weird. They never mentioned Ernie, of course, because they had no way of knowing that he was part of the story. But they had mentioned Don Carrigan, and that had sealed Ernie's fate as surely as if they had read his obituary on air.

To make matters even worse, he was in pain from the damn dog bite from the other night. He had taken some antibiotics that he'd had lying around the house, but they didn't seem to be doing the trick. Maybe the dog had rabies, and that would kill him and solve his problems.

The Carrigan revelation left Ernie with very few options, which his instincts immediately laid out for him. He could do nothing, and hope his employers hadn't seen the story, but he knew very well that they didn't miss anything. And even if they didn't know about it yet, they would soon. There would be follow-up stories, and maybe a trial, and the name Don Carrigan would become widely known.

He could go to the police, rat out his employers, and try to get into a witness protection program. He couldn't quite see himself in such a program, living out his years in some cookie-cutter suburban house in the middle of nowhere-land. But that really didn't matter, since he couldn't rat out those employers enough for the police to protect him.

The fact was that he didn't know who those employers were.

He knew Carl, the man who gave him his assignments. But he also knew that Carl was not the man's real name, and he did not even know how to contact him. Carl did the contacting, when he had a job that needed doing. But Ernie didn't have any way of knowing if Carl was the top guy; in fact, he suspected that he wasn't.

Squealing on someone without being able to tell the cops who he was squealing on, or where that person could be found, did not exactly guarantee a witness protection ticket. So that option was closed to him.

Another possibility was to hope Carl contacted him, and then to confess his sins and rely on Carl's understanding and compassion. Carl somehow always knew how to find him, which until now was a good thing. Ernie didn't spend more than a few seconds on this approach; Carl had already demonstrated that understanding and compassion was not part of his makeup.

The fourth option was the one Ernie would take. It included no guarantee of success; in fact, its ultimate failure was all but inevitable. But it might buy some time, and allow Ernie to live another day.

Ernie would run.

I'm not big on experiencing stuff.

I understand that this sets me apart from most of humanity, but I'm okay with that, because I think that logic is on my side.

For example, last summer Laurie roped me into going apple picking with her and Ricky at a farm in upstate New York. So we bathed ourselves in completely ineffective antimosquito spray and went out in ninety-degree heat to take fruit that had reached the second stage of rotting off trees.

I pointed out that there were supermarkets where we could get any kind of ripe, clean apples we wanted in air-conditioned, mosquito-free comfort, but was informed that we'd be missing out on the "experience."

Today's similar experience is driving to a Christmas tree farm to pick out a tree and cut it down for use in our house. It's absolutely freezing out, so Ricky and I take turns swinging the damn ax, trying to keep warm. Laurie takes a cell phone video of us doing it, probably so she can post it on Facebook and humiliate us. That doesn't bother me; if she puts it on my page, Ricky is the only one who will see it.

We finally finish beating the hell out of the tree, getting it out of the ground and then strapping it to the top of our car.

"You sure that will hold?" Laurie asks.

"Sure it'll hold," I say, even though the extent of my Christmas tree car-strapping knowledge is skimpy at best. "I don't think it will," Ricky says, based on his well-documented years of experience in tree transportation.

Of course it doesn't hold; it starts to slip off twice on the highway, and we have to pull over and restrap it. We had left a sharp edge in the tree trunk where we cut it, and it wound up scratching the car trunk. I hope Laurie doesn't see it; she might not appreciate the irony of trunk scratching trunk.

"It scratched the trunk," Laurie says, pointing.

I nod. "I know, but it's worth it, because we're having so much fun." I don't mention that since Laurie keeps the tree up until the end of January, by the time we're finished with this one it will belong in the Petrified Forest.

We stop at a store to buy a new stand and extra lights, and in the process we walk by at least fifty perfectly cut trees that they are selling, with home delivery included. "We could have gotten a tree here, Mom," Ricky says.

"Your father likes to cut down his own," she says.

"When I was a kid we used to chop down trees in the morning, and then chew on the bark for breakfast," I say. "That's why I never had a cavity."

"You make up a lot of stuff," Ricky says.

So I'm not necessarily into experiencing things when there is an easier way to get them done, but the one thing I love doing, and have always loved doing, is going to live sporting events. There is something about sports stadiums that gets to me; even driving by empty ones gets me excited. I take

Ricky to as many games as I can, in all different kinds of sports, and I'm happy to say that he seems to share my love for it.

I would say that it's obvious he is my son, except for the fact that he likes picking apples.

When we finally get home and drag the stupid tree into the house, we find the initial discovery documents that Hike has dropped off. I settle into the den and prepare to read them, a prospect I always dread.

Reading discovery for the first time reminds me of a show Laurie occasionally watches; I think it's on the Food Network. A couple of wannabe chefs get into a cooking contest with each other, and some judges eat the food they've prepared at the end to determine who did a better job.

But just before the time clock starts, the chefs open a box which contains all the ingredients they will have to use to make their dishes. This is it; this is what they will be forced to work with.

Reading discovery documents reminds me of that show. I am about to learn the facts of the case as the prosecution sees it, and more important, I will find out what ingredients they will be using to make their case. I won't get any choice; the chefs and I have to make do with what we are given.

In this case the ingredients are skimpy but powerful. Carrigan has a history of some violence. After two terms in Iraq, he was stationed domestically and got into a couple of fights. The implication is that although he wasn't court-martialed, both he and the government came to the mutual agreement that his military days were over.

Once he was a civilian, Carrigan was arrested for getting into a few more fights in various places. The charges were all dropped, although one of his adversaries apparently wound up in a hospital. There are reports that Carrigan was, and no doubt is, suffering from a substantial case of post-traumatic stress disorder.

The evidence connecting Carrigan to the murder of Steven McMaster is simple and circumstantial, but powerful. A woolen cap was found in the garage of McMaster's house, where the man was apparently accosted. The hat contained a number of hairs, as hats are wont to do, and the DNA of those hairs matched Carrigan's.

Additionally, Carrigan kept a locker at the facility which provided food and shelter to the homeless, and one of the items found in that locker was a ring that Karen McMaster has identified as belonging to her deceased husband.

Game, set, and match.

The documents contain other investigative work that the police did at the time, but it is obvious that once the DNA match was made, they didn't consider it a whodunit.

In terms of the facts of the crime, McMaster's neck was broken, a fact that the police found consistent with Carrigan's military training and combat experience. McMaster's wife was out of town, but when she couldn't reach him, she called a friend to check on the house. It was the friend who discovered the body.

According to the wife, a large amount of jewelry was taken, as well as a considerable amount of cash. None of the stolen merchandise or cash was ever recovered.

A warrant went out for the arrest of Carrigan, but he had moved out of his most recent apartment, and was nowhere to be found. He had only a couple of distant relatives, and they disclaimed any knowledge of his whereabouts. So he was not found until I blabbed his name in the newspapers.

These are not great ingredients for Chef Andy to work with.

The parking lot was an aging five-story structure.

Parking was free, part of an effort by the city of Passaic to get more people to come and spend their money at the downtown stores. It had never worked; the malls of nearby Paramus were far more appealing.

So the lot was rarely crowded, and the top floor was always virtually empty. There was no reason to drive up there if there were spots available on floors below it. Also, the top floor was uncovered rooftop parking, and no one would want to leave their car in the baking sun all day in the summer, or risk it getting stuck in snow in the winter.

The shooter had been assured that the sightline was sufficient and that there were no security cameras. The target location was the front of a restaurant three blocks away, a distance that for a shooter of his talents might as well have been five feet. There would be little chance of him missing.

The shooter arrived at the parking lot at 1:15. Based on frequent observation, the target would leave the restaurant between 1:25 and 1:30. He was not there every day, only when he had business at the nearby courthouse. Court resumed at

2:00 P.M., and as an attorney, he had to be in place when his case was called. But he was going to be there this day; his case was next on the docket. The shooter had confirmed that.

The target's name was Ronald Lester, and among his specialties was family law. That was a dubious claim, since most of his work was in the area of divorce, which meant he was involved in the dissolution of families. But Lester handled other matters as well, and he was considered the dean of New Jersey lawyers, mainly because he had practiced for thirty-five years and counting.

The weather on this day was ideal for the shooter's task: a bright sunny day requiring him to bring sunglasses, but with no wind and obviously no precipitation.

By 1:20 he was in place. There were no bystanders, but even if there were it is likely that his car would have shielded him from being seen. In any event, if there were any chance of his actions being observed, he would have aborted and waited for another day.

But all was perfect; today would be the day.

At 1:27 Ronald Lester walked out of the restaurant with a colleague, and at 1:28 he was dead of a single bullet to the heart.

Chaos erupted in front of the restaurant, as everyone sought cover, not knowing whether other bullets were to follow. The shooter did not pause to admire his handiwork; he quickly put his rifle back into its case, loaded it into the trunk of his car, and drove down the five floors and out into the street.

But it was not correct to say that he left no trace of his presence behind.

He failed to retrieve his sunglass case.

find myself to be of two minds," Carrigan says.

This is in response to my asking him how he is doing when he is first brought into the lawyer's meeting room. I've asked a lot of jailed clients how they are doing; it's a clever conversation starter that I use. But his answer is a first for me; most of my clients usually opt for "terrible," "miserable," or "shitty."

"How so?" I ask.

"I simultaneously do not want to be convicted of this crime, yet I have little concern for what might happen to me. Maybe my wanting to prevail is an involuntary need to regain some long-lost dignity."

I nod. "I wouldn't describe your dignity as lost. But for now, let's concentrate on the part of you that doesn't want to be convicted."

"Fair enough."

I tell him what I've learned by reading the discovery documents, and the circumstances of the crime he has been charged with. I'm not great at reading faces, but his looks almost amused as he listens to what I have to say.

"So I made off with large amounts of cash and jewelry?"

"That's what they're contending."

"I must have invested the proceeds badly," he says. "Very badly."

"So you had nothing to do with this?"

"Absolutely nothing."

"What about the other violent incidents?" I ask.

"Guilty as not charged. But I was definitely involved. I understand that it demonstrates a propensity towards violence. I was trained to be violent."

"The documents also say you are suffering from PTSD," I say.

"The documents are correct."

"I need to know more about it. It can contribute to our defense."

He shakes his head. "No. I'm not going to say that I killed this person because the demons made me do it. They did not, and I did not."

I nod. "Fair enough. But I still want to know more about it."

"Why?"

"Because I need to know everything. I'm your attorney; if you know something, I have to know it. It's the only way I can be prepared." Then, "It's the way I was trained."

He smiles. "Okay, but no PTSD defense. If we go that route, I'd just as soon say I pulled the trigger."

I hadn't said how McMaster had died, and the fact that Carrigan assumed it was by a gunshot makes me feel better about him. Of course, he could have said that deliberately for just that purpose, but I don't think so. "McMaster's neck was broken," I say.

He frowns. "That's not good. Deadly hand-to-hand combat was part of my training, and I remain very good at it."

"There are two main pieces of evidence tying you to the crime. The first is that a hat was left at the scene; the theory is that it fell off during a struggle in the garage, before he was forced to go into the house to open the safe. It included strands of hair that have been identified by DNA as yours. Any idea how your hat got there?"

"None."

"Think about it. Because those were definitely your hairs, which means it was likely your hat."

"I will. What was the second piece of evidence?"

"You have a locker at the shelter where you have some meals?"

He nods. "I do."

"A ring was found in there which has been identified as belonging to the murder victim."

"I've never seen any such ring. I don't own a ring."

"Then think about how it could have gotten there. Now, back to the PTSD. Tell me about it."

He shakes his head. "You'd get a slanted view. I can send you to someone who knows more about me than I do."

He gives me the name and number of a shrink at the VA hospital that he used to see, and signs a short letter authorizing her to talk to me. The truth is that I don't see how it will be useful at trial if it's not the centerpiece of our defense, but I was telling Carrigan the truth. I like to accumulate all the information I can, and then some of it will come in handy, and some of it won't.

At this point I've sort of eased into the case, without making an affirmative decision to do so. I basically like Carrigan, not something I can say with all of my clients. I have no idea if he committed the crime; he probably did, based on the DNA evidence.

There could be extenuating circumstances; maybe his mental challenges are such that he is not even aware of what he's done. But I'm feeling like he's entitled to a real defense, if for no other reason than it's the best way I can think of for getting to the truth.

I have reached a point in my career where I have only been defending innocent clients. It's nice to have that freedom, but in this case I'm treading close to the edge. I'm not sure about Carrigan yet, but I'm hopeful, and that is going to have to be enough.

So I guess I have a client.

The legal world of Passaic County, New Jersey, is grinding to a halt today.

A beloved lawyer, Ronald Lester, was gunned down by a sniper's bullet in front of a local restaurant near the courthouse. "Beloved" and "lawyer" are not words that are commonly grouped together in a sentence, but Lester certainly fit the bill.

He practiced mostly family law but was what might be called, to use a medical term, a general practitioner. He dabbled in criminal and civil law, and even did some estate and probate work. But the point is that he did everything with a smile, and very few people walked out of court considering him an enemy, even when he represented the other side.

I wasn't close to Ronald, but I knew him well enough. He was actually closer in age to my father, Nelson, who was himself a legend in legal circles. Nelson was the county prosecutor, and when Ronald was starting out he briefly worked in the prosecutor's office. My father sort of mentored him, and they stayed close until my father's death. Ronald always called me "kid."

Everybody is here at the service: lawyers, court staff, police officers . . . everybody, including me. Many of the judges also found reasons to empty their docket for the day, and they are here as well. It's a deserving tribute to a life well lived.

There is unfortunately an undercurrent of concern, if not fear, among the people gathered here. There is something about a shooting by an apparent sniper that inspires an extra dose of terror. There feels like no way to protect oneself; the bullet can come at any time, without any warning, or any ability to see it coming.

But the word I hear is that law enforcement doesn't think Ronald was shot randomly; only one bullet was fired and it hit him in the heart. They traced the source of the shooting to a parking garage three blocks away, meaning that the shooter was a remarkable marksman. If he wanted to hit other people, he could have.

After it's over, and we've listened to a bunch of great stories extolling Ronald's many virtues, many of us gather outside to reflect on what has happened.

Pete Stanton is here, and I ask him if the police have any idea who did this. He's the captain of the Homicide Division, so if anyone would know, he would.

"Yeah," he says. "We know."

"Who is it?"

"Why? You looking for a client?"

"Come on, Pete."

"I can't tell you yet. We'll be going public soon. We don't want to scare him off yet; it will make him harder to find."

"Can you tell me how you know?"

He looks at me for a few moments, considering it.

"If you tell anyone, we'll be going to your service next week."

"I won't."

"He left something at the place he shot from. An eyeglass case; at that hour the sun would have been in his eyes, so he must have put on sunglasses."

"You can trace it back to him?"

He nods. "We got a print."

"Really? That's something that even you shouldn't be able to screw up."

Laurie can be remarkably persuasive.

    I don't mean in dealing with me. She has a myriad of tools at her disposal that makes any dispute between us far less than a fair fight. Any courtroom ability that I might have to argue, badger, and convince does not successfully translate to the home front.

Laurie's persuasive talents extend way past the domestic arena. She has a way of convincing people to do stuff that I just don't have, but at least we are collectively smart enough to realize this and utilize it to our advantage.

If we are going to attempt to get Carrigan acquitted of the murder of Steven McMaster, we are going to have to immerse ourselves in the details of it. The first step in that is to attempt to talk to McMaster's widow.

Since Carrigan is accused of making her a widow, and we are on his side in the dispute, one might think that Mrs. McMaster would be reluctant to talk to us. That's why Laurie was the one assigned to convince her, and she pulled it off without a hitch.

And that is why we're going to see her now. It's not at the

Short Hills house where the murder occurred; for all I know she sold it so as to rid herself of the horrible memory. She told Laurie she was staying "in the city," so that's where we are headed.

Northern New Jersey has a lot of cities. Paterson, Englewood, Hackensack . . . each one qualifies as a city. But when Jerseyites mention the city, we mean New York. In fact, we mean Manhattan.

Mrs. McMaster's apartment is on Park Avenue and Eighty-Second Street, which is not the most convenient place to get to. We take the George Washington Bridge and then the FDR parkway. If the real FDR had to contend with this much traffic on the way to his meetings, he wouldn't have given the Pearl Harbor "Day of Infamy" speech until December 10.

We finally pull into a parking lot two blocks away from our destination, just off Madison. I ask the attendant how much it will be and in answer to his question, I tell him we'll be under two hours.

"Sixty-two bucks," he says.

I shake my head. "You don't understand. I don't want to buy another car; I want to leave this one here."

"Yeah," he says, and hands me a ticket. He is clearly not an aficionado of parking lot humor, which is a shame considering his chosen occupation.

We enter the lobby of Mrs. McMaster's building and the doorman calls up and announces our arrival. Then he listens for a moment, says, "Very well," and tells us, "Twenty-fourth floor."

"Which apartment?"

He frowns slightly and repeats, "Twenty-fourth floor."

It turns out that twenty-four is the highest number on the elevator, which means she has the penthouse apartment, and when we arrive we see that there is only one door, which means she has the entire penthouse floor. I'm sensing the presence of some money here.

The door is opened by a woman who is clearly some kind of housekeeper/maid. She is wearing a sort of uniform, mostly white with some dark blue trim. Her skirt looks like one enormous doily; I shudder to think how many normal-sized doilies were killed in the making of that garment.

She greets us with a smile and tells us that Mrs. McMaster will see us in the den. The foyer itself is enormous; I think the Knicks could practice in here. We could probably wander around for the entire afternoon trying to find the den, which would cause me to have to take out a mortgage to pay for our parking costs.

Fortunately, the doily lady brings us to the den and opens the door. The lady of the house is indeed waiting for us in there.

She walks over to us, a half smile on her face that implies she knows a secret that we don't. "Karen McMaster," she says, extending her hand.

We introduce ourselves and decline her offer of something to drink. She asks for tea, and the doily lady is back with it so quickly that it must have been brewed and waiting just in case.

"Thanks for seeing us," Laurie says.

"A friend told me that I shouldn't, that I would in effect be helping the enemy. You are the enemy, aren't you?"

"That's not how I would describe us," Laurie says. "We want

to find out the truth, and we want to see the real killer punished."

Karen McMaster raises her tea cup in a toast. "Here, here," she says.

"What kind of work did your husband do?" I ask.

She smiles. "I never really found the right word for it. He was a supplier of food to grocery stores. If you ever bought something in a supermarket, chances are one of Steven's trucks or ships was the reason it got there. He would always call himself a grocery store clerk, because he made sure the shelves were stocked."

"And the business has continued on?" I ask.

She nods. "Oh, yes. Steven had very good people under him."

"And you have no involvement?" Laurie asks.

"Well . . . I own it," she says, as if the answer was an obvious one.

Laurie says, "If it's not too difficult, what can you tell us about the night your husband died?"

"I'm afraid not too much; the police know more than I do. I tried to avoid hearing details."

"You were out of town?" I ask.

She nods. "I was here, in this apartment. There was a charity dinner coming up, and I was attending to the details. Steven had a foundation that supported Meals on Wheels; he gave them so much. That night I kept calling him, but he didn't answer, the home phone or cell. I knew something was wrong; he was never out that late."

"What did you do?"

"I called my friend Susan Zimmer, our neighbor. She sent her husband Walter to the house, and . . . he found Steven.

He called the police, and then they called me and broke the news. As you can imagine, I was beyond upset."

For some reason I've never trusted it when people tell me how upset they were or are about something. Being upset feels like something that should naturally reveal itself; to describe it feels like an attempt to convince, or even brag.

I'm basically not liking Karen McMaster, though I can't quite put my finger on why. I don't think it's because she's richer than I am; I think it's more because it feels like she is so studied and prepared that it doesn't leave room for any "there" there.

For example, if she really does charity work, it strikes me that she's more interested in broadcasting that fact than in actually helping the charity. I'm sure my reaction is unfair, but I don't care; I'm still not going to ask her to be Facebook friends.

But I certainly don't have any reason to think she wasn't upset to find out that her husband was lying dead in their house with his neck broken. "The police said you identified your husband's ring?" I ask.

She nods. "Yes, it was definitely Steven's. I had it made for him by our jeweler; I gave it to him for his thirty-fifth birthday. He hardly ever took it off."

"One last question," Laurie says. "Before you knew that there was a suspect in the case, and well before the arrest was made, did you have anyone in mind that might have been the perpetrator?"

"Oh, no. No."

"No enemy your husband might have had? No one who might profit from his death?"

"No," she says with certainty. "No one. Everyone loved

Steven." Then, "But no one more than me." She says that with either sadness or fake sadness; your guess is as good as mine.

On that note, we thank her for her time and start the long trek across the foyer, so we can go downstairs and bail out my car.

It's one of the saddest calls I will ever make.

I have to call Edna, who used to be my secretary but has since self-elevated her title to office manager. Edna took on the office manager's responsibility for two reasons: she informed me it called for an increase in pay, and also because since we almost never have any clients and therefore never go into the office, it's a pretty easy place to manage.

I haven't spoken to Edna in a while; for the last few months our relationship has consisted of me mailing her checks, and her cashing them. Check cashing is an area in which she has always been totally reliable.

This call, coming out of the blue like this, is going to be particularly painful for her. So I decide to get it out there right away, in effect, ripping off the Band-Aid. "Edna, we have a client."

I can't tell if it's a gasp I hear, or a sharp intake of air. But since Edna's youthful years are well behind her, I'm briefly worried. Once she composes herself, she says, "I knew that's why you were calling. As soon as I saw your number on caller ID, I was positive."

"I felt I should be the one to tell you."

"Any chance you'll plead it out?" she asks.

"None. Our client says he's innocent."

"That's what they all say."

I tell Edna that we are going to dispense with the team meeting this time, at least for now. Sam, Hike, and Laurie are all aware of what's going on, and all that is left is to notify Marcus Clark. He'll help Laurie in the investigation side of things. I always leave it to Laurie to contact Marcus, because he likes her, and also because I am scared to death of him.

When I get off the phone with Edna, Laurie asks, "How did she take it?"

"She's upset, but she'll step up," I say. "It's not like she does any actual work even when we have a client. I guess it's just the idea that she might have to do something that's scary."

Sam calls to give me an update on his research into McMaster and Carrigan. "I'll email it," he says, "but you want me to give you the basics now?"

"Sure."

"Steven McMaster grew up in Vermont and went to Princeton. I don't see any grad school; he went into his father's food service business. Grew it big time; the guy was loaded. Married to Karen McMaster, who is a bit of a society type. His death hasn't slowed her down much; she's still in the press a lot. She's supposed to be dating already, but that could be newspaper gossip. I could tail her if you want."

"That's okay, Sam. No stakeouts necessary yet."

"Carrigan grew up in Dayton, Ohio. Graduated from Ohio State, where he played football. Seems to have been a backup, but got in the game occasionally, mostly on special teams.

Became a teaching assistant and then an English professor there, but enlisted in the army when Iraq blew up. His father was a Green Beret, and he became one as well."

"Any family?"

"Not anything close that I can tell. His parents died in a car crash when he was nineteen. No siblings, never married."

I thank Sam and ask him to send me over the reports. Knowing Sam they will be very detailed.

I update Laurie on the information Sam provided, and she mentions correctly that we need to plan our investigative strategy. It's time to take our growing canine family for a walk, so we put leashes on Tara, Sebastian, and Zoey, and head out to kill two birds with one stone.

"We've got to go at this from both angles," I say, and even though I have no doubt that she knows what I mean, I continue anyway. "We have to prove that Carrigan didn't do this, and at the same time try to find out who did. Or at least who might have."

"It's fresh ground," she says.

"What do you mean?"

"Based on the police reports in the discovery documents, they never conducted a truly full-scale investigation into McMaster's death. The DNA evidence immediately established Carrigan as the killer, and they were quite willing to accept that. Not that I blame them. But all they really did after that was check off some boxes. They weren't trying to find anything, because in their minds they already had found it."

"Good point," I say. "We also have to look into Carrigan's life, especially including where he was and what he was doing around the time of the murder. This is a guy living on the street with his belongings in a plastic bag; he didn't take an Uber out to Short Hills and ask the driver to wait while he robbed and murdered McMaster."

"But his hat was there," she points out.

"That doesn't mean his head was under it."

She smiles. "You're getting into this."

"It's Christmas."

Another smile. "And tonight we decorate the tree." I can't help but moan at hearing that; I know I should appreciate the whole "togetherness" aspect of it, but it takes so long and is so boring.

And the worst part is if some of the lights don't work; they call on me to fix them, because I'm the man of the house. "Man of the house" is not a role I'm well suited for.

"I don't know if you're aware of it," I say. "But there's a bowl game on ESPN tonight. Toledo against Wyoming."

"Do you realize that except for people who live in Toledo and Wyoming, you will be the only person in America watching that game?"

I nod. "I consider myself to be representing New Jersey; it's a heavy burden."

"Don't worry; you're off the hook. Ricky and I have decided we are going to decorate it without you."

"Why?" I ask. As soon as I do, I regret it. I should just accept my victory and move on; more conversation can wind up getting me back to putting trinkets on the damn tree.

"Because all you do is complain. And half the ornaments you put on fall off."

"I can live with this," I say. I could go on and say I am hurt by being excluded, but I don't for two reasons. First, it's not true; I'm delighted. And second, if I feign being insulted, they might reconsider their decision.

So for tonight it's just me, Toledo, and Wyoming.

As the saying goes, "Are you ready for some football?"

Ernie Vinson was not aware that he was literally hiding in plain sight.

For the time being he was staying at a Holiday Inn just off the 95 Freeway in New London, Connecticut. It had a couple of advantages, one of which was that it was well off his normal beaten path, which would mean that Carl would have no reason to look for him there.

The other positive was that it was a short distance from Uncasville, which is where the Mohegan Sun Casino was located. Ernie had a very substantial amount of money, and he liked to play roulette. So it was worth the risk to go there. He had grown a beard, not a full one yet, but it was coming in, and he felt it made him even harder to be recognized.

This was not the final stop, of course. Ernie was trying to figure out exactly where that should be. Carl had a long reach, and he would be coming after him. Ernie knew that his transgression was too significant to be forgiven.

Ernie was thinking an island, maybe Aruba or Barbados. He really didn't know anything about those places, having never been there, but he always wanted to try them. He'd research it, and he'd pick one, and once he established a fake identity, it would be his home.

So for now he was holed up in the Holiday Inn using a fake name, with occasional trips to the casino. He figured he'd stay there for another week or so, and then make whatever move he was going to make.

But for now, at least, he felt that he was safe.

He was wrong.

The fact was that Carl had him under surveillance, as he did with all the people who worked for him. He had planted a GPS device on Ernie's car, and was capable of monitoring Ernie's cell phone, which, like all cell phones, also contained a GPS.

Carl knew all about the situation with Don Carrigan, and assumed that the publicity would cause Ernie to run. Carl had other things on his plate, and for a few days was content to just monitor Ernie's comings and goings around the Holiday Inn in Connecticut.

But there was no way that Ernie would stay there forever; he would instead go someplace that he felt would make it more difficult for Carl to get to him. So that created some urgency; Connecticut was a lot easier to reach than some of the other places Ernie might come up with.

So while Ernie was at the Mohegan Sun, gambling in what he considered safe anonymity, Carl entered Ernie's room at the Holiday Inn and waited for him to return.

Ernie had no luck that night; the roulette wheel was not being kind to him. For him gambling was a diversion, not in any way an addiction, so he was able to walk away without chasing after his losses. He was disciplined in his gambling, and in this case that discipline shortened his life by an hour or two.

He saw Carl when he entered his room, but had no time to react. Carl didn't talk to him, didn't explain why he was about to be killed. Carl was not the type to take unnecessary chances, and every moment that Ernie was alive increased the possibility that he would find a way out of his predicament.

And in any event, both men knew exactly what was happening and why. Ernie had committed the cardinal sin, and it was an unforgivable and soon to be fatal one at that.

So Carl simply shot him twice in the heart, the second time clearly unnecessary. But he had an effective silencer on his gun, so he was not concerned about anyone hearing the attack and reacting.

He simply left Ernie's body on the floor, stepping over it on his way out.

I did have a hat like that. I think it was probably stolen."

Carrigan is reacting to the photo of the hat that I've just shown him, and which was in the discovery documents. It's a plain knit hat, the stretchy kind that you can pull over your ears or part of your face in the winter.

It's not the kind of hat that people would go out of their way to steal; I would imagine you could get one for a couple of bucks at a Walmart. I have a flash forward of me trying to convince a jury that some thief "probably" stole it, and the picture is not a pretty one.

Laurie has come with me to the jail for this meeting. She is showing more personal interest in this case than any I can remember. I don't know if she believes in Carrigan, wants to believe in Carrigan, or just feels responsible for my taking on the case.

"Tell us the circumstances," I say.

"It was a while ago, maybe last spring. It was a warm night, so I probably wasn't wearing a hat at all, though I had a couple of them. I'm not sure where I was, probably down the shore."

"Down the shore where?" Laurie asks.

"Would have been Bradley or Belmar. There are comfortable places there to sleep under the boardwalk, and the police don't hassle you."

Carrigan describes living under the boardwalk casually, as if it's no big deal or hardship. I'm not sure that's what the Drifters had in mind when they came up with their song.

"Keep going."

"One night . . . I don't wear a watch so I don't know what time it was, but it was probably two or three in the morning . . . I woke up and a guy was grabbing at this plastic bag of my stuff. He pulled it out, but then he came at me," he says.

"Came at you how?" I ask.

"With a knife. I saw a glint of light on it in his hand."

"Did he come at you because you woke up and were moving towards him, or do you think his plan was to stab you all along?" Laurie asks.

"I can't answer that. He would have had no reason to kill me if I was asleep, but it's unknowable now."

"What did you do?" I ask.

"I chopped him in the neck, and then chopped down on his hand. It knocked the knife out of his hand, and he started making gurgling noises, from me hitting his neck."

"And you had been sleeping? You wake up fast."

He nods. "I was well trained, and he clearly was not. In general, I'm not a good guy to mess with. Anyway, he took off, and then I realized he took the plastic bag with him. He got away in a big car, like a minivan or something."

It's not a particularly credible story, and that's being kind. A guy pulls up in a minivan for the purpose of robbing and maybe killing a homeless man who is completely unlikely to have anything of value? A jury would laugh me out of court, and yet he tells it in a believable way.

"So the hat would have been in that bag?" Laurie asks.

He shrugs. "I can't say for sure, but that's my best guess. Not much for you to work with."

I nod. "Not much at all. Any chance you could identify the guy? Did you get a license plate or anything? Would you know him if you saw him again?"

"No, no, and no. Sorry."

"Any idea why he would have wanted to hurt you, once he had the bag of your stuff?"

A shake of the head. "No, but there are some messed up people out there. And they think some homeless man, laying in the street asleep, is about as easy a prey as they're ever going to find. This particular guy found out differently."

"How often does that happen to you?" Laurie asks. I can see the intensity in her face, and I would bet anything she's thinking about how unfair it is that people have to live the way Carrigan is describing.

"I get hassled a lot, but you mean attacked in a serious way? Just twice; the time I told you about, and the time Zoey took a piece out of that guy. How is Zoey doing, by the way?"

"She's doing well. Getting along great with Tara and Sebastian, no negative issues at all. Laurie took her to the vet, and everything checked out okay. She should be delivering her puppies in about three weeks."

"I'd love to see a picture; I'd love to have a picture."

"Of Zoey?"

He nods. "And of the puppies when they're born. Weird how much I miss her," he says.

I nod. "Believe me, I get it."

"What will you do with the puppies?"

"Find them great homes. We're good at that."

He nods. "Good. Thank you. I can't understand why you both have done so much for me, but please know that I appreciate it."

Before we leave, I give Carrigan his homework assignment. "Here's what we are up against: your DNA was on the scene, and the hat that was there must have been yours. So there are two possibilities. One is that the person who stole your hat happened to be the same person that committed the murder, and he happened to leave that hat on the scene."

He frowns. "Seems like a bit of a long shot."

"The longest," I say. "The other possibility is that you were set up, that the hat was taken strictly for the purpose of leaving it at the murder scene and framing you."

"Also unlikely."

"Yes, but we still have to choose door number two; we have no other options. So what you need to do is think of who might have a grudge against you, strong enough to frame you for a murder. It has to be someone who would also be willing to break a man's neck in the process."

"I don't know who would hold such a grudge."

"These violent incidents that you had after you got back from Iraq, maybe some of the people you beat up?" Laurie asks.

"They were in-the-moment flare-ups, not the type to leave lingering bad will. But I'll try to think about it."

"Good. Try real hard," I say.

The news is dominated by the police revelation of the suspect in the sniper shooting of Ronald Lester.

The name is Chuck Simmons, and though pretty much no one had heard of him as of yesterday, everyone knows him now.

His sketch is on every newscast, as well as a brief bio. He's a forty-nine-year-old veteran of Desert Storm, and hints are dropped that his military function was that of a sniper. The local authorities won't confirm that, but neither will they deny it. The Defense Department has gone way out on a limb and issued a "no comment."

The main pertinent fact about Simmons is that he went through a bitter divorce four years ago, and his wife Greta's attorney was none other than Ronald Lester. The media has gone from speculation to certainty that this was revenge for what they call Lester's total victory in the courtroom.

Simmons's life apparently spun out of control, and as far as his ex-wife and few friends knew, he'd dropped out of sight. But now he is back with a vengeance, and there is a full-court press out for his capture.

By now everyone having any connection to the law enforcement community knows that Simmons left an eyeglass case behind at the location from which he fired the shot. The police couldn't be positive that the shooter left the case, it could have been another member of the public who had parked his car there, but the connection between Lester and Simmons's divorce case was too direct for it to be considered a possible coincidence.

In a way, the news causes a collective sigh of relief among the local citizenry. The idea of a sniper randomly targeting people is far more terrorizing than that of that same sniper going after a person that he thought wronged him, in order to exact revenge. All of those who never had anything to do with Simmons, and that includes just about everyone, can relax.

I, for one, can breathe easier when I walk into and out of the courthouse. I still feel a bit nauseous when I'm there, but it's because of my distaste for lawyering, rather than fear of being on the receiving end of a bullet.

The Carrigan case is totally off the media radar screen; until Simmons is caught even a breakout of World War III will not receive significant attention. I'm fine with that; while I often use the media to my advantage, right now I have no need or ability to do so.

I go to Charlie's for the first time in a while and am surprised to see only Vince there. Since it's *Monday Night Football*, Pete's absence is unusual to say the least.

"Where's Pete?" I ask.

"You didn't have the radio on coming over here?" he asks.

"No."

All he does is point to the TV screen. Rather than showing

pregame shows, they are broadcasting the news. And the banner, breaking news headlines across the screens, says it all:

"Greta Simmons killed in sniper shooting." "Ex-wife of murder suspect is second victim."

"Holy shit," I say, because I am most eloquent when I am surprised.

"She got shot walking out of the gym she goes to," Vince says.

As I watch, it's obvious that the circumstances are the same as with Ronald Lester. She was killed by one perfectly placed bullet, fired from a significant distance. The shooter, certainly her ex-husband, melted away before anyone could even figure out where the shot came from.

Once again, people are going to react with horror mixed with relief. Simmons is out for revenge, perhaps he's gotten all he is after, but in any event the average person is safe.

If you're not in Simmons's crosshairs, then life will go on.

While our operating assumption is that Carrigan was framed by someone out to get him, it doesn't really stand up to logical scrutiny. And since juries are often into logical scrutiny, we're in big trouble.

How would the murderer, the person with this intense grudge, even have found him? Carrigan was living on the street; one couldn't exactly google his address. And he already was living a miserable life; would someone have felt it necessary to try and make it worse?

I don't buy it, and I'm the one trying to sell it.

But there are other logical weaknesses that work in Carrigan's favor. How did he get to Short Hills? And why pick that location? There are wealthy people that are vulnerable to robberies much closer; even Paterson has them. Hell, I'm one of them.

And what did he do with the money? He doesn't seem to have blown it on fancy living, so where is it? And was this a one-time robbery? There's no evidence that Carrigan committed any other thefts.

But there is a great deal I don't know about our client; for all I know he's been traveling cross-country on a bank-robbing spree. Which is why I am heading to the VA hospital in East Orange to meet with Dr. Lucia Alvarez.

Dr. Alvarez was Carrigan's shrink when he got off active duty. She treated him for PTSD and his letter to her allows and encourages her to share details of his treatment and condition with me. I don't think he was thrilled to do so, but I insisted, and I think in his mind it was far better than having to tell me about it himself.

I would imagine that Dr. Alvarez is swamped with patients suffering ailments similar to Carrigan's, but she greets me with a smile and a very calm demeanor. Her office is small and nondescript, with a desk, chair, couch, and small table. I don't know if she uses the couches for her patients, but I quickly sit in the available chair.

"Thanks for seeing me," I say. "I assume you got Don Carrigan's letter authorizing you to tell me about his case?"

She nods. "Yes, and I called him at the prison, just to confirm. It's an unusual situation; I'm never comfortable talking about my patients."

"I understand. I don't really have an agenda here; I just want to learn whatever I can about Don to aid me in defending him. All I know is that he was in Iraq, suffers from a form of PTSD, and has claustrophobia. They're giving him Xanax in the prison to control attacks."

She nods. "Good. But it still must be difficult for him. I think the best way to do this is for you to ask me questions, and I'll respond as best I can."

"Fair enough. Let's start with whatever you can tell me about his service in Iraq."

"I'm afraid not much," she says. "Much of it is classified,

which says a lot about the type of missions he was on. Not for the fainthearted, I assure you."

"He would have been well trained for them, right? For the most part whatever he faced he would have expected?"

She nods. "The training assured that he would be competent to handle the assignment; there is no such assurance that the ultimate effect on him would not be profound."

"So he never discussed with you what he did over there?"

"He did not. I doubt he will ever speak about it."

"It left him homeless and on the street," I say.

She frowns. "I know that now; all I knew then was that he stopped coming to see me. I tried to locate him, but couldn't."

"This happens often?" I ask.

"Far too often. What happens is that soldiers who live through war trauma internalize the idea that they have changed, that they are 'different,' just from the act and intensity of making it through. What they don't know, really can't know, is that they have been permanently altered, that the changes will not be likely to wear off. And because they are military, because they are tough, they think the opposite is true, that they can get through anything. They believe they will survive these new difficulties just through force of will."

"So it doesn't wear off?" I ask.

"It does not. Typically it's not until they try 'normal' life that they experience how much they have changed, and how they can't find their place in the normal world anymore. Life can seem anything from meaningless to unbearable, and that is not even getting to the guilt of having survived when others, their friends and colleagues, have died."

"Why claustrophobia?"

"It's actually quite common as a manifestation of PTSD. This probably had something to do with the type of missions that he was on; he likely was in confined areas. Now he can feel trapped in situations that wouldn't affect you and me at all, but his terror is very real."

"Can that terror cause him to react violently?"

"Yes, within limits. I remember there was an incident at a small apartment he was renting. He had a panic attack and broke a table, as well as causing other damage. He was evicted, and moved into a motel. Sometime after that he obviously opted for the street, voluntarily or not, but I am not privy to the facts of that."

"You said within limits. He is charged with lying in wait to commit a robbery, and then breaking the victim's neck."

"With the caveat that anything is possible, I don't believe it for a second," she says.

"Will you testify to that?"

"Of course. Don Carrigan is an honorable man, as well as a hero. He did what his country asked him to do, and he has suffered for it. The act that you are describing is not consistent with his character or mental state, and I will state that in any venue you'd like."

That's good enough for me, and I'm feeling relieved that she confirmed the instincts about Carrigan that both Laurie and I have.

"He's very attached to a dog that he found," I say. "Her name is Zoey."

She nods. "Not surprising at all, and I'm glad to hear it. Dogs can be a big part of PTSD recovery. They are helpful with relaxation and provide comfort and companionship. Most important is the sense of responsibility he would feel to the dog; it would help prevent his shutting down and disconnecting from the world."

"That seems to be what happened," I say. "The dog is pretty tough also. She bit the guy that attacked Carrigan."

She smiles. "Where is Zoey now?"

"We're caring for her. She's pregnant."

"He'll probably ask without prompting, but keep him informed of her progress. Show him photos if you can. We want him to stay engaged."

"Will do."

"Thank you for helping him."

"Thank you for helping him and many others like him," I say.

"Unfortunately, in Don's case my outcome was not a desirable one. Maybe you can do better."

Hey, Andy. I just got the police report," Ralph Brandenberger says, calling me on my cell.

"What police report?" I ask, but if he responds, I can't hear him. There's a barking explosion in the background; such is his life as the man who runs the local animal shelter.

"About that homeless guy and the dog . . . from the other night. Whenever there is a bite involved, I always get the report."

"Right," I say, suddenly interested. The report wasn't in the discovery because it has nothing to do with the murder Carrigan is accused of. But I should have been asking about it because I just realized in the moment that it could be important. "I'd like to see it, Ralph."

"No problem. You want to pick it up, or should I mail a copy to you?"

"I'll be right over."

I've been thinking about the attack on Carrigan that night in the wrong manner. For one thing, I haven't viewed it as significant. I didn't question the fact that it wasn't included in the discovery documents, because I basically agreed that it wasn't related to the McMaster murder.

If I've thought about it at all, it has been in viewing it as potential evidence that he is not prone to unnecessary violence. All he did was defend himself from the attacker; he could have gone further and inflicted serious damage on the man. He was certainly provoked and just as certainly had the physical ability to have killed the guy.

But what I should have been focusing on was the existence of the attack itself. What was the guy hoping to get from Carrigan? He certainly had nothing of value. Could he have been hoping to do more? Could his plan have been to kill Carrigan?

Why would someone do that?

There's always the chance that the attacker was a deranged murderer who liked to prey on the helpless, but it seems unlikely. A more realistic scenario is that the guy was targeting Carrigan, for reasons unknown.

And if Carrigan is to be believed, and it is becoming increasingly likely in my mind that he is, then this is the second time he was attacked. The first time was a knife-brandishing assailant who stole some possessions, including the hat.

I don't know the frequency in which the homeless are targets of unprovoked attacks, but the fact that it's happened twice to my client is a red flag that I am going to investigate. If our hypothesis is that Carrigan is the target of a frame-up, then we can't reject the possibility that the same people could also be targeting him for robbery or murder, and maybe both.

Ralph has the copies of the documents waiting when I arrive. He asks, "How is the dog doing?"

"Doing well, Ralph, thanks."

"What about the homeless guy? Is he still in the picture?"

Obviously Ralph is not a ravenous consumer of the news; he doesn't know that Carrigan has been arrested. "He's definitely in the picture," I say.

I call Laurie and tell her I'll be home in a little while with the new documents, and she says that by then she and Ricky will be finished with the tree. They decided that this tree is bigger than previous years' trees, so the four million ornaments and lights they put on the other night left it looking a little barren.

They've since bought more; I would be surprised if a sequoia could stand up under the weight. I do know one thing; if they've added any more lights, then when they turn them on, planes will start landing in our living room.

Once I get home, we all have dinner and then I take Tara, Sebastian, and Zoey for a walk. For a dog carrying around a bunch of other dogs inside her, Zoey gets around pretty damn well. She can certainly run rings around Sebastian, but then again there are file cabinets than can run rings around Sebastian.

I love walking with the dogs at this time of year. For some strange reason I like the frigid air, and the dogs clearly prefer it to the heat of summer. But I also like the Christmas lights on the houses, and have since I was a kid.

When I get back, Ricky is already in bed, and I go to perform the "tuck in" ritual, which is a particular favorite of mine. We always take five minutes to talk about whatever Ricky wants to talk about; usually around this time of year it's whether the Giants will make the playoffs.

But this time he asks me how "Mr. Carrigan" is doing. I

don't know if he fully understands what is going on; it seems like he knows that the police think he did something wrong, even though Ricky believes he didn't.

If I'm not careful, there will be another defense attorney in the family. That is the kind of development for which the term "God forbid" was coined.

"He's doing okay, Rick," I say, not exactly a full blown answer to his question.

"Does he miss Zoey?"

I nod. "Very much. But he knows we'll take good care of her until he can see her again."

"Will he live with her over the garage?"

"We don't know that yet."

"I hope he does. Just don't let them live on the cold street. Okay, Dad?"

"I promise."

He smiles, having accomplished his conversational mission. I wouldn't be surprised if Laurie put him up to it.

f I were grading police investigative reports, I'd rank this one as borderline pathetic.

The officer who chronicled it, Sergeant Nathan Robbins, made that clear with the work he put into it; he did everything but write a cover letter saying, "I completely do not give a shit about this investigation."

The attempted robbery, or assault, or whatever, of Don Carrigan that night was of no particular concern to Sergeant Robbins. I can't judge whether Carrigan's status as "homeless" contributed to that attitude, but I wouldn't be surprised.

Perhaps if Carrigan had a tattoo on his forehead that identified him as a former Green Beret, things might have been different. Or perhaps not.

In fact, the ironic reason that the report was filed at all was probably because of Zoey's involvement. The video is said to show her biting the assailant, and the man pulling back in pain. I assume that Robbins must have realized that at some point some charges or lawsuits could be filed by somebody, so he had better document it all, rather than just move on.

But for such a skimpy report, there are a whole collection of things that interest me. For one, there is the video itself, a copy of which is included in these materials. It's in the form of a DVD, which I pop into my computer, first calling Laurie in to watch it with me. I am nothing if not a romantic.

The video shows Carrigan and Zoey lying on the ground; they are in the same place that I had seen them the day before, when I gave him the money and the PetSmart card.

A heavyset man walks into the frame and toward Carrigan. I'm already surprised; Carrigan told me the man was driving a large car, possibly an SUV. But this guy is walking, not driving a vehicle.

The man leans in, as if talking to him; in the darkness it is hard to tell if he's carrying a weapon. In any event, he clearly did not get the reaction he expected.

Carrigan immediately went into action and kicked the guy in the chest, from a prone position. Almost simultaneous to that, as if they had prearranged the choreography, Zoey bit the guy, and he recoiled.

And I think, though I'm not sure, something went flying out of the guy's hand.

"That's a gun," Laurie says. She stops the image, goes back and forth a few times, and finally says, "I'm positive it's a gun." I still can't tell, but I'll take her word for it.

Suddenly, a black SUV pulls up to where this is all happening, with the passenger door already open. "He wasn't alone," I say, stating the obvious. The only alternative is that he was driving the car from outside of it, telepathically.

We can only see the side of the SUV; the license plates are completely out of the video. I have no idea what the make of the car would be; I'm not into cars at all. It's possible that someone else could figure it out, should that become necessary.

The assailant retreats, stopping to pick something off the ground. "He grabbed the gun," Laurie says. Carrigan seemed unafraid and was moving toward the guy, but he got into the passenger side of the SUV, closed the door, and the car drove off. Carrigan had no way to chase him if he wanted to.

End of video.

"You're sure that was a gun?" I ask.

"I am."

"Then why didn't he use it? He was a good seven feet from Carrigan at the point he picked it up. Why not turn and fire?"

She smiles. "My job is to tell you what happened. You're in charge of figuring out why."

The video now dispensed of, I start in on the written documents, and it's here that we catch a real break. Among the few pieces of evidence that Robbins preserved is a piece of cloth, probably from the sleeve of the assailant.

With blood on it.

file a motion with the court to have a DNA test on the bloody sleeve.

I ask that it be done on an expedited basis. There is no way that request will be granted, especially since the assault that night really has nothing whatsoever to do with the crime with which Carrigan is charged.

So I also ask for a piece of the evidence, with enough of the blood on it that it can be tested. That is within my right, and the judge orders it. The prosecution has the right to sit in on any testing I do, but they decline, for two obvious reasons.

One is that they don't see how it has anything to do with their case, and the other is that they have preserved the majority of the material, so they could conduct their own tests at a later date if for some reason they wanted to challenge whatever result I come up with.

I ask Hike to pick up the piece of the sleeve that we're being given, which is at the evidence room in Passaic County. I tell him to bring it to me at the state lab in Newark, where I will be kissing the ass of one Horace Persky.

Horace and I have done mutually beneficial business in the past. He is said to be a genius at what he does, but since I'm far from a genius at what he does, I have no way to judge the accuracy of that assessment.

Horace is the number two person at the lab, and has been for as long as I can remember. Three "number ones" have come and gone during his tenure, but each time he has turned down the opportunity for promotion. His expressed reason, which I have no cause to doubt, is that he doesn't need the aggravation.

On a number of occasions I have needed lab work done on a very expedited basis, and Horace always comes through for me. Coincidentally, it comes at a time when he needs tickets to a particular sporting event, and I've come through for him.

Hike brings me the sleeve in an evidence bag, and I give it to Horace with the comment that I need it as soon as humanly possible. I really don't, but since I'm going to have to pay for this big time, I might as well make some demands of my own.

His response is to nod and say, "Giants-Eagles is a big one this Sunday, huh?"

"Sure is."

"Giants win and they make the playoffs."

"Sure do. You know, Horace, I was just thinking. I have two tickets to the game lying around which I can't use. Any chance you'd want them?"

"I might," he says. "What yard line?"

"I don't know yet. They're lying around at a ticket broker."

We consummate the deal, as we always do, and I leave him to do his work, while I call my scalper to get ripped off on the two tickets. Then I head off to see my client again at the jail.

As I always do when I visit a client in jail, I ask how he's doing and whether I can do anything to make his life more comfortable. Carrigan always shrugs it off with an "everything's fine." Considering he was lying on frozen cement in front of a pawn shop and wondering where his next meal was coming from, he's probably telling the truth.

I give him a picture of Zoey, sitting on a recliner chair and looking regal. He smiles when he sees it. "She looks happy," he says. "I hope I get to see her again."

"So do I," I say. Then, "I saw the video of the attack on you, when she bit that guy."

He smiles. "She seemed to take a pretty good chunk out of him. I rewarded her with a biscuit, which probably wasn't the right thing to do."

"You handled yourself pretty well also."

"Yeah."

"Laurie thinks the guy had a gun."

Carrigan nods. "He did."

"Why didn't you tell me that before?"

"You didn't ask; we didn't even talk about that night. What does it have to do with the murder I'm supposed to have committed?"

"So a guy comes after you with a gun, and you don't think it's worth mentioning?" I ask.

"Andy, we live in different worlds. If he shot me, I would have mentioned it."

"Did he say anything?"

"Yes. Something like 'get up and come with me,' or 'let's go,' or words to that effect. I'm paraphrasing, but I would think with reasonable accuracy. We didn't have a long conversation. He made his demand, and I successfully resisted."

"When he backed off, he picked up the gun and took it with him," I say.

"Yes. I recall that."

"Why didn't he shoot you?"

He shrugs. "You'd have to ask him that. But I don't think he had any intention of shooting me. If he had, he wouldn't have had to come so close in the first place. He could have shot from ten feet away, without waking me up and with little chance of missing."

"So he wanted you to go with him?"

"Apparently."

"Any idea why?"

He shakes his head. "Not the slightest."

"You also didn't tell me he wasn't alone, that there was someone else driving the SUV."

"I refer you to my previous explanation about you not asking me. Can I in turn ask why this is important?"

"Here's how these things work," I say. "Everything is important, until it isn't."

He stops to consider this for a moment, then, "Your current world, and my former one, are not so different after all."

"In both, it is you that is facing the risk."

"They give us an hour's access to the computers in the prison library," he says, "though they rather rigorously manage what we can access. I've been reading about you."

"Uh, oh."

"As you know but won't admit, your record is stellar. But there's one newspaper article that talks of you as only being willing to represent people you are convinced are innocent."

I nod. "I'm lucky to have the resources to be able to stick with that."

"You believe in my innocence? On a gut level?"

"I didn't; now I do. Laurie has all along."

He nods. "Your gut is right. But there's something you

should know. With the way . . . with the way I am, I am not living my life out in a cage. There is no way, and there is no amount of medication that could make that palatable."

I don't want to think about the implications of that, and I don't want to focus on the fact that I don't blame him.

The hunt for the sniper doesn't seem to be going well, but that hasn't stopped the media from obsessing about it. There are any number of rumors and false alarms about where the elusive Chuck Simmons could be; psychics have even weighed in to report that he has killed himself, has escaped to Mexico, and was spotted at a Giants game.

On a local level, it's been similar to when that plane went down somewhere in the Pacific, with no trace of where it crashed. Even with no new news, they kept finding new angles and new so-called experts to talk to. It seems like every psychologist in America has opined on Simmons, why he has done what he's done, and what he's likely to do next.

But eventually they are going to run out of stuff to write, which is why there are fortunately new murders and disasters to step in and fill the breach. The one that is being reported this morning is the shooting death of Ernie Vinson.

While it took place at a Holiday Inn in New London, Connecticut, it gets coverage here because Ernie is a local New Jersey guy. It wouldn't be correct to describe him as a favorite son, or even a respected citizen. Ernie's fame comes from the fact that he is, or rather was, a gangster. He was an enforcer in the Joseph Russo crime family.

Mob killings are big news because they could lead to mob wars, which are even bigger news.

The details are understandably sketchy, both because the murder was just discovered and because the police are unlikely to be sharing anything significant with the media at this point. All that the media knows is that the killer was believed to be a professional. I suspect that in this case that means he was efficient in the manner of the killing, and probably that he was smart and experienced enough to have dodged video camera surveillance.

Hike calls with the first piece of good news we have received; the change of venue motion that he filed has been granted. It doesn't change the facts of the case, or even really the dynamics of the trial, but it will be a hell of a lot more convenient.

Of course, the downside to it is that we'll have a judge who knows me. Where judges are concerned, to know me is to dislike me, since I don't always do everything by the book, and they generally worship the book. On the other hand, if we tried the case in Essex County, whichever judge we got would learn to dislike me by the time we got through jury selection.

My feeling good about this news lasts for about twenty minutes, and is brought to a crashing halt by another phone call from Hike. "This is bad," he says.

Coming from Hike, "this is bad" does not necessarily portend anything serious, because he thinks everything is bad.

But this time he's correct. "They have a witness who claims our client admitted to the McMaster murder. The guy says Carrigan bragged about it."

"Who is he?"

"Someone who apparently met Carrigan at a soup kitchen, or a shelter, or whatever the hell it is. It's in downtown Paterson, same place where they found the ring. We just got discovery on it."

"Get it to me, please."

"Will do."

This has the potential to be a major problem, depending on the credibility of the witness. If we're contending that Carrigan was framed for the murder, and that's our most likely way for claiming how the hat got left at the scene and the ring was in the locker, then this new witness could be part of the frame. At least that is how we will try to spin it.

I've dealt with jailhouse snitches a lot, and they are not exactly the most reliable witnesses. Usually they see their testimony as a way to lessen their own sentences, and very often they are correct.

I've never had any experience with soup kitchen snitches, so I'm breaking new ground here. They might have their own reasons to lie; I would guess money being right up there. But each case is different, so we'll see.

I tell Hike to file a motion seeking to interview the witness, whose name is Jaime Tomasino. It won't work; in criminal cases the defense does not have an automatic right to depose an adverse witness. But I believe in giving everything a shot.

In typical fashion, the prosecution did not include any information about Tomasino, such as his address, because they don't want to give us a chance to get at him before trial. This does not present much of a problem, because of the existence of Sam Willis.

So next I call Sam and ask him to try to track down Tom-asino. He's got an unusual name, so I would think Sam would have a good chance of learning things about him, even without any more information. I specifically say that I'd like a photo and an address. Then I head into the bedroom to tell Laurie what has happened.

This proves rather difficult to accomplish, because she's on an exercise bike, pedaling away, and wearing headphones. I assume she's listening to music; she says that doing so pro-pels her to greater cycling heights. We have different tastes in music; my choices invariably lull me to sleep.

I make a hand motion indicating that I need to talk to her, and she holds up one finger, in effect telling me she'll be with me in a minute; she just needs to finish the program. One minute becomes five, as I stand here like a lazy idiot watch-ing her exhaust herself. Five minutes watching a biker doesn't feel as long as five minutes actually being on a bike, which feels like five decades, but it still seems to take forever.

Finally she stops pedaling and takes off her headphones. "Good ride?" I ask.

She's getting her breath. "Great ride."

"Yet you remain in the exact place you started."

She nods. "That's the beauty of it."

I tell her the news about Jaime Tomasino, the witness that the prosecution has uncovered. "Have you talked to Carrigan?" she asks.

"Not yet; we just got the discovery. But his position is that he didn't commit the murder, so he certainly won't say that he told Tomasino that he did."

"But he might say whether or not he knows the guy."

That's a good point, and I'll certainly ask Carrigan about

it. Laurie gets off the bike, and I follow her into the kitchen. I'm going to have a cup of coffee while she makes herself some kind of healthy shake, composed of every revolting green vegetable known to humanity. She also adds some kind of powder, which I have to assume is a crushed and dried version of a revolting vegetable.

Based on the way we exercise and eat, if Laurie doesn't outlive me, there is no justice in the world.

Over the sound of the blender I hear the phone ring, and I go into the den to answer it. It's Horace Persky, from the state lab. "How's it going?" he asks, which is Horace-speak for "Did you get the Giants tickets?"

"It's going fine. You're on the forty-five-yard line, club level."

"Sweet," he says. "I got the DNA results on the bloody cloth. I'm emailing them to you, but I thought you'd want to know this right away."

That sounds intriguing. "You got a match? Whose is it?"

"None other than Ernie Vinson."

"The Ernie Vinson who just turned up dead in the hotel room in Connecticut?"

"The very one."

Wow.

I'm not ready to call this a significant and connected development, but I'm tempted.

Not long after Ernie Vinson attempts to attack or kidnap Don Carrigan, he turns up dead. I don't believe in coincidences, but it's possible that these two things are actually unconnected.

I say this because Ernie Vinson was no Boy Scout; he was a mob-connected enforcer. That is among the more violent careers, and the dangers involved in holding such a job no doubt would be off the actuarial table charts. If you're applying for life insurance, and you're mob-connected, you should lie about your occupation on the application. So Vinson's murder could easily have nothing whatsoever to do with Don Carrigan.

But of course the two events could actually be related to each other, and I have to look into that possibility. If we can make the connection, which is a long shot, that would be huge for us.

More interesting to me is the question of what the hell Ernie Vinson would have wanted with Don Carrigan. Vinson was a violent guy, but he operated with a purpose. He wasn't, at least to my knowledge, someone who randomly killed for kicks. He killed on orders or for money, or both, and that doesn't seem to fit with Carrigan's status in life.

My first call is to Sam Willis, to get him to use his computer magic to learn whatever he can about the last days of Ernie Vinson. "I'm on it," he says.

"Also, Vinson had an accomplice the night he attacked Carrigan. There was someone else there, driving a dark-colored SUV. I'd really like to know who that was. Can you access Vinson's phone records?"

"Why do you insult me?" Sam asks. He knows that I am aware he can get phone records as easily as I can get food out of the refrigerator.

"Sorry," I say. "But maybe he talked on the phone to the guy who helped him. It would be a big help if you could narrow down the possibilities."

"I'm on it," he says again. There is literally nothing I could ask him that wouldn't draw an "I'm on it."

I next dial Pete Stanton, who thinks I am calling about the Carrigan case. "Leave me alone" is his friendly conversational opener. "I have nothing to do with the case. I just made the arrest for the Essex County cops."

"I'm calling about Ernie Vinson," I say.

"He's dead."

"I was hoping to get better information than that. Like who killed him, and why."

"All I know is what I read in the papers. But he was a mob killer, so I assume he was killed by another mob killer. That's usually how it works."

"Any idea why?" I ask, though I already know this conversation is going nowhere.

"I'm going to go out on a limb and say that the other mob killer wanted him dead."

"You're an outstanding source of information."

"Hey, he worked for Joseph Russo. Why don't you ask him?"

"I think I will," I say.

"I was kidding."

"I wasn't."

"Are your affairs in order?" he asks.

"I laugh in the face of danger."

"You're about to get your chance," he says. "I should mind my own business, but you want me to go with you? I could do it unofficially."

I appreciate the offer. Pete knows if he's with me, because he's a cop, Russo would never try anything. "No thanks, Pete, I got this."

"Yeah."

As soon as I get off the phone, I head down to the Tara Foundation to speak to Willie Miller. It's the dog rescue operation that we run, and Willie is my partner in it. He and his wife, Sondra, do all the work, something that makes me feel guilty much of the time. But they love doing it.

Willie also spent seven years in prison for a murder he did not commit, and I got him off on appeal. In the process we won him a fortune in a civil suit, which is why he can happily work at the foundation for no pay.

While in prison he used his considerable skills in karate to defend another inmate from an attack by three assailants out to kill him. Willie put the three of them in the hospital, earning the eternal gratitude of the inmate he protected. Willie's actions were especially noble because he had no prior relationship with the inmate; they had never so much as spoken to each other.

That inmate was Joseph Russo. And Willie's actions earned an actual sense of gratitude in Russo that caused Russo to tell him that if Willie needed anything, at any time in the future, Russo would be there for him.

I've used the "Willie connection" to get to Russo a number of times since then, and it has worked out well. But my relationship with Russo has grown a bit more complicated recently. Russo had been the number two man to Dominic Petrone until my efforts sent Petrone to prison, where he will spend his golden years.

Russo was thus elevated to the head of the family, and all reports are that he has consolidated his power in the interim. So he either hates me for putting away his mentor, or is grateful to me for securing the top job for him. Or something in between.

He's let me live since then, so that's a good sign.

Willie is talking to potential adopters when I arrive, which can always be a volatile situation. Willie does not think that every home is an appropriate one for one of the dogs under our protection and he's not hesitant to so inform the applicants in rather direct terms.

I say hello to Sondra, and she tells me she heard about Zoey from Laurie. "You might want to let her come here," Sondra says.

"Why?"

"Because you and Laurie are working on the case, and when she has the puppies, that's going to be a full-time job. Plus, we have better access to the vet."

I hadn't thought about that, but she's probably right.

They're here with the dogs all day, and they could take Zoey and the puppies home at night. Plus we have a vet on call twenty-four/seven for the foundation, which might be needed.

"Thanks, Sondra. Let me talk to Laurie about it."

At that moment the office door opens and a middle-aged couple, stunned looks on their faces, walks out. They head for the door, dogless. They clearly had not passed the "Willie Miller" test and were told so with no chance for misinterpretation.

Willie comes out and says, "Hey, Andy."

"What happened with them?" I ask, meaning the departed couple.

"They were going to tie the dog up in the yard when they were out."

I can't help but smile with relief that Willie didn't kill them both. "What did you tell them?" I ask.

"That they weren't going to do that with one of our dogs, and that if I found out they did it with any dog at all, they'd hear from me." Then, "So what's up?"

"I need to see Joseph Russo."

"Sure, no problem," he says, as if the request is nothing unusual at all. "When?"

"Whenever," I say. "Sooner the better."

Danny Costa was scared for so long, he had forgotten how it felt not to be scared.

That fear had progressed through three stages, each one stronger than the one before it.

The moment it began was that night when they went after the homeless guy. Danny had literally gone along for the ride; Ernie Vinson was paying him good money just to drive his SUV. All Ernie told him was that they were going to tie the guy up and put him in the back of the car. Danny didn't know why, or what would happen after that.

He didn't want to know.

But then it went wrong; amazingly, the guy was more than Ernie could handle, and the dog bit him. Danny didn't know why Ernie didn't just shoot the guy, but he was afraid to ask.

So they drove off, and when Danny had dropped off Ernie at home, Ernie made him swear he would not tell anyone what happened. Danny knew what Ernie was capable of, so there was no way he would disobey. But Ernie's words were not what scared Danny.

It was his eyes.

Danny could see in his eyes that Ernie himself was afraid.

He had never seen it before, and it shocked him. He had never known Ernie to be afraid of anything; if Ernie was afraid, then there were some very dangerous people involved.

That was the first stage of Danny's fear. The second came when he couldn't reach Ernie by phone and no longer saw him around. He went to his house, but he was not there either. To Danny, this meant that Ernie was on the run, or worse.

But the third stage, which left Danny nothing short of petrified, was when he saw the TV report that said Ernie was found dead in that hotel. There was no question in Danny's mind that it was a result of that night with the homeless guy, but he had no idea why.

He wished he had asked Ernie more about what was going on, though it was not Ernie's style to have confided in him. And in a way, he was almost glad not to know, because the knowledge might have made him feel even worse.

There was literally nothing Danny could do, other than hope that the killers had not gotten Ernie to mention Danny's role that night. If he hadn't, Danny was safe. If he had, then Danny was toast. Because if Ernie could not stand up to them, if Ernie was that scared of them, then Danny had no chance.

He was a dead man.

He couldn't go to the police; he had absolutely nothing to tell them. They wouldn't have had any reason to believe that Ernie's death was related to the homeless guy, but even if they entertained the possibility, Danny had no information to help them connect it to Ernie's killers.

So for now all Danny could do was wait . . . and hope.

And try not to panic.

Uncle Marcus is in the kitchen."

I've just showered and gotten dressed when Ricky comes into the bedroom and drops that bomb on me. Laurie has obviously arranged for Marcus Clark to come over, as he is working with us on the investigative aspects of our case.

I'm not sure what to do. The kitchen is where the coffee is, but Marcus is in the kitchen. It's not an easy decision. I need coffee, but not having coffee is not going to kill me. Marcus could certainly kill me. I'm not scared to death of missing out on coffee, but I am scared to death of Marcus.

On the other hand, I've spent a lot of time with Marcus and he's never killed me. Not once. In fact, on more than one occasion he's saved my life. Marcus listens to Laurie, and Laurie wants me to be safe and alive.

I need more time to think about this. It's happened so suddenly. Usually I know when I'm going to see Marcus, so I have time to mentally prepare. It's not fair that I have to wake up to this.

Maybe I should send Ricky downstairs to get me some coffee. That would possibly humiliate me in front of my son, and Laurie would see through it. But it is definitely a viable option.

I've made my decision: I'm not going. Coffee is not good for me anyway; I think I saw a study on it recently. I have to start taking better care of myself; my body is a temple.

"Andy, can you come down?" Laurie yells from the kitchen. "Marcus is here."

Now I am stuck.

"Mom's calling you," Ricky says.

"Thanks, Rick, I heard her. How come you're not in school?"

"Christmas vacation started yesterday. We're off for two weeks."

"That's ridiculous. In my day, Christmas vacation was like an hour."

So I head down to the kitchen, fearless as always. There, sitting at the counter island and drinking my coffee, is Marcus. He even looks scary in this setting; he would look scary in a tutu dancing at the Met.

"Hey, Marcus."

"Unhh," he says, in a burst of eloquence. Marcus says very little, and what little he says is indecipherable to all but Laurie.

They have a few sheets of paper in front of them, no doubt related to the case. "Marcus has been tracking down the people that our client has had violent incidents with," she says.

"Good. How many are there?"

"Six."

"Six? And he's never been charged with any of them?"

She shakes her head. "No, but keep in mind that for the most part he hasn't been tangling with Boy Scouts. He's been arrested a few times, but the charges were dropped. Nobody on either side pressed charges."

"Okay. We need to talk to all of them."

"Not as bad as it sounds," Laurie says. "Two of them are in jail, one lives on the West Coast, and one is dead."

"Any chance the dead one is Ernie Vinson?"

"No." Then, "Do you want to talk to them yourself?"

"Might as well; I've got nothing else to do today. Let me go down to the jail and show the names to Carrigan; maybe we can decide whether to talk to them based on what he knows and remembers about them."

The doorbell rings and when I open it I see Sam Willis standing in the rain. "Got something for you," he says. "I figured I should bring it over."

"Come on in. What is it?"

He hands me an envelope. "An address for Jaime Tomasino and a photograph. As soon as I get more information, I'll get it to you."

"Great. You want some coffee?"

"You have chai tea?"

"Chai tea? You think you wandered into Starbucks?"

Once we're in the kitchen and Sam, Marcus, and Laurie have exchanged hellos, I open the envelope. There's a photograph of Jaime Tomasino, just as Sam promised.

"Is this a driver's license picture?" I ask.

"Yup."

"How'd you get it? Never mind, don't tell me."

"Okay."

"I officially have no idea that you can get into the motor vehicle bureau's computers."

"You want me to get rid of any speeding tickets for you? By the way, I think it's great that you're an organ donor."

I'm about to answer when the phone rings, and Laurie picks it up. After saying "Hello," she just listens for about twenty seconds and says, "Okay." It's a stirring conversation.

She hangs up and says, "Willie's going to pick you up in ten minutes. You're going to see Joseph Russo."

"I guess I do have something else to do today."

Usually when I am facing something that could involve personal danger, Laurie insists that Marcus go with me. She knows that when it comes to potential violence, Marcus can handle pretty much anything, and I can handle pretty much nothing.

But the Joseph Russo situation is different. Marcus could protect me in the moment; he could protect me in the moment from an alien invasion. But Russo has an endless supply of dangerous people in his employ, and if he was set on getting to me, he would know that Marcus could not be there forever.

Besides, I'll have Willie with me, and Russo is in Willie's debt. The fact that he's agreed to talk to me is evidence of that.

I call Hike and tell him to get the names of potential grudge holders from Laurie and talk to Carrigan about them. Then I take a few sips of coffee and wait for Willie.

Willie pulls up on time, and Sondra is with him. Laurie is going to drive her back to their house with Zoey. I give Zoey a hug goodbye; I'm going to miss her, but she's much better off at Willie and Sondra's, at least until she has the puppies.

Once we're in the car I ask where we're going to meet Russo.

"At his house," Willie says.

"Did he sound pissed or friendly when you told him I wanted to talk to him?"

"Friendly. Joey always sounds friendly; he's a good guy."

"Willie, he deals in drugs, prostitution, extortion, and has had people murdered. He's a good guy?"

He nods. "Except for that stuff."

The media coverage of the sniper shootings had died down.

Not surprisingly, the public terror had gradually gone from fear to concern to a vague unease. By this point it was mostly gone, since it had been weeks since the last shooting.

The general theory, which the police privately did not disagree with, was that Chuck Simmons had gotten his revenge and gone underground. Part of the reason that law enforcement felt that way was the fact that the manhunt had been so intense; if Simmons was still out and about and planning additional shootings, he would surely have been caught already.

Someone who was uncomfortably close to the situation, and who was seriously afraid he might become a victim, was Drew Stroman. Stroman was Greta Simmons's boyfriend at the time of their divorce.

Greta had been separated from her husband for a few months by the time she met Stroman, and he was not a factor in their marriage breaking up. Nor was he named in any of the legal complaints; in every sense he had nothing to do with anything that happened between husband and wife. And their relationship hadn't lasted; they'd been broken up for months by the time Greta was killed.

But still he worried. There was always the chance that Simmons was misinformed about his role and held a grudge against him, especially since he had been there to show his support for her during the trial.

For all Stroman knew, Chuck Simmons could hold him responsible for the loss of his wife and what he knew of his life. It was unlikely, and people told him that he was safe, but he worried that he could be the next target.

So for weeks Stroman tried to limit his movements; he stayed indoors as much as he could. And he followed the media stories voraciously, hoping to see that the police were making progress, or even better yet had made an arrest. But he also read those same articles hoping not to see his name mentioned. He was included in some stories, but usually with the helpful disclaimer that he had met Greta Simmons after her separation from her husband.

As the public fear died down, so did Stroman's. He still remained concerned and careful, but he was slowly starting to get on with his life. He was himself newly married, and the situation had understandably caused a strain on his wife as well. He resolved finally to put it behind them.

That resolution came to an end, as did his life, when Drew Stroman got off a bus near his house in Wyckoff and a sniper's bullet crashed into his chest.

J oseph Russo lives in the Riverside section of Paterson.

It's a modest house in what is likely the most crime-free neighborhood in the United States. Guys like Russo must be in it for the power; it's not like they use their money to buy fancy stuff. And Russo, like Dominic Petrone before him, doesn't travel or take vacations. If you go to Aruba, or St. Martin, you can swim at the beach without fear of banging into Joseph Russo.

Russo would actually look a bit out of place on the beach. He's about five foot ten and well over three hundred pounds; I wouldn't want to be the lifeguard called upon to pull him out of the water. A tugboat would be more appropriate. But I don't think I'll mention that when I see him.

There are two large bodyguards sitting on the front porch when we arrive. That doesn't deter Willie, who bounds up the steps like he's Sylvester Stallone in Philadelphia. I take it a little slower, but I don't want to fall too far behind Willie. He is my protective umbrella.

The guards don't move a muscle; they just let us enter through the front door. They have obviously been alerted to our arrival. Once we get inside, there is another scary-looking guy waiting for us. He simply points to a door off the foyer and says, "In there."

Willie doesn't miss a beat; he just walks to the door and opens it, with me in tow. It turns out to be a small dining room off the kitchen, and Russo is at the table eating breakfast. He's almost done, and there are three plates of mostly eaten food. Russo does not deny himself nourishment.

Russo stands up, a big smile on his face. "My man," he says. Even though there are two of us here, I notice his use of the singular "man." It's fair to say that I don't have Willie's status with him.

"How's it going, Joey?" Willie says, as they embrace. Willie almost disappears into the enormous mass that is Russo.

Russo turns to me and says, "He's the only one who can call me Joey."

"He's a lucky guy," I say.

"And I call you wiseass."

I nod. "The name seems to fit."

The other times that Russo, Willie, and I have gotten together, Russo has told me some version of the time Willie saved his life in prison. He usually implies that he could have handled the three guys on his own, and I don't mention that I find it highly unlikely, especially since the attackers had makeshift knives. But he always credits Willie with a courageous intervention, worthy of his gratitude.

This time he skips the story, since he probably remembers that I've heard it a bunch of times, or maybe he just doesn't want to spend a lot of time with me. Instead he says, "What's your problem this time?"

I don't mention that "my problem" last time resulted in his

boss going to prison and his moving up to head of the family. That seemed to work out pretty well for him, but I avoid pointing it out.

"No problem; I just need some information."

Russo turns to Willie. "He thinks I'm here to give him information?"

"Andy's a good guy," Willie says.

"Willie likes you."

I nod. "And I like Willie."

"So what do you want to know?" Russo asks.

"Whatever you can tell me about Ernie Vinson."

"He's dead."

"I already knew that. I'm hoping for a little more detail. Favorite color, hobbies, who killed him, that kind of thing."

"How the hell would I know?"

"He worked for you."

Russo shakes his head. "Used to work for me. He quit to go on to bigger and better things, thought he'd make more money and be more important." He laughs. "How'd that work out for him?"

In the moment it dawns on me that Russo might have had him killed for walking out on him. In that case it's unlikely that Russo will break down and tearfully confess.

I decide to switch topics. "Have you read about the homeless guy, Don Carrigan, who was arrested for a murder in Short Hills last year?"

"Was I mentioned in the story?"

"No."

"Then why would I read it?" he asks.

I'm tempted to ask him how he knows if he's mentioned in a story without reading it, but I stifle my curiosity. Maybe he has intelligence briefers who come in every morning with a report on current events, like the president.

"Well, a few weeks ago Carrigan was lying on the street in the middle of the night, and a guy came along and threatened him with a gun. He wanted Carrigan to come with him in an SUV that someone else was driving."

"So?"

"So the guy with the gun was Ernie Vinson."

He does almost a full double take in response, which in Russo's case means that he turns his head so quickly that only three of his four chins have a chance to follow. "How do you know that?"

"DNA," I say.

He shakes his head. "Goddamn DNA; they never should have invented that shit."

"Except for Facebook, it's the worst invention of all time," I say. "But it was definitely Ernie Vinson."

"Going after a homeless guy?"

"Yes."

He pauses for a few moments, as if for the first time in the conversation he cares about what he is going to say. "Okay, here's the story. Vinson came to me a while back, maybe a year, maybe a few months more. He says he wants out, that something has come up where he can make big money.

"I don't ask what it is," Russo continues. "Because I don't give a shit what it is. He's a stand-up guy, not a brain in his head, but a stand-up guy. When he worked for me, if I told him to walk in front of a train, he'd walk in front of a train.

"So he came to me like a stand-up guy and said he wanted to leave. So I said, 'Don't go near my territory,' and he said it had nothing to do with my territory. So I said 'Go ahead, make your money.'"

"Do you know what he was doing?"

"No. That's the last I heard of him until I heard he was dead."

My tendency is to believe Russo, at least to the extent that I no longer think he was the one that had Vinson killed.

I haven't learned much, and the little I did learn makes it even more confusing. If Vinson suddenly had gotten a job that was making him a lot of money, what could he have possibly wanted with Don Carrigan?

Maybe it was the same talents that Carrigan used to fend off Vinson that made him appealing in the first place. Maybe somehow Vinson was going to attempt to utilize Carrigan's unique military training to help him commit some kind of violent act.

But I have no idea how Vinson would have known about Carrigan's abilities, where Carrigan was, or how he would have expected to get Carrigan to cooperate.

Which brings me to Jaime Tomasino.

I had sent Hike to ask Carrigan about the people that might have a grudge against him.

He's done that, and in the process Carrigan gave him a couple of additional names to consider. But I deliberately didn't want Hike to mention Jaime Tomasino to Carrigan; I want to do that myself. I want to see and measure his reaction.

Tomasino is the individual that the prosecution has put forward as a witness; he will apparently testify that Carrigan confessed the McMaster murder to him.

"Do you know someone called Jaime Tomasino?" I ask Carrigan, once we're settled in.

He thinks for a few moments, as if trying to place the name. Or maybe's he's pretending to be trying to place the name; I'm sure I wouldn't be able to tell the difference. "I don't think so," he says. "Who is he? Where would I know him from?"

"The soup kitchen you ate some meals at."

"Oh, then it's possible I know him. Most people that go there don't give their names. I mean, you have to give your name when you sign in, but you wouldn't use it in conversation. I talked to a few people there, but I don't think I knew any of their names."

"He says that you admitted to him that you killed McMaster."

He reacts in surprise and then shakes his head. "That's ridiculous. I didn't kill him, so why would I say that? And if I had killed him, why would I say that?"

"Any idea why he would claim that you did?"

"No, but that's more your area than mine. I assume he had something to gain by lying, maybe some financial inducement. Money is in rather short supply among soup kitchen patrons."

"Was there anyone there you would describe yourself as friendly with?"

He shakes his head. "No, it's not a large room, and it's usually crowded. Not someplace I'd want to hang out in, for obvious reasons."

I take out the driver's license photo that Sam gave me, and I place it in front of Carrigan. "This jog your memory at all? This is Tomasino."

He shakes his head. "I can't say I've never seen him, but I'm good with faces. If I talked with him at any length, I'd remember. So if I spoke to him at all, the conversations would have been brief and inconsequential. But I don't think I did."

"Okay," I say. "I'm going to try and talk to him."

I start to stand but stop when he starts talking again. "You know, I didn't believe it, but you may be right."

I never tire of hearing that I'm right, so I sit back down. "What do you mean?"

"Your hypothesis that I've been framed. I didn't think so; my view was either that the DNA testing was wrong, or that somehow my stolen hat happened to wind up in the possession of the actual killer. Having said that, I never did come up with an explanation for the ring in the locker."

I know where he's going, but I let him finish.

"But if someone is putting this Tomasino guy up to lying about me, then it has to be more than that. There really has to be someone behind it, someone probably with money to spend."

"Did you ever think about becoming a defense attorney?" I ask.

He smiles a sad smile. "Yeah, it's at the top of my bucket list. Would I be allowed to practice outdoors?"

I leave the jail and head for the soup kitchen, which is called "Welcome Home." It's three o'clock in the afternoon, so I'm hoping to get there when it's not yet in the middle of the dinner rush. I doubt they have early bird specials.

It's a combination shelter–soup kitchen and it's located just off Market Street, not far from Eastside High School. I graduated from Eastside, yet as I pass by I notice that strangely there is still no statue of me commemorating that fact.

When I enter I'm struck by how clean the place is. It looks very much like a school cafeteria; there is a long counter where people push their trays along as they are served by other people behind the glass partitions, which are there to cover the food.

There are long tables set up end to end horizontally across the room; without counting I'd say they can seat at least eighty people. Of course, right now there are no people and no food; this is not meal time, so there is no reason for anyone to be here.

Probably there are people in the shelter section of the operation, so I set out to find out, but I'm stopped by the sound of a door opening. I turn and see that about twenty people are exiting a room. They barely glance at me and just head for the door to the outside.

The last person out, a tall guy probably in his early fifties, sees me and asks, "Can I help you? We don't start serving until five o'clock."

"I'm here for conversation, not food," I say.

He smiles. "For that we're open all day. I'm Sean Aimonetti; I'm the director here. And you are . . . ?"

He offers his hand and I shake it. "Andy Carpenter. Just curious, is that a class you were teaching?"

"It was an alcohol counseling session. Dealing with alcoholism is a specialty of mine, so I do double duty here. Now, how can I help you?"

"I'd like to talk to you about a case I'm working on; my client has been here."

He nods. "Right, Andy Carpenter. I thought I recognized you; I've seen you on television."

"I'm even better looking in person," I say. I've had a lot of cases that have gotten significant media coverage, so he probably has seen me in reference to an earlier case. I haven't been on television on this case yet, emphasis on the "yet."

Another smile. "Six of one, half a dozen of the other. Is this about Don Carrigan? Are you representing him?"

"I am."

"The police have been here; I've answered their questions. And they brought a search warrant to empty out his locker."

"Did you get to know Don at all?"

He shakes his head. "No, not really. We have a lot of people coming through here."

"Do they come through mostly anonymously, or do they provide information about themselves?"

He shrugs. "We ask for information; sometimes they provide it, sometimes they don't. Sometimes it is accurate; sometimes it isn't. Providing information is not a requirement to receive food and shelter."

"Another person's name has come up in connection with the case. He's a patron here as well and he claims to have been a confidant of Mr. Carrigan. One Jaime Tomasino."

"I don't know him," he says. "But James might."

"James?"

He nods. "James Lasky. He's much more involved with the clients here. We don't invade their privacy, but we do need to make sure there are no disruptive issues. Unfortunately mental illness can be one of the causes of homelessness, and those suffering from it often don't get the treatment they need and deserve. But we need to make sure no clients endanger any of the others or our staff."

"And James Lasky oversees that effort?" I ask.

"He does."

"Can I talk to him?"

"I think he's next door in the shelter. Let's go."

Before we do I ask where Don Carrigan's locker is. "Is it over at the shelter?"

"No, as I understand it, he came here only for food; he did not spend his nights here. So it would be in that room over there; let me show you."

He leads me to the room, and there must be a hundred lockers. I walk along them, checking them out. "Can I take some photos of this room, so I can refer to it?"

He shrugs. "Sure."

I do so and then say, "Time for Mr. Lasky."

The shelter side of Welcome Home is not unlike the kitchen side.

It's a series of cots, almost like an army barracks, but with at least ten feet of space separating each one. There are lockers along the back wall, and bathrooms along the side wall. The place is very clean and well kept, with a general feel of dignity for the "clients." I'm impressed by the work these people are doing in caring for those who are far down on the luck totem pole.

There are five or six patrons sitting on the bunks; I assume it doesn't fill up until nighttime, or maybe after the dinner next door. My further assumption is that the shelter clients are also food clients, but I don't know that for sure.

Sean Aimonetti leads me into a back office where a man in his midthirties is talking on the phone. Based on his side of the conversation, it seems to be a matter concerning laundry, maybe the cleaning of the sheets and bedding.

About thirty seconds later he gets off the phone, and Aimonetti introduces me to James Lasky. "This is Andy Carpenter, James. He's a lawyer with some questions that you could probably answer better than me."

"Let's hear them; I've got a lot to do."

Aimonetti says he's going to leave the two of us alone, which is exactly what he does.

"It's about two of your clients, Don Carrigan and Jaime Tomasino."

He nods. "I heard about Carrigan . . . too bad. I know both of them. Carrigan never stayed overnight; Tomasino used to."

"But not anymore?"

"Not for a while," he says. "What do you want to know?" Everything about him—his body language, his tone of voice, his facial expression—all seems designed to tell me how busy he is and how little time he has to give me.

"Did they have a relationship?"

"What does that mean?"

"Did they talk to each other a lot?"

"I think so. I mean I don't know if they were buddies, but it strikes me that they did. I wouldn't swear to it. Carrigan usually wasn't much of a talker, but Tomasino was."

"You keep track of these things?" I ask, surprised at his answer.

"I don't keep records about it, but I keep my eyes open. I have to anticipate trouble, which is why we don't have much of it."

"What can you tell me about Tomasino?"

"What do you mean?"

"If he doesn't come here anymore, do you know where he's living?" I already have that information from Sam, but I want to see if Lasky is going to be forthcoming.

"No," Lasky says.

"Do you know what his occupation was, or is?"

"No."

"Would you call me if he comes in again?"

"No. These people deserve privacy like everyone else."

I thank Lasky, though he basically gave me nothing, and I leave.

On the way home, I try to sift through all of this. Basically it comes down to who I believe and who I don't believe.

Carrigan falls into the "I believe" category. Part of the reason for that is he is my client, so I have to start with a trust in what he is telling me. If he's lying, we're going to go down in flames. But I also have come to trust him.

He could have told me that he knew Tomasino, but that he never confessed to him. But he was adamant that he didn't know him, and I take that at face value.

So that leaves the people I don't believe. Obviously Tomasino falls into that category, and he can't be just wrong, he has to be lying. A murder confession is something that would make an impression; one would accurately remember if he heard it or not.

Tomasino said he heard it; Carrigan and I say not.

Lasky falls into a slightly different category. He thought that Tomasino and Carrigan had talked on occasion, but wouldn't swear to it. So he's of no value to me, and more likely to be called by the prosecution than by us.

Unfortunately, one thing the prosecution doesn't need is another compelling witness.

The prevailing wisdom was that Chuck Simmons had run out of people to shoot.

He had gunned down his ex-wife, her boyfriend, and her divorce attorney in relatively rapid succession, and to that point had escaped unscathed. The police had no idea where he might be, and though they weren't saying so publicly, they even recognized the possibility that he had taken his own life, having accomplished his mission.

There would seem to be two other people who should have been in danger, based on Simmons's actions to date. They would be his own attorney, in the event that Simmons felt he was poorly represented, and especially the judge who presided over the case, and who made the adverse rulings.

But for various reasons, which the media had pointed out with great frequency, those two people had nothing to worry about.

Simmons's lawyer was in the clear because he didn't exist. Simmons had represented himself, despite the advice of everyone, including the judge, that he hire competent counsel. He didn't listen, evidence in the current public's mind that he is as stupid as he is crazy and violent.

The judge, Alan Yount, was also not a viable candidate to be Simmons's next victim. Judge Yount was off the hook because he was already dead. He died a year earlier of a sudden and massive heart attack.

No one suspected that Judge Yount's death was suspicious in any way. Unless Simmons spent years somehow forcing the judge to smoke and pig out on fast food, he was in the clear.

But since the media needed angles to keep the story going, they focused some attention on Judge Yount's son, Eric Yount, who also happened to be a judge. The younger Judge Yount was a federal superior court judge in the Southern District of New York, and was an expert in business and financial cases.

Judge Eric Yount agreed to do one interview on CNN, during which he claimed to have no knowledge of the Simmonses' divorce case whatsoever. He correctly pointed out that his father, as a family court judge, handled thousands of similar cases over the course of his career.

Additionally Eric was long out of the house, through law school, and a judge himself when the Simmons case was heard. His father had never even mentioned it to him in passing, probably because there was nothing extraordinary about it.

The interviewer pointed out that Simmons himself obviously found it very extraordinary, so much so that he had killed three people as a result.

Judge Eric Yount expressed his sympathy for the victims and their families, voiced his hope that the police would soon get their man, and then said he was done talking about the case.

It had nothing whatsoever to do with him.

According to Sam's information, Jaime Tomasino lives just off of Grand Avenue in Englewood.

I'm on my way there now with Laurie. I'm going because I want to question him, and Laurie's coming along because she wants to make sure that Tomasino doesn't punch me while I'm talking.

I tried to talk her out of coming. "There's no reason to think it will get violent," I said. "I just want to talk with him, and I'll be charming while I do it."

"Andy, you can be really annoying when you talk," she said, but I didn't ask for examples.

Before we go I bring a small recording device that I often use; I want to preserve any comments Tomasino makes for, if not posterity, then trial. It's legal to do so, though not considered very ethical for a lawyer; there's sort of an unwritten rule against secretly recording witness interviews. I'm not even a big fan of written rules, so I pretty much ignore unwritten ones.

As we approach Tomasino's small house, the front door

opens and a man comes out. Based on the photo we have, I'm pretty sure it's him, but not positive.

"Let's find out," Laurie says, but I hold her back.

"Let's see where he's going first." I'm not sure why I want to wait; I suppose it's that when I see where he's headed it will represent a piece of information. To a defense attorney, to any attorney, information is the currency of the realm.

He starts walking down the block, and we follow at a decent distance behind. He doesn't seem to be heading for a car, which is good, because by the time we got back to ours we'd have lost him.

After about four blocks he turns into a restaurant called Manulo's Steakhouse. Laurie and I walk to the window in time to see the maître d' lead him to a table for two, though he removes the other set of silverware.

They seem to think that no one will be joining Mr. Tomasino, which is factually incorrect. I'll be sitting across from him in a matter of moments.

I tell Laurie I want to do this alone; I think it will go better one-on-one. "You can watch through the window and shoot him if things get rough," I say.

There is a menu on the window, and I see that steaks go as high as forty dollars. Not quite New York prices, but a hell of a long way from the Welcome Home soup kitchen.

I turn on the recorder, then go in and walk right past the maître d'. It's a nice restaurant, well appointed, but at this early hour there are only four tables occupied, one by Tomasino. The music in the background is Sinatra singing "Someone to Watch over Me."

"Hey, aren't you Jaime Tomasino?" I ask as I reach his table.

"Yeah. Who are you?"

"Andy. Andy Carpenter! Don't you remember me? We went to different schools together." As I'm talking, I sit down on the chair opposite him.

"What the hell are you talking about?" he asks.

I pick up the menu and glance at it quickly. "Hey, not a bad menu. You going to have the filet? I thought you were more into soup? Anyway, I hear you know Don Carrigan."

"Who's that?"

"You don't know Don Carrigan?"

He pauses to remember, and seems to. "Oh, yeah. Carrigan. The guy who did that murder. Who are you?"

"I'm his friend. I'm trying to help him, but not if he's guilty."

"They told me not to talk to anybody."

"Who? The prosecutors?"

"I don't want to say. You should take off."

"I just have a couple of questions, then I'm out of here. Carrigan told you he killed that guy?"

"Yeah. He bragged about it."

"You sure it was the same Carrigan? Short black guy?"

He hesitates. "Yeah, that's him."

There aren't many more beautiful sentences I've heard in my life than Tomasino saying, "Yeah, that's him," thereby proclaiming that the tall white Carrigan is a short black guy.

No matter how much someone paid Tomasino to lie, they are not getting their money's worth.

I could confront him more, but I have to be careful here. The last thing I want is to scare him and have him go back to the prosecutor, or whoever paid him to rat out Carrigan, and describe the conversation. I don't want anyone to know that he couldn't identify Carrigan; I want the pleasure of doing that in court.

"So you don't want to talk to me about this?" I ask.

"Right. I want to have dinner."

"Okay, I understand. Enjoy the steak, although I see quite a bit of soup in your future."

When I get outside, Laurie says, "That was quick. Did you find out anything?"

I nod. "I did. He's lying, and he's being paid to lie."

Tonight is finally Christmas Eve, so Laurie, Ricky, and I wrap the gifts for under the tree.

Laurie handled getting Ricky's gifts, so my one job was getting something for her. I don't usually do well in these kinds of situations; Laurie is tough to buy for.

She's big on experiential stuff, but if I'm going to share in the experience, it's got to be something I'll find bearable. I don't want to get stuck apple picking or tree cutting again.

I think I've solved the problem beautifully, if I do say so myself. I've gotten all of us a trip to Tuscany. Neither she nor Ricky has ever been out of the country, and I know she's wanted to go to Italy for a long time. I think Ricky will get a lot out of it as well. I was in Italy once when I was a teenager, and I loved it.

We go to sleep early because we know that Ricky will be deliberately making noise to wake us up at the crack of dawn. This is Ricky's third Christmas with us, and by now his excitement about this day is clear. Laurie and I never used to give holidays like this that much thought, but we enjoy it much more now that we can see it through Ricky's eyes.

I do, of course, have a bone to pick regarding the holiday; the NFL doesn't have a single game scheduled. How come Thanksgiving has three games and Christmas gets shut out? Sometimes, depending on the day Christmas falls, the NFL will have a game or two, but today being Friday, there's not a single one. I am outraged.

Fortunately, the NBA treats Christmas like their biggest day of the year, and they have five excellent games scheduled back-to-back. Ricky and I will watch most of them together, allowing me to see the games and get credit as an involved father. Two birds with one basketball.

It's a very enjoyable day with family. Everybody was very happy with their gifts, including me. I got a new iPad, and since I never had an old iPad, I'm looking forward to Ricky teaching me how to use it. Laurie and Ricky loved the Italy trip idea, and she has already gone online and ordered about two thousand guide books.

I'm a lucky guy, and I'm smart enough to know it. I think on and off about the Carrigan case throughout the day; I can't help myself. But basically I keep it in the back of my mind, ready to move to the front tomorrow.

Unfortunately, I'm not going to be able to wait until to-morrow, because soon after Ricky goes to sleep, Marcus calls and Laurie tells him to come over. He's got information that he believes we'll want, so she figures we might as well hear it now.

Marcus and Laurie perform a quick hug-and-kiss "Merry Christmas" maneuver, and when I wish Marcus the same, he gives me a holiday grunt. It warms my heart, but not enough for me to add a hug and kiss.

Marcus has been running down all the various people on

our list of potential grudge holders against Carrigan. It includes the people that Carrigan has had violent encounters with since leaving the service, as well as a couple of people in the service that he considered potential enemies.

I let Laurie do the talking to Marcus, because she is the only person in the room who can understand his responses. The truth is that when he talks, which is rare in itself, I find myself looking for subtitles.

But I can get what he's saying by listening to Laurie's responses, and what I understand is that he has narrowed it down to four possibles. He doubts that any of them have framed Carrigan, but these are the four most likely.

I tell Marcus about Tomasino, and the strong probability that he was paid to lie. I ask him to factor this in, and eliminate any of the suspects who would not be in a position to put up the money. I also ask him to remove those who would not likely have the smarts to conceive what is becoming a complicated criminal conspiracy.

This prompts him to remove three people from the list, leaving just one. "You know where he is?" Laurie asks.

"Yunh," Marcus says. It's accompanied by a slight nod, so I'm assuming the answer is yes.

"Right now?"

Another "Yunh."

"So let's get him out of the way. You need me to come along?"

Laurie can provide armed backup and has faced dangerous situations many times as a police officer. Since the guy is a drug dealer, I'm expecting Marcus might consider bringing her along.

Of course, I'm wrong.

"Nenh." Accompanied by a negative shake.

"You ready?" Laurie asks, this time directing the question to me.

"For what?"

"To check out the drug dealer."

"Nenh," I say, but she and Marcus seem to take that as a yes. I've got to learn to enunciate better, but it's tough since grunting is not my native tongue. I can't claim that it's unseemly to visit a drug dealer on Christmas, since for Laurie Christmas doesn't end until February, and by that point Carrigan's trial will be over.

So it appears I am not going to be able to watch the Houston Rockets play the Minnesota Timberwolves tonight.

Jimmy Greer is a young, successful entrepreneur.

According to Laurie, translated from the mouth of Marcus, he's not more than thirty, but has firmly established himself as a top executive in his fields. His fields are drug dealing and prostitution, and business is great.

The fact that Greer even exists is a commentary on the reign of Joseph Russo. When Dominic Petrone was in charge, he ruled these areas with an iron hand. It isn't that Russo is more tolerant; it's more that he's less organized and probably less greedy. So he doesn't watch as closely or come down as hard on transgressors, and people like Greer fill the breach.

Greer's office is on the outskirts of downtown Paterson, near the Great Falls in Passaic. It's not far from Hinchliffe Stadium, a decaying building that used to hold events ranging from old-time Negro League professional baseball to high school football games to car races to boxing matches. I played baseball there a number of times, but I wasn't any better there than I was anywhere else.

The stadium has recently been designated as a historic landmark, and there are always efforts to raise funding to renovate it. I hope they're able to; it makes me feel old to look at it in its current state.

But Greer probably isn't interested in hearing the history of the stadium; he's interested in making money. In his business the nighttime hours are the most important, which is why Marcus is sure he will be at the storefront that serves as his office, even on Christmas night.

There are quite a few people hanging out on the street when we pull up. I can see everybody staring at us even before we get out of the car; we are an unfamiliar intrusion in an area where anything unfamiliar is considered potentially dangerous.

It's a relatively warm night, so though people are wearing coats and jackets, they have obviously decided to finish off Christmas hanging out and being sociable. But there is one garbage can with a fire in it, and people standing around it taking in its warmth. I expect that any moment I'll run into Rocky Balboa.

Marcus nods toward a storefront, and I assume the man standing in front of it smoking a cigarette is Jimmy Greer. He's a pretty big guy, maybe six foot two and two hundred pounds. Based on his build, when he's not peddling drugs and women, he might well work out a lot.

Jimmy had a run-in with Don Carrigan a couple of years ago in a bar. Jimmy was smaller time then, with no organization to command. Carrigan saw him providing drugs to kids that seemed underage, and he intervened.

Jimmy didn't appreciate the intervention and they took their dispute outside. It didn't go well for Jimmy; Carrigan broke his nose and knocked out two teeth. Both men were taken into custody and released without being charged. As the winner, Carrigan would have been the most likely to feel the brunt of the justice system, but by then the cops had a good idea what Jimmy was about, and they were fine with him getting beaten up.

Jimmy had vowed revenge on Carrigan, which is basically why we're here. He now has more money and resources, so that revenge could theoretically be more easily exacted. And since robbery arrests are also in Jimmy's glorious past, by robbing McMaster and framing Carrigan, he could have accomplished a double triumph.

We get out of the car, Marcus casually and me reluctantly. I always seem to get into these situations, but I never get used to them. I'm nervous to the point where my throat is constricted, which is a problem, because if we count on Marcus to do the talking, we'll be here until baseball season starts.

Jimmy is talking with a man larger than he is, but I detect a dynamic in the body language between them that says Jimmy is the boss, and the other guy is the subordinate. We walk right up to them, and the other guy seems to back away, thereby confirming my body language assessment.

"What do you assholes want?" Jimmy asks. As affable conversation starters go, this was not a promising one.

"We want to talk to you about Don Carrigan," I say.

"Who's tha—" he starts to ask, before the memory seems to kick in. "What about him? He's in jail for murdering that rich guy, right?"

In addition to the guy talking to Greer when we walked up, other people are in listening distance of our conversation, and everybody seems interested.

"Maybe we can talk somewhere more private?" I ask.

A hint of a smile comes across his face. "Yeah, we can go to a private place. Sure."

I think I see him make eye contact with others on the street as we all turn and walk into the building. I'm not liking this at all, but Marcus seems fairly sanguine about the whole thing. Marcus has the amazing ability to be simultaneously unconcerned and totally ready for anything. I retain the opposite ability to be obsessively concerned and helpless in anything remotely resembling an emergency.

We go into the storefront and then through a door along the back wall into what is apparently Greer's office. He goes behind his desk and sits down. There are no other chairs in the room; obviously Greer doesn't care if his business associates are comfortable. "Why do you care about that asshole Carrigan?"

"He's accused of robbery and murder. I'm trying to find out if he did it." I pause for effect, then, "Or if you did." I am blunt like that because my goal in situations like this is not to find out information, but rather to make an assessment. Greer is not going to confess, and he's very unlikely to make a slipup that would reveal his guilt. I just want to get a feel for whether or not he could have, and might have, pulled this off. That way we will know whether to investigate him more intensively.

Greer's reaction is to laugh. "You think you can come in here, to my place, on my turf, and accuse me of murder? Is that what you think? Let me tell you something, if I want to go after Carrigan, I don't kill some rich guy and set him up. I kill him."

As unpleasant as Greer is, what he is saying makes logical sense; I'm afraid I don't see him as having the subtlety necessary to have pulled this off.

Suddenly, the door that we came through opens and three men come in. They are either tough guys, or doing a good job pretending to look tough. One of them is the guy Greer was talking to when we pulled up.

Greer laughs again. "These assholes accusing me of murder. They come into my place and accuse me of damn murder."

He is talking to the three newcomers, and the assholes he is referring to are me and Marcus. Greer is clearly wounded by the insult of my accusation, as if he has spent his life doing all he can for the betterment of society. He continues, "Maybe we should show them what we think of them coming in here like this."

I think I see the three guys start to move toward us, but they stop frozen in place because Marcus is holding a gun on them. I didn't see Marcus draw the gun; it just seemed to appear. Marcus is not someone you want to run into at high noon at the OK Corral.

"Wall," Marcus says; at least I think that's what he says. I'm not sure if anyone else understands, because nobody moves or reacts.

Marcus has the gun in his left hand, and he walks over to one of the guys and with his right hand turns him and throws him against the wall, face-first. The sound of the guy's head hitting the wall is thunderous. If he's an NFL player, I'm thinking he's going to go into the concussion protocol and come out of it maybe three years from Wednesday.

"Wall," Marcus says again, and the other two guys now fully understand and join their buddy in turning and facing the wall, placing their hands against it. Marcus quickly frisks them and removes five guns from the three guys; apparently one of them felt that only one gun was enough. All the time he is doing this, Greer is frozen in place, smart enough not to attempt to intervene.

Marcus next does the worst possible thing, next to walking out and leaving me alone with this group. He hands me the gun. I don't do well with guns, but he says, "Watch," and points to Greer, which I assume means I'm supposed to hold the gun on Greer.

I do that, and if I were Greer I would be concerned, because my hand is shaking so much I could easily press the trigger by mistake.

My vantage point and peripheral vision is such that I can see everyone in the room. Marcus turns the three guys around, and it's fair to say that they look disapproving of what has happened so far. But now neither Marcus nor they have guns, and they are three and he is one.

Because of that they are both emboldened and stupid.

Not necessarily in that order.

Marcus makes a motion that they should come and get him, which is what they proceed to do. At least two of them do; the guy whose head hit the wall at warp speed still has the dazed look of a guy whose head hit a wall at warp speed. It has either rendered him incapable of action or knocked some sense into that head. Either way, he is not engaging.

The other two guys make two mistakes. The first one is not running out the door they came in. Their second mistake, at least the way I see it, is not arriving at Marcus at the same time. One of them gets there about two seconds before the other. Two seconds in Marcus-time is an hour and a half to anyone else.

Marcus completely dismantles them. He hits the first to arrive with an elbow in the head, and the poor guy topples over like he's the seven pin and Marcus has just converted a spare. The other guy arrives those two seconds later, which is not enough time for him to see what happened to his buddy and reassess his involvement, should he have been bright enough to make the effort.

Marcus is ready and waiting for him. He kicks him in the groin, and when the guy screams and doubles over, Marcus uppercuts him and literally lifts him off his feet. Gravity asserts itself and the guy lands on top of his fallen colleague. If they ever come to, they will forever envy the guy whose head hit the wall.

I hand the gun back to Marcus, and then I turn to Greer. "If I find out you were involved in this thing, I'll be back. And next time I won't go so easy on you."

We leave and go straight to the car. People on the street are staring at us, probably surprised that we are walking out intact, and not being carried out in bags. They obviously don't know me and Marcus.

The good news is that three shitheads got their asses kicked and Greer got humiliated. The bad news is that I don't think there's any chance he had McMaster killed or framed Carrigan.

But it was a holiday night I won't soon forget. As the song goes, "It's Christmas time in the city."

Judge Eric Yount couldn't seem to avoid the subject, much as he wanted to.

An obscure case that his father handled quite a few years ago, the divorce of Chuck Simmons and his wife, is all anybody wanted to talk about. His father has passed away, which is probably the only reason he was not on Simmons's target list. But that, Eric tried to tell people, should be the end of it.

Maybe it should have been, but it wasn't. Eric Yount had by this point come to characterize his friends and acquaintances into two groups. One consisted of those who talked to him about the sniper situation, and the other included those who would have liked to talk to him about it, but were hesitant to do so.

Even among his colleagues, there was no escape. On this day, Eric was having lunch with a close colleague and friend, Judge Lawrence Alexander. They were the two business and financial experts on the court, and handled almost all of those cases that came along. Judge Alexander was about to start an important patent case and Judge Yount was a couple of months away from a major merger dispute. They kept apprised of each other's cases, in case one of their caseloads got crowded to the point that the other would ever have to step in and take over.

Those issues were what Eric Yount preferred to be discussing, but Judge Alexander kept mentioning things about the sniper case, and Eric's peripheral involvement in it. They'd discussed it many times before, but clearly the case had a fascination that even seasoned judges found irresistible.

But it was dying down a bit. There had not been a shooting for quite a while, mainly because there seemed to be no one left to shoot. With no new leads appearing as to Simmons's whereabouts, Eric could feel a slight lessening of interest among those he interacted with.

Eric and Judge Alexander had a tradition which they'd been following at their lunches for almost three years. Eric would bring a deck of cards, and they'd cut them to see who would pay for the lunch, high card eats for free.

It had no real effect on their personal economics, both because the lunches weren't particularly expensive, and over time the number of victories for each side evened out. On this day, Eric drew a ten, and Judge Alexander a jack, so Eric paid.

Eric asked for the check, in a bit of a hurry. He had a couple of hearings on his docket for the early afternoon, nothing crucial but it would be unseemly for everyone to be there and the judge to show up late.

They left the restaurant, Eric walking out first. Judge Alexander said something to him, and he turned to respond. Just as he started doing so, he saw a glint of metal in the window of a building across the street.

It wasn't that Eric was afraid, but something made him move to his left. An instant after he did so, the shot rang out, missing Eric but hitting Judge Alexander in the chest.

He was dead before he hit the cement.

No one had expected Chuck Simmons to exact revenge on the son of the judge who handled his divorce case. The media went crazy when the news broke. Demands were made, by the public and politicians alike, for the capture and arrest of Chuck Simmons.

In a particularly inappropriate and irresponsible response, media outlets started speculating on who could possibly be next. The bailiff who was there during the Simmons divorce trial? The court clerk? The court reporter?

And what about other family members? If the judge's son could be a target, what about the lawyer's brother? Or the ex-wife's mother? It all seemed ridiculous, but so had the idea that Judge Yount's son might be in danger.

As for that son, immediate and intensive security was ordered for Judge Eric Yount, and it would remain in place until Chuck Simmons was in police custody, or dead.

Andy, can I come over? I've got something you'll want to hear," Sam says.

He's calling at seven thirty in the morning, so it is obviously something he considers important.

"Sam, you're welcome here anytime, but I can actually hear words over the phone. Talk some, and I'll show you how it works."

"It's easier in person, but . . ."

"No, whatever you say. Come on over." I'm actually anxious to hear this, since Sam prefers giving bad news, or no news, over the phone. If he wants to come to the house, especially at this hour, he must think this is really good.

Laurie immediately starts getting ready to make waffles. Sam loves waffles, though what he really loves is maple syrup. Sam would willingly eat horse shit if he could pour syrup on it. It will only take about ten minutes for Sam to get here, but it's not a waffle problem, because Laurie won't be baking or churning or whatever you do to make waffles. All she'll do is take them out of the freezer.

Sam arrives promptly and heads straight for the kitchen table. One of his talents is that he can talk with a mouthful of waffles. "I went through Ernie Vinson's phone records," he says to Laurie and me. "You guys are going to love this."

Sam has a tendency to dramatically draw these things out. "Let's hear it," I say.

"You want the good news, or the great news?"

"In any order you want, but it would be good if the news started flowing sooner rather than later."

"Okay, let's start with the good. I think I know who was driving the SUV the night Vinson tried to mug Carrigan."

"Who?"

"A creep by the name of Danny Costa."

"Why is he a creep?"

"He's been in and out of jail. Twice for drugs, once for passing a bad check. Nothing big time, but not an asset to society."

"How do you know it's him?"

"I don't for sure, but I've narrowed it down, and he's the most likely candidate. He had three calls with Vinson that day, and two the day after. And he drives a black SUV, four years old."

"You know where he lives?"

He takes another forkful of waffle before nodding; a little syrup is dripping down his chin, but I don't want to slow things down by pointing it out. "Yup."

This is a terrific piece of information, and if it's only the good news, I am very much looking forward to finding out what Sam considers great.

"Now for the great news," Sam says, right on cue. "I went back a long way in Vinson's records, looking for something that might ring a bell. Guess who he spoke to two days before Steven McMaster was killed."

"Tell me."

"You don't want to guess?"

"Sam, tell me now or you've sucked down your last waffle."

"Okay, you ready? Vinson spoke to none other than Karen McMaster. He called her and they spoke for almost three minutes."

Boom.

This opens up an entirely new aspect to the case, and I'm embarrassed to say that I haven't contemplated it before. The person who had the most to gain, at least financially, from Steven McMaster's death was his wife, Karen.

If I was going to follow the best advice anyone ever gave anyone, "follow the money," I should have at least considered the possibility that she was involved. But I never did.

Of course, it's possible she had nothing to do with this, even after Sam's revelation. But Ernie Vinson was not chairing some charity dinner that Karen McMaster was involved with. He was not a member of her book club, nor did they attend polo matches together.

Ernie Vinson was a thief and a murderer; he was a former enforcer in Dominic Petrone's and then Joseph Russo's families. I cannot think of a single reason for him to have had contact with Karen McMaster. And when you add in the fact that it was just before her husband's murder, the coincidence meter explodes.

"Sam, when you're finished with your waffles, find out everything you can about Karen McMaster."

Zoey is officially a mother of six puppies.

Willie called to give us the news this morning, and I'm on the way over to see the new family. But the vet said that mother and puppies are in great shape.

Sure enough, all looks good, and the puppies are already adorable. Zoey seems exhausted, which makes perfect sense, but she's comfortable. Bringing her here was a good idea; Willie and Sondra are in a much better position to take care of her.

I hang out for a while, petting her and the other dogs, and then unfortunately have to go back to real life. Real life means thinking about the case, and trying to come up with an approach that can be productive.

My operating theory is that Ernie Vinson killed Steven McMaster.

It seems to make sense considering the facts currently at our disposal. The fact that I am not close to getting it admitted at trial, or getting a jury to believe it, does not worry me, at least not yet. We're going to investigate and get more facts to prove our hypothesis.

I'm also assuming that Vinson is the guy who tried to attack Carrigan originally, when he stole his hat to place at the scene, thereby using Carrigan's DNA to implicate him. Of course, it's always possible that he was attacking him for other reasons, and just liked the hat enough to wear it to a murder, but that seems unlikely.

It's the reason for the second attack on Carrigan, on the night Zoey bit him, that I don't understand. What would he have to gain from that? Was he trying to kill him? And the same question arises: What would he have to gain from that? How was Carrigan a threat to him?

And why now? It's been a long time since the McMaster murder. If Carrigan was a threat to Vinson, then why did he wait so long? And how did he even know where he was? Carrigan was on the street; Vinson couldn't google his address or look him up in the phone book.

And to make matters more confusing, Carrigan had the impression that Vinson was attempting to kidnap and not kill him. Vinson had already discovered that Carrigan could be dangerous and was very capable of handling himself in a violent situation, so why would Vinson take that chance? He could have just driven up and shot him from the SUV.

These are questions I need to answer, and quickly, because the trial is approaching. Which is why Laurie and I are going to see Danny Costa.

Laurie and I discussed whether she or Marcus should be the one accompanying me when I visited with Danny. We checked, and he has a rap sheet of small, non-violent crimes, so we're not that concerned he is dangerous. We chose Laurie because she can serve as my protector and wouldn't be as intimidating to Danny as Marcus would be. Godzilla isn't as intimidating as Marcus.

Danny Costa is a combination gas station attendant and

used car salesman in Garfield. It's a large service station that does mechanical work and body work, besides selling gas. It also has a group of about ten used cars to the side of the place, with prices written in large letters on the windshields.

Marcus has checked out Costa's role here, and it consists of pumping gas and doing the limited work involved with selling the used cars. Costa has someone to help him man the pumps, so he is free to deal with anyone showing up interested in buying a car.

For some reason, probably to preserve jobs, New Jersey is the only state in the country to prohibit self-serve gas pumps. Oregon had been the other one, but they have recently abandoned that law, and now New Jersey stands alone.

Laurie and I pull up and park near the back of the station. We park there so that Costa will not easily know which car is ours. We don't drive a fancy car, it's a Subaru Forester, but it's nicer than the junk that they have on sale. No sense making Costa suspicious as to why we're here.

Laurie waits outside while I go in to find Costa. When I do, I say, "My wife and I were interested in that 2011 Chevy. Can someone show it to us?"

"I'm your man," says Costa.

We go outside and Laurie joins us. "This is my wife, Laurie. This is Mr. . . ."

"Costa," he says. "Danny Costa."

"Hi, Danny. My name is Andy."

We walk toward the car I had mentioned. "You've got a good eye," Costa says. "This is a terrific car. Only fifty-one thousand miles, and gets twenty-six to the gallon." As we reach the vehicle, he pats the hood, as if complimenting it for being such a terrific car.

"I don't know," I say. "What do you think, honey?"

"I think we should ask our questions, sweetie," she says, ice in her voice. Laurie doesn't have as much fun with this stuff as I do.

I point to a black SUV parked nearby. I believe it's Costa's car. "How about that one? Is that for sale?"

"No, that's mine." He indicates the row of cars that we're standing by. "These are the ones that are for sale."

I point to the SUV again. "Look, honey. Isn't that the car we saw Ernie Vinson riding in that night?"

Until this moment we weren't positive that Costa was the one driving Vinson that night, but Costa's facial reaction to my question erases all doubt. And that expression conveys one thing: fear.

"Hey, what's going on?" he asks.

"We're here to ask you about Ernie Vinson, and what happened that night with the homeless man on the street."

"I don't know what you're talking about," he says. "You don't want a car; I've got a job to do here."

"Danny, we know two things with absolute certainty," I say. "You were the driver for Ernie Vinson that night, and this car does not get twenty-six miles to the gallon."

"Who are you?"

"We represent the homeless man that you tried to kill."

"I didn't try to kill anybody. How did you find out about me?"

"Here's the way this is going to work, Danny. We're going to ask the questions. If we like the answers, we won't go to the police. If not, we will. But if we do that, everybody finds out, even the people you're afraid of. It's really pretty simple."

"I didn't try to kill anybody."

"What were you doing there?" Laurie asks.

"Ernie asked me to give him a ride. He said he had a quick job, and he'd pay me."

"How much?"

"A grand. I didn't know what he was going to do."

"What was he doing?" I ask.

He shrugs. "Just grabbing the guy."

"Why?"

"I don't know; he said I wouldn't be a part of it. But then the guy turned out to be pretty tough, and that damn dog bit him."

"What happened then?"

"We drove away, but then he said to go back. He needed to get that guy; I don't know why. I mean, it was just a bum."

"So you went back?" Laurie asks.

"Yeah, but there were cops there. That's when Ernie got really scared. He tried not to show it, but I could tell. He told me not to tell anyone what we did that night, not a word."

"Who was Ernie afraid of?" I ask.

"I don't know; I swear. But Ernie was a tough guy, the toughest I know. If he was scared like that, then there was some dangerous shit going on. And then . . . well, you know what happened to Ernie. I never saw him again."

"Did Ernie say anything else that night? Anything that maybe surprised you?"

He thinks for a few moments. Then, "After he got bitten and we drove off, he was like talking to himself. And he said, 'That's twice I missed that son of a bitch.'"

We have nothing else to ask Costa, so I kick the tires of the Chevy a few times just to show Laurie that I know what I'm doing, and then we leave.

I didn't tell Costa that I might be calling on him to testify at trial, since that would send him running. He's going to resist when and if the time comes, because he won't want his name to be out there.

But I have ways to convince him.

I can prove that Ernie Vinson is the man Zoey bit. He has his DNA on the bloody sleeve that was at the scene. Once we had our DNA results proving that, I withdrew my request that the state have the same test done. I'll reinstate it later; the longer the prosecution is unaware of Vinson's involvement, the better for me.

I can also prove that there was a connection between Vinson and Karen McMaster. Sam has gotten the phone records, and when the time comes I will subpoena them through normal channels. Again, I don't want to do that yet, because I don't want to tip off the prosecution.

I can't prove that Vinson was the one who stole Carrigan's hat, or previously attacked him. I have no doubt in my mind that this is the case, but unfortunately my mind won't be one of the minds on the jury.

Of course, I also can't prove that it was Vinson that murdered Steven McMaster. I believe that he either committed the murder himself, or directed someone else to do it. I also believe that whoever did it planted Carrigan's hat there.

I don't know if Carrigan was chosen specifically for this purpose, or was just in the wrong place at the wrong time and made an easy target for a frame. I suspect it is the latter because I haven't yet found any previous connection between Carrigan and either McMaster or Vinson.

It is also obvious that Vinson was just the hired help. He left Joseph Russo because he had a better job, a chance to make much more money. That in itself is evidence that he was not calling the shots.

More proof lies in what Danny Costa told us about Vinson's fear of someone as yet unidentified. Vinson had been sent to do something to Carrigan and he had failed. He feared that his failure would prove fatal, and he was right.

Vinson was working for scary, powerful people, and for some reason those people had Don Carrigan in their sights. Maybe it was just as a patsy, someone to pin the McMaster murder on. But they had already accomplished their goal; why send Vinson back for round two?

The important thing to uncover now is the reason that Karen McMaster was in contact with Ernie Vinson at all, but specifically why that contact came two days before her husband was murdered. Actually, the *how* might be more interesting than the *why*.

I can believe that Karen wanted her husband dead; I just don't know how she would have found the person to make it happen. There has to be a third party who knew both of them and made the connection.

Sam Willis comes over to give Laurie and me his report on Karen McMaster. The police, based on the discovery documents, did very little work in that area. Ordinarily the spouse has to be eliminated as a suspect early on, especially when that same spouse stands to become single and very wealthy.

But Carrigan was such an obvious choice as the perpetrator

that the cops did little more than cursory work, and what they did uncovered nothing untoward. Karen was a grieving widow who was out of town when the murder happened. She was in the clear.

"Karen McMaster grew up in Nanuet, in Rockland County," Sam says. "She went to Syracuse and majored in interior design. Once she got out of school she moved into the city and got a job at an ad agency, working as an assistant designer for commercial shoots.

"She then moved out of that and started doing her own interior decorating. That's how she met Steven McMaster. Based on the timing, they hit it off right away, which must have made things a little uncomfortable."

"Why?" Laurie asks.

"Because they were both married at the time. Within a year they had divorced their spouses and married each other."

"What a beautiful story," I say. "Love conquers all."

"It certainly improved her lifestyle," Sam says. "McMaster was already loaded. He took over his father's business and built on it. By the time they got married he was worth fifty million dollars."

"What about when he died?"

"Estimate is two fifty." He shakes his head in amazement, then says, "From delivering groceries."

"People gotta eat," I say. "If not for guys like that, you'd be sucking down imaginary waffles, dry without syrup."

He nods at the sad truth of my statement. "Anyway, there was a lot of stuff in the media about their marriage being in trouble. Apparently, Mrs. McMaster was more into high Manhattan society than her grocery clerk husband, and it created a rift. She seemed to be spending most of her time in their

Manhattan apartment, while he hung out in Short Hills. His company office was in Montclair."

"Were either of them fooling around?" I ask.

"I can't say one way or the other. But I can say that the grieving widow did not wear black for a year and hibernate. She was almost immediately seen in the company of one Craig Kimble."

"I think I heard of him," I say. "He's either a rich guy or a relief pitcher for the Red Sox."

"The pitcher is Craig Kimbrel," Laurie points out, elevating herself to an even higher level in my estimation.

"This is the rich guy," Sam says. "Buys companies, either builds them up or strips them down, but sells them at a profit. Also doesn't worry much about legalities; he's always accused of reneging on deals, stealing patents. They take him to court and he wears them down with an army of lawyers."

"An army of lawyers," I repeat. "Like me and Hike. Are Karen and this Kimble guy still together?"

"Doesn't seem like it. My best guess is they split up about four months ago, because she's been seeing other rich guys since. Not that she needs the money."

"I think we should talk to Kimble," Laurie says.

"You got a number, Sam?"

"Of course. You want his private cell phone?"

I can't help but smile. "Why not?"

I dial the number Sam gives me, and it's picked up after one ring. "Craig Kimble?" I ask.

"Who wants to know?"

"My name is Andy Carpenter. I'm a lawyer and—"

"Is there anyone in this country who isn't a lawyer?"

"We do breed a lot," I say. "I want to talk to you about Karen McMaster."

"What about her?"

"I wasn't clear enough. I want to meet and talk to you about Karen McMaster."

"What about her?"

"It's about her husband's murder. When is a good time for you?"

"I don't know anything about it. I'm busy, and—"

"I could ask the judge to issue a subpoena; I doubt he'll factor in the fact that you're busy. So if you spend fifteen minutes telling me what you don't know, we could bypass that."

He relents and says he'll meet with me tomorrow in his Manhattan office. That will give me time to do a Kickstarter campaign to raise money for the parking.

Don Carrigan seems genuinely happy that Zoey gave birth to the puppies.

I stopped off to tell him the news on my way to Kimble's office, and he broke into a wide grin on hearing it. It's the first time I've seen that expression on his face, which is a shame in itself. He deserves better.

"What will happen to the puppies?" he asks.

"We'll take care of them, probably for a couple of months, and then find them good homes. Placing puppies is easy; everybody wants them."

"Good to hear."

"Let me ask you a question," I say. "You told me once that people in your situation, I mean homeless, rarely use your names, even when talking with each other. Just how rare is it?"

"Pretty rare," he says. "I don't want to overstate it, and often we'd use first names, but in that situation, in my situation, identity becomes less important. It's just about getting through the day."

"So you specifically rarely told anyone your last name?"

He nods. "Close to never. Why?"

"I'd love to know how Ernie Vinson knew where you were."

We talk some about the state of his case, which takes the smile off his face. Carrigan is a smart guy who could see through my bullshit even if I attempted to give him any, which I don't. I am always honest with my clients about our chances of success, which means in this case that I have little good to say.

As I'm getting ready to leave, I ask him if he needs anything to read. He declines, saying that the prison library has books, magazines, and newspapers. "I've been reading about that sniper," he says.

I nod. "Not a good situation. They don't seem to be making progress."

"I know Chuck Simmons, the guy they think is doing it."

I'm surprised to hear this. "How?"

"We crossed paths in the service, and then he stayed in my apartment for a couple of weeks after his marriage went south."

"Why did he stay with you?"

"Because I ran into him, and he needed help. He was in a bad way. All he talked about was his ex-wife, and how they robbed him. That's when I could understand him."

"What do you mean?"

"His drinking was pretty much out of control. I tried to talk to him, but he wouldn't hear me. And I'm not the best one to do mental health counseling, you know?"

"You think he's doing the shooting?"

He shrugs. "I wouldn't have; he seemed like a good guy. But he was pretty upset, and it probably ate at him all this time. It's too bad."

"Any idea where he could be?"

He shakes his head. "Not really; I think I heard at one point he was hanging out in Garfield, but that could have been wrong. Sorry. I hope he's okay, and if they find him, I hope they're okay. He's a very tough guy on the rare occasions that he's sober; he wouldn't go down easily."

I leave Carrigan. The only positive aspect I can think of to any of this is that if they catch Simmons, Laurie can't ask me to defend him, because I'm already defending Carrigan.

Kimble's office is on Fifty-Seventh Street near Madison Avenue. I'm going to have to pull into another ridiculous parking lot because if I instead decide to look for the nearest free spot on the street, I'll have to park in Rhode Island.

Kimble's company is called CK Enterprises, and it occupies one floor near the top of the building. When I get off the elevator I am immediately blinded by gleaming steel; everything is shiny and modern. On the wall across from the elevator is what seems like a real street sign that says I am on "K Street," an obvious takeoff on the famous lobbying street in DC.

I tell the receptionist that I'm here, and I am told to take a seat. Twenty minutes later, another young lady, who could be the receptionist's twin sister, comes out to tell me that Mr. Kimble will see me now.

I expect to see someone who seems to be really busy, thus showing that he has very little time for me. Instead, Craig Kimble seems completely relaxed and calm, greeting me with a smile and handshake and offering me something to drink.

Sam mentioned that he has some serious lawsuits he is defending; in fact, he said because of his rather aggressive business practices, he always has serious lawsuits he is defending. But he certainly does not give the appearance of being under any strain.

"So what do you make here?" I say.

"Money," he says, and then laughs, although I'm sure the answer was accurate. Then, "I have a bunch of companies, but I don't maintain an office at any of them. I hire good management, I pay them well, and then I let them run their companies. I only step in when I have to. They get rich and I stay rich."

"You want to buy a small New Jersey law practice?"

Another laugh, followed by, "Now what about Karen McMaster?"

"I'm representing the man wrongly accused of her husband's murder."

He nods. "Yet another wrongly accused man." I'm pretty sure he's being sarcastic, but he says it straight.

"You dated her after Steven was killed?"

He nods again. "And before. They had what could be called an open marriage. It was especially open on Steven's side; he had a pretty good-sized stable going. For Karen it was just me, or at least I think so."

"So her grief when he was killed was short-lived?"

"I wouldn't put it that way; I think she loved the guy. I definitely know for a fact she didn't want him dead. Why should she? She had a good life going."

"She's a lot richer now."

He nods. "True. But for Karen it's not only about having money; it's about showing people that she has the money. She could do that married to Steven, and she can do it now."

"What made you split up?"

"None of your business, but nothing relevant to your case."

"Are you still in touch with her?"

"We're still friends, but that's all. Karen doesn't shed friends.

She's a warm person, plus she never knows when they might come in handy. Especially me."

"Why especially you?"

"The more money one has, the more potentially handy they can be. But don't misunderstand, I really do like Karen."

"You ever hear her mention a guy named Ernie Vinson?"

"Name sounds familiar, but I don't think it's from her. Wasn't that the mob guy who was killed a while back? Or am I thinking of someone else?"

"That's him."

"Karen wouldn't associate with a guy like that. Way beneath her social class." He laughs. "She would consider Prince Charles beneath her social class."

I ask a few more questions, none of which get me closer to any evidence that Karen McMaster had her husband killed.

As I'm leaving, I thank Kimble for his time.

"No problem," he says. "Compared to most of my lawyer meetings, this was relatively pleasant."

On the way home I call Sam and tell him to find out who, if anyone, Kimble called when I left his office. I basically want to know if he is going to warn Karen McMaster that I'm causing trouble.

It wouldn't prove anything if he does call her; he indicated they are still friends. And it wouldn't mean either of them is guilty of anything; even innocent people would want to know if someone is looking into their life.

But it's information that I'd like to have.

Any information is information I'd like to have.

I t was a conversation Judge Linda Abernathy was not looking forward to.

As chief judge, it was Judge Abernathy's job to assign cases. The close-knit group of judges in her court system was devastated by the shooting death of Judge Alexander, but they needed to move on. So that is what she was trying to do.

As one of two financial experts among the court judges, it would be Judge Eric Yount who would normally be called on to take over Judge Alexander's cases. But this situation was nowhere near normal.

For one thing, Judge Yount had been Judge Alexander's closest friend on the court. They were contemporaries, had been confirmed close to the same time, and had the same area of expertise. It was natural that they would become close, and they had.

Another incredibly complicating factor was that Judge Yount was the target of the shooting. Had he not turned when he did, he would have been the victim, and this meeting would be with Judge Alexander. Judge Yount was understandably racked with guilt about it, and had confided in his colleagues that he was undergoing therapy to help deal with it.

To make matters even more difficult, the security around Judge Yount was intense. Just because Simmons had missed him the first time, there was no reason to believe he'd give up. Simmons was apparently deranged enough to blame Eric Yount for how he believed his father wronged him. So the son, Eric, was now essentially a prisoner; he spent all of his time either in his home or in the courthouse.

He was advised not even to walk near windows; it was a terrible way to live, and the restrictions would relax only when Simmons was caught. The strain on his wife, Nancy, was immense and taking its toll on her.

Of course, the situation would have been devastating even without all these complicating factors. A judge had been shot and killed; that just does not happen in this country and cannot be tolerated. The system is not built to handle it. More important, the people affected are not built to handle it.

So Judge Abernathy called Judge Yount into her office; she was intent on treating the court calendar as business as usual, even though they both knew that was impossible. "We need to talk about Lawrence's caseload," she said, referring to the late Judge Alexander by his first name.

Yount nodded his agreement. "By all means."

"I'm attempting to get another judge transferred in here, and there is one awaiting confirmation, but we have to deal with what we have now. I will also say, and I mean this sincerely, Eric, if you feel you need to take a leave of absence, I will support you unconditionally."

"I appreciate that more than you could know," Yount said, "but . . . and I don't want to sound corny, but if I do that, if we change the way we do things, then he wins."

"Okay."

Yount said, "And if I back off now, Lawrence will be up there laughing at me."

Abernathy smiled. "He probably would at that." Then, "You're familiar with the patent case that was next up for him? The Baxter Optics case? It's scheduled for this Monday, but I can move it back."

He shrugged. "I've started looking at it already, so I'll be prepared. It's not that complicated; Baxter is being sued by a small optical supply manufacturer in a patent dispute over a new type of contact lens. The issues are fairly straightforward."

"There's potentially a lot at stake," she said.

He smiled. "What else is new? It will take my mind off life."

"So you want it?"

Another smile. "Not particularly, but just try and take it away from me."

I'm back at the Welcome Home shelter to do what I should have done the first time.

I've spent most of my time trying to figure out who actually murdered Steven McMaster, and not enough trying to prove that Don Carrigan didn't.

Part of the problem is Carrigan's lifestyle. He was homeless and living on the street; I can't show that he was at a charity dinner the night of the murder, or that he was playing poker with his buddies.

But maybe I can show that he was at Welcome Home, if not at the exact hour of the murder, then maybe close enough to reduce the window of time available for him to have gotten to Short Hills and done the deed.

Once again Sean Aimonetti, the director, is there to greet me with a smile. "Haven't we done this already?" he asks.

I return the smile. "I'm retracing my steps. I left my wallet somewhere."

"I emptied it. I thought it was a donation."

The banter out of the way, I ask him if people who show up for food or shelter sign in each time when they arrive.

"They're supposed to," he says. "We encourage it, but it's

not a rule or a requirement. We try not to do anything which will discourage attendance; the important thing is to get these people fed and protected."

"Do you save the log-in books?"

"Yes."

"Can I see one in particular?"

"I really think we have done this before, because once again I'm going to take you over to the shelter and turn you over to James Lasky. He's in charge of all of that stuff."

We head over there, but one of the workers says that Lasky won't be back for a half hour; he's at one of the other shelters. I hadn't realized that Welcome Home had more than one location, but Aimonetti tells me there are four.

While I'm waiting, he shows me around the place and describes how it works. It's all very remarkable and staffed with very extraordinary people. By the time he's finished, I've written a check for a fairly substantial donation; that way maybe I can feel extraordinary too.

It doesn't work . . . I don't.

Lasky finally comes back and seems less than thrilled to see me. He again broadcasts the fact that he has a lot on his plate, and my presence interferes with his cleaning it. But Aimonetti asks him to help me, and I say it won't take long, so he nods grudgingly and asks what I want.

"I want to see your log-in books for a specific week," I say, specifying the week of the murder.

"Why?"

"So I can see who logged in." I'm not going to tell him why because I don't want word of this getting back to the prosecution, in case it doesn't show what I want it to. The other unspoken reason for my refusal is that it's none of his business.

I tell him the week I'm looking for, and he heads into what appears to be a storage room, though I can only see it when he opens the door. It's a good five minutes before he comes back, carrying a very large book. "Here it is," he says.

I walk over to a table about fifteen feet away and set it down. I want the message to be clear that I don't want anyone looking over my shoulder, and it seems to have worked because no one walks over with me.

The book covers a month, which includes the week in question. It's fairly straightforward, so much so that even I can understand it. Each day has four pages, one for each meal, and one for overnight shelter.

That's the good news. The bad news is that Carrigan signed in for dinner five days that week, but the night of the murder wasn't one of them.

What I am holding in my hand is evidence for the prosecution to use; hopefully they won't be smart enough to do so. But his failure to sign in that night means he had ample time to get to Short Hills and commit the murder. It isn't proof of anything, but at the very least it looks suspicious.

Even to me.

There's a court session this morning that will accomplish absolutely nothing.

It's to go over some of the pretrial motions submitted by both sides. The only ones that have any chance of being granted are the ones that are of no consequence.

Our key motion consists of trying to get the judge to rule that the hat containing the DNA samples not be admitted as evidence because of chain of custody issues. I have as much chance of winning that one as I have of making the NFL Pro Bowl as an offensive tackle.

The absolute worst part of the day is when it is revealed that the judge assigned to the case is going to be unavailable, and Judge Henry "Hatchet" Henderson will be taking his place. He is not called "Hatchet" because of his calm and affable demeanor.

Hatchet hates lawyers in general, and me in particular. He thinks I'm a wiseass and bring disrespect upon any courtroom I enter, showing that Hatchet may be tough, but he's not stupid. But I'm not alone in incurring Hatchet's wrath. His attitude toward lawyers is similar to Michael Corleone's attitude toward Barzinis and Tattaglias: he will tolerate them and let them live, until he won't.

The prosecution's main motion, which will also fail, is to get the judge to forbid us to challenge the DNA evidence. They do this because we declined to conduct a Kelly-Frye hearing, which specifically challenges the science.

I didn't ask for it because Kelly-Frye hearings always lose, and they lose because the science of DNA works. I hate it because it almost always cuts against the defense, but it works. But it doesn't mean we won't challenge it on other grounds, including chain of custody. Just because Hatchet didn't rule out the hat on those grounds does not mean we can't challenge it.

Carrigan is with Hike and me the entire time, and it gives me a chance to ask him about the sign-in process at Welcome Home. "Did you always sign in?" I ask.

He nods. "Pretty much. If there was a long line to sign in I might not have, but basically I always did. I figured if they were feeding me for free it was the least I could do to sign in like they wanted."

I don't ask him about the night in question because if he didn't commit the murder, there is no reason he would remember it. It would have just been another day in a life in which specific days didn't have a hell of a lot of meaning.

At the end of the hearing, the prosecutor, Raymond Tasker, walks over and shakes my hand. "Waste of time, huh?"

"At least you got to meet Hatchet."

He nods. "I've heard stories. Hey, you got a second to chat about something?"

I find that whenever people ask to chat, it means it's about an issue of some importance. They use "chat" because it conveys that the conversation will be casual and insignificant, which means they want to make you think that and throw you off. Consider that another life lesson presented free of charge by Andy Carpenter.

I say goodbye to Carrigan and Hike and I go with Tasker to an anteroom. Once we sit down, he asks, "I assume you still don't want to plead it out?"

"That's your version of a chat? No, we do not want to plead it out."

"What about if I made the offer too good to turn down?"

"I make it a habit never to turn down offers that are too good to turn down, but goodness is in the eye of the beholder. In any event why would you want to do that?"

"I want his accomplice," Tasker says.

"Excuse me?"

"You want my operating theory of the case? It might be slightly different from the one the jury hears."

"I'm honored," I say.

"We have more than enough to nail your client. He was on the scene, the DNA proves that, the ring further implicates him, and he's proficient in hand-to-hand combat. He's a neck breaker, and the victim died from having his neck broken."

"That's your theory?"

"Part of it. The rest is that Carrigan didn't do it by himself; he wasn't even the driving force, literally and figuratively. He got recruited by someone and driven to the scene. The recruiter came away with all the money and none of the police focus. We don't see any signs that your boy went on any kind of a spending spree. Maybe he stuck the ring in his pocket."

"So you are willing to make the deal so good it can't be refused if Carrigan gives up the recruiter?"

"Correct," he says.

"There's just one flaw in your theory," I say. "It's ninety percent horseshit. Carrigan wasn't recruited, he wasn't on the scene, and he didn't commit the murder. The ten percent you got right is the fact that he never went on a spending spree; there never was anything to spend."

"If you think you can sell that to a jury," Tasker says, "you'd better be even better than people say."

I smile. "Once I turn on the charm, I'm dazzling."

Kimble didn't call Karen McMaster after you left his office," Sam says.

We're meeting in my office. I'm here because I asked Edna to come in to copy a bunch of documents, and this is where our copy machine is.

When I showed her the documents, she asked, "All of these?"

"Yes, Edna," I said.

She looked at them and said, "Some of them have writing on both sides."

"Yes, we call them two-sided documents. It's a legal term." She has gone off to get started, and based on her traditional document copying speed, I'm hoping to get the copies before the judge sentences Carrigan.

I had asked Sam to keep track of Kimble's phone, just to see if he was still close enough to McMaster to warn her that I had suspicions about her.

Sam continues, "Actually, I should qualify that. He didn't call her from his private cell phone, the number you called him on. It's always possible that he made it from a company phone. I could check her phone records, but if I had to guess, I'd say he didn't call."

"Did he call anyone?"

"Not for at least two hours, and then he only called his home and one of his companies on the West Coast. Nothing suspicious."

I'm not terribly surprised; I had no reason to doubt that Kimble and Karen McMaster had gone their separate ways. I'm actually a little disappointed; if he called, she might start feeling pressure and might make a mistake. But there are other ways to apply pressure.

"There's one other thing you might want to know; I'm not sure if it means anything."

"What is it?"

"Well, I looked closer at Karen McMaster's phone records. One of the things I wanted to check was if Kimble had called her at all recently. He hadn't."

"Okay."

"But I got deep into the records, and I saw some other calls she had made and received the day her husband was murdered. One of them could be interesting."

"How so?"

"Well, that night she got a call from a number registered to someone named Carl Betters. I got his address and other personal information off the phone company records."

"Who is he?"

"He's nobody; he doesn't exist. Not at that address or probably anywhere else. I've seen fake records before, and this one is fake."

"What time did she get the call?" I ask.

"Ten oh eight."

"What time did she call the neighbor to go check on her husband?"

Sam takes some papers out of his briefcase, and quickly moves through them to find what he's looking for.

"Ten seventeen."

"How long was the call with Carl Betters?"

"Thirty-eight seconds."

There could be a number of benign explanations for this, but I don't buy any of them. Maybe the person who called her wants to keep his or her privacy by using a phone registered in a fake name. Maybe the person isn't fake and does exist, but Sam just can't locate him or her. Maybe the person who called dialed a wrong number.

I'm not in the business of believing in benign explanations or coincidences. I think this call was to tell Karen McMaster that the deed was done, and that she should put in motion the process of her husband's body being discovered.

"We need to find out whose phone that is," I say.

Sam shakes his head. "Can't be done. I'll find out how the bills are paid, but you can be sure the owner doesn't blow it by writing a personal check from his real account. This is an elaborate fake."

Edna comes into the room carrying a fairly large stack of paper. "Here they are," she says, and then coughs a few times.

"Are you okay?" I ask.

"I think I breathed in too much ink toner fumes. It can be very dangerous."

"You should take tomorrow off and suck up as much oxygen as you can."

She nods. "Good idea. You know where to find me if you absolutely have to."

Edna leaves, but her last comment gives me an idea. "Sam, you can't find out whose phone it is, but can you find out where it is?" Every smartphone has a GPS in it, which is why the phone company computers can see where it is at all times. Anything the phone company can see, Sam can see.

He thinks for a minute. "I don't know why not. It's not a burner phone; some of them don't have a GPS in them. This is a real phone, just registered to a fake name."

"So let's see what you can find out. If you can pull this off, there are a half dozen waffles in it for you, soaked in maple syrup."

"Vermont?" he asks.

"Is there any other kind?"

T he good news is that Sam thinks he knows where the cell phone owner lives.

The bad news is that it is a high-rise apartment building on Broadway and Eighty-Eighth Street called the Montana. "It's a rental building with a hundred and fifty-six apartments on twenty-six floors," Sam says.

"Any of them rented to someone named Carl Betters?" I ask, since that's the pseudonym the cell phone guy used.

"No. So he could be going by his real name, or more likely a different fake. By the way, rentals are seven thousand and up a month, so this guy has some money to spend."

The more we talk it out the more we realize how difficult it is going to be to locate our man, assuming it is a man. First of all, the names on the apartment rental list are not going to be particularly revealing, since our boy would likely be using a fake name. Even worse, for all we know he's in town from Topeka, and is staying with an old college buddy.

Second, there is absolutely no guarantee that he is involved in our case. Simply because there was a call from that phone to Karen McMaster the night of the murder does not exactly a slam dunk case make.

Just the fact that we're basing our hopes on this shows how weak our case currently is. Even if the guy is the leader of the Taliban, it's a long way from proving Karen McMaster guilty, or Don Carrigan innocent.

Compounding the problem is that there is a short delay involved in Sam getting into the phone company computers and then locating where the phone is at any particular moment. It's not like a radar screen where he's following a blip; if it were we'd have a better chance.

We come up with a plan of attack. Sam is going to spend the next four or five days tracking the locations of the phone, seeing if we can detect a pattern. If the phone shows up in a particular place at a particular time with some frequency, then we can take advantage of that pattern.

It will still be hit or miss, but we might have more of a chance of hitting.

In the meantime, I need to focus on trial preparation. I have Hike resubmit the request we had put in for the bloody sleeve to be DNA tested. Once we had our own results, we had withdrawn the request, since we didn't want the prosecution to know about Ernie Vinson.

But now we have no choice but to reinstate it; not doing so now would risk not having the results in time for the defense case. Which would unfortunately also mean that we would not have a defense case, since right now we are relying on reasonable doubt, and only Ernie Vinson's involvement has a chance of providing that for us.

We don't yet subpoena Karen McMaster's phone records,

which we know will reveal that she spoke to Vinson two days before the murder. We are going to make that request at the last minute, since getting the phone records can be done very quickly, unlike the DNA.

A lot of what we are doing runs into the difficulty of trying to prove a negative. It seems improbable that a person with Carrigan's limited resources and mobility made it out to Short Hills to commit the robbery/murder, and then got back without being seen.

It's also hard to believe that he stole all that money and jewelry, and then is in the situation he is in today. But who's to say? Maybe he spent a week going to the track every day and blew the whole thing. How can we prove that he didn't?

Also, Tasker has revealed that he might posit the idea that Carrigan had an accomplice, in fact a boss. He'll say that Carrigan merely committed the crime at his boss's direction. So even without being able to say who the boss is, just the concept of it solves Tasker's problems.

He can say it was the boss who drove Carrigan out there, and the boss who took the money and jewels. He might even say that he stiffed Carrigan out of his share, which is why there is no evidence that Carrigan went on any kind of a spending spree, and why he is still on the street.

After four days of monitoring the GPS in the cell phone, it appears that we may have caught a break. The owner of the phone has had lunch three of the four days at a nearby restaurant called City Diner. Twice he's gone there at 12:30, once at 12:40, and once at 1:00.

So Laurie and I come up with a plan that may or may not work. The good news is that if it doesn't, we won't have done any harm. The bad news is that merely not doing harm is going to keep Carrigan in jail for the rest of his life.

It's going to require the whole team to execute it, so I call everyone in for a meeting.

Even Edna.

This morning I'm taking the team out to breakfast for a test run.

Not the whole team is here; Sam will be manning his computer when the real thing happens, and Marcus will be outside, waiting to follow the suspect if we can identify him.

I'm also not going to be an active part of this because I've had a lot of media exposure, and we are afraid I might be recognized by the suspect. I don't know that he would make the connection and thereby be scared off, but it's not worth taking the chance.

So the breakfast group consists of Laurie, Edna, Hike, Willie, and his wife, Sondra, who is pitching in as well. I've helped with the logistics, but Laurie did most of it. Sam wanted to be included for the breakfast rehearsal because the place is alleged to have terrific waffles and syrup, but since he won't be here during the main event, I told him he couldn't.

The group is spread around the room. Willie and Sondra sit at one table, Laurie and Edna at another, and Hike sits by himself. This covers the entire room, including the row of booths, but that's not why we did it in three tables. We just felt it wasn't fair for anyone to have to sit with Hike.

From these positions, at least one member of the group will be able to see every other table in the restaurant. When we get the suspect to unknowingly reveal himself, we have a pre-arranged signal, and the person in the best position will surreptitiously take a photograph of him.

Not everyone will be able to be at the same tables during lunch, when it will be busier, but they'll arrive early and come as close as they can. They should be able to improvise; I've molded them into a crack, highly trained outfit.

Sam is going to text the entire group when it shows up that the cell phone is in the restaurant. He'll know it on approximately a seven-minute delay, and since no one eats lunch in seven minutes, that should be fine.

The first day goes by without the cell phone entering the restaurant. As does the second, and the third. Our team is putting on weight eating a big lunch every day, but making no progress whatsoever.

I call a meeting at the house the night of the third day. We're getting nowhere and the trial is getting close. It might be time to come up with a new strategy.

Sam gives a report on what he's seen regarding the phone movements. "He's been out and about some," Sam says, "but not at lunch time. It's not like he's gone anywhere else to eat; he must be eating in the apartment."

"Is there any pattern to where he's going these other times?"

Sam shakes his head. "Not so far. I haven't run down what the places are that he's gone to; I've got the addresses, but that's all. I'm just looking for consistencies so you can set up shop and catch him. But he hasn't gone to the same place twice."

"Maybe we can call him, pretend to be someone else, and

get him to reveal who he is. Or lure him to a place we choose. Like a hoax," Hike says.

I shake my head. "No, we might spook him. We don't call the number until we can take advantage of it for sure."

No one else has any decent suggestions. Willie and Sondra are pleased with the way things are going; they like the pasta. Edna sort of doesn't know what to make of it, though on balance she's not happy. She likes lunching with Laurie, but having to be there every day makes it feel like work.

Hike got a look into the kitchen, pronounced it unsanitary, and thinks we're all going to get food poisoning. Marcus doesn't have anything at all to say, which is a real news event.

Since we can't come up with a new strategy, we agree to continue with the old one.

We're making real progress.

Carl met the shooter at the designated place and time, 11:00 P.M. at a warehouse in Paterson.

They had not communicated in weeks; the shooter was a pro and did not need the constant attention that Ernie Vinson had needed. Which Carl appreciated; even though he had only three people in his immediate employ, it was enough to make him realize he wasn't the management type.

Carl liked to handle things himself, and he was very capable of doing so. Steven McMaster had found that out the hard way. As had the aforementioned Ernie Vinson.

Carl arrived on time, but the shooter was ten minutes late. There were few things that Carl disliked as much as being kept waiting; it was disrespectful and Carl didn't see himself as someone to be disrespected.

When the shooter arrived, he was greeted with, "You're late."

He looked at his watch and shrugged. "Ten minutes."

"It's disrespectful," Carl said.

"Sorry. No disrespect intended."

"You've been busy."

The shooter nodded. "You've been reading my press clippings?"

"I have. I read where you missed the judge."

"It happens," the shooter said. "Damages my reputation."

"Now the security around the judge's kid is airtight. Nothing can happen to him."

The shooter nodded his agreement. "Then, you have my money?"

Carl just pointed to a briefcase sitting on a carton, and the shooter asked, "That's it?"

Carl nodded. "That's it."

The shooter walked over to the briefcase, pressed the buttons on the side, and the click indicated that it was open. He lifted the lid and there was the money, stacks of hundreds, neatly bound with rubber bands.

It was the most beautiful and last sight of his life.

Finally, on the seventh day of what is feeling like a ridiculous lunch stakeout, the text comes from Sam.

"He's in the restaurant."

I am in a Starbucks across the street, the same location I have been in for the last seven days. I'm not sure if Guinness tracks it, but I believe I have broken the world's weekly indoor caffeine consumption record.

Next it is my turn to text; the time is 1:11 and my text says I will call the suspect's cell phone at 1:15. We're relying on our cell phone clocks, so we should be synchronized, or at least very close to it. I don't have to tell them that I will text again fifteen seconds before my call.

Fifteen seconds before 1:15 I text the warning and then dial the suspect's number on a burner phone that Sam provided. This way there will be no caller ID showing up. The hope and plan is that he will answer the phone, and one of our team will see him and take his picture. I will hang up, so he shouldn't be too suspicious.

I don't hit send until the exact moment that my cell phone digital timer says 1:15.

And then I wait.

It takes twenty seconds, but it feels like an hour and a half. Laurie's text says, "I got him."

Then, from Hike, "Me too."

I respond with, "Have a nice lunch." As we had previously discussed, I want them to finish their lunch, not all get up abruptly and walk out. The suspect may find it curious that he got a hang-up call as it is, and I don't want him to think anything in the restaurant is suspicious.

We've changed our plan; Marcus is not there to follow the suspect. At this point it's unnecessary; we know where he lives and hopefully pretty soon we'll know who he is, so we can follow him at any time we want.

Over the course of the next half hour, Laurie, Edna, and Hike leave the restaurant and head for my office, where they will meet up with Sam. I'm still in Starbucks sucking down lattes, waiting for Willie and Sondra to leave, but an hour goes by, and they are still not out.

I hope nothing has gone wrong and that they just want to finish their pasta.

Finally, after another interminable twenty minutes, I see them leave the restaurant. I leave the Starbucks and head for the office; I can hear sloshing noises in my stomach.

We arrive at the office at the same time. When we open the door, Laurie says, "We were getting worried about you."

"Sorry," Sondra says. "Willie had an idea."

I don't like the sound of that, but based on their demeanor it doesn't seem like whatever the idea was degenerated into a disaster. "What was the idea?" I ask, cringing.

Sondra takes a cloth napkin out of her pocket and reaches into her pocketbook with it. She pulls out a water glass, carefully holding it by the top edge. I'm assuming it came from the restaurant. "This should have his fingerprints on it."

"That was his?" Laurie asks, and doesn't wait for the obvious answer. "Is there any chance he saw you take it?"

Willie shakes his head. "He was out of the restaurant already. Nobody saw me take it. I'm pretty good at this; I had a lot of practice back in the day."

"That's great," I say, and I mean it. If we don't get prints off the glass, there might be DNA. Either way, there is no downside, and potentially substantial upside. "Who's got photographs?"

Laurie and Hike both say that they do, and I have them email them to me. Fortunately they are both of the same guy; it would have been just our luck to have two people coincidentally answering phone calls at the same time.

I've never seen the guy before, and neither has anyone else in our group. He looks tall and heavyset, though it's hard to gauge his dimensions in the photographs, especially because he is sitting down.

Sam goes to his office to print out the photographs. With any luck we'll have an ID on him before long, and with more luck he won't turn out to be a pastor in from Kansas for a religious convention. As it is, we've put in a lot of effort to ID this guy, when the extent of his involvement, as far as we know, is a thirty-eight-second phone call to Karen McMaster.

I'm hoping that whoever he is, he's listed in the phone book under "murderers."

t's bad enough talking at Charlie's, but at least there you buy the beer and burgers," Pete says. "Now you're bothering me at work?"

I've come to see Pete at the precinct; I called and told him I need his help. Not surprisingly, he's reacting with characteristic warmth and sensitivity.

"If you help me on this, it's possible you will wind up making a legitimate arrest of an actual criminal, which would bring your total to one."

He seems to notice for the first time that I have brought a shopping bag with me. "What is that? I hope it's not your lunch, because you've only got five more minutes."

"Okay, I'll try and make this simple enough for even you to understand, which will be a challenge. There's a person that I believe to be a perpetrator of a crime." I take out the photos and put them on the desk. "Here are photos of him." Then I take out the glass, handling it carefully. "And I believe his fingerprints are on this glass."

"You've got a picture and a print? I'll call the SWAT team; let's go shoot him."

"I'm serious, Pete. If you can find out who it is, I believe it will be a very good thing for the society you are sworn to protect. If it turns out that I'm wrong, then no damage has been done."

"You going to tell me what it's about?"

"Once you tell me who it is."

"You're a pain in the ass."

There is a knock on the door and an officer opens it. "We need to talk," he says to Pete.

Pete goes outside with him, leaving me alone in the office. He comes back less than a minute later. "Meeting's over," he says.

"What's the matter?"

He thinks for a moment, then says. "The media knows already, so it can't hurt to tell you. A body has been found in a warehouse off Market Street."

"Will you take care of this?" I ask, pointing to the photo and glass.

He seems about to say something insulting, then decides he has no time. Instead he picks up the phone. "Get forensics in here . . . there's a water glass on my desk. I want them to get prints off of it."

"And the photos?" I ask.

He nods. "When I get back. Can I go now?"

"Thanks, Pete."

"Yeah. Let's do this again real soon."

On the way back home, I hear on the radio the news of the murder. There are very few details being made public other than the location of the warehouse and the fact that the victim was an adult male.

When I get home I suggest that Laurie, Ricky, and I go out to dinner. Jury selection starts tomorrow, which means

I am about to go into what I call the "trial zone," from which there is no escape.

We go to a Japanese restaurant in Fort Lee where they cook the food at your table. Ricky loves it, particularly when the chefs display showmanship with the use of their knives. It's a nice break and one that I certainly needed.

When we get back I take Tara and Sebastian for their walk and settle into the den to go over the trial documents again. Unfortunately, no matter how many times I read them, they don't get any better.

Jury selection is the part of a trial that I most dislike.

Actually, that's not completely true; waiting for the verdict is the aspect I hate the most. But the time on verdict watch is passive, so there is nothing I can do. Of the parts of a trial that I can impact, jury selection is the worst.

It's a crapshoot; it always has been and it always will be, no matter how vigorously so-called jury selection experts try to inject science into it. So I'm never confident, nor am I pessimistic.

And the worst part is that there is no positive or negative reinforcement until the end of the trial. The truth is that I can speculate, but I really don't know how I did in jury selection until the dreaded verdict watch is over.

Most of the people in the courtroom share my dislike of the process. I'm sure the opposing counsel feels similarly to me, and the other members of the court, like the judge, bailiff, and court clerk, have to be bored to death.

The citizens in the jury pool fall into two categories. Most of them don't want to be there and are thinking of some way to prevent being chosen. The ones who do want to be there must spend all their time trying to figure out how not to get excused, so that is probably stressful.

The only person who absolutely always likes the process is the defendant. That is because he or she has been stuck in jail for a pretty long time, and that can get rather boring. The courtroom atmosphere is live theater and serves to demonstrate that somebody is finally paying attention to him.

This time the selection mercifully takes only two days. We wind up with an evenly divided gender split, and a diverse racial group. I'm happy with it, or I'm not . . . I'll let you know.

I haven't heard anything from Pete regarding the photograph or fingerprint of our cell phone suspect. I know he's got a lot on his plate dealing with the recent murder, so as a good friend I'll give him until tomorrow.

Then, if he still hasn't gotten me my information, I will never buy the lowlife another beer as long as he lives.

Tomorrow Tasker and I will be delivering our opening arguments, so I will be preparing tonight. I would guess that I prepare less than most lawyers in that I absolutely never script anything out. I know all the points I want to cover, but I want to do so in a way that sounds spontaneous.

Spontaneous, I've come to understand, sounds sincere. And as some wise man once said, if you can fake sincerity, you've got it made.

By eleven o'clock I'm ready to go to bed, and then the phone rings. It's the assistant warden of the jail. "You should get down here," he says. "There's been a medical incident concerning your client."

I rush down to the jail and am directed to the medical ward. The doctor on call, Dr. Diane Ranes, comes out to see me. "I guess the best way to describe it is a psychological episode," Dr. Ranes says. "In layman's terms, he freaked out. It's not uncommon with his condition; I'm not sure if he has been taking his medication regularly, but it's more likely the stress of the impending trial contributed to it."

"What did he do?"

"Started throwing things in his cell, screaming, clawing at the bars. Fortunately we were able to subdue him and administer a sedative. We'll increase the Xanax dosage, at least in the short term, but we don't want to overdo it and turn him into a zombie."

"I agree," I say, because I don't know what else to say.

"Prison and claustrophobia do not mix," she says.

"He doesn't belong here at all."

She smiles. "I'm afraid I can't help you with that. All I can do is try and deal with his symptoms while he's here."

"Thank you. Can I see him?"

"He's sleeping."

"Will he be able to go to court tomorrow?"

"We won't know that until tomorrow. I'm hopeful; at least he didn't physically injure himself."

I nod. "If he can't make it, I'll get a continuance."

I turn to leave, since there's nothing left for me to do here. I'm prepared for court tomorrow, or whenever the trial begins.

It's been a while since I've felt this kind of pressure. I have got to get this man out of here.

First of all, ladies and gentlemen, I want to thank you for your service."

That's how Tasker begins his opening statement; it's what all lawyers, including myself, say in our opening statements. We say it even though we know that a number of those jurors providing this service are doing so because they couldn't figure out a way to avoid it.

Carrigan has made it into court, so no continuance request was necessary. He gave me a weak smile and nod when I asked how he was doing. If I'd gone through what he did, and was medicated like he is, the only way they could get me out of bed would be with a shovel.

Laurie came into court today to provide moral support for our client. She gave him a reassuring hug just before the judge entered. I heard her say, "Andy's the best. You'll see."

"Believe me, the last thing I want to do is give you a lecture on the law," Tasker continues. "I sat through many of them in law school and I know they can be torture. But I do want to talk to you briefly about circumstantial evidence.

"Most people hear that phrase and they think that such

evidence is suspect. It's not. Circumstantial evidence can be as powerful and every bit as compelling as direct evidence.

"Not every crime is committed in daylight, with a bunch of eyewitnesses watching. Not every crime is recorded on video, or uploaded to YouTube. And the crime you are going to hear about in this courtroom had no such witnesses, and no such video. So you will hear mostly circumstantial evidence, but I predict you will have no doubt that what you hear will remove any reasonable doubt in your mind as to the guilty party.

"The classic example of circumstantial evidence is the following: You go to bed at night and notice that there is no snow on the ground. You wake up in the morning and there is six inches of snow on that same ground. You therefore know, beyond a shadow of a doubt, that it snowed during the night. You know this even though you didn't actually see the snow fall. What convinced you was circumstantial evidence.

"Donald Carrigan is not a master criminal, not even close. He's not even very good at it. He robbed and murdered Steven McMaster, and then made mistakes that implicated himself so clearly that the truth of what happened could not possibly be missed.

"Donald Carrigan was trained to kill, and he killed in exactly the manner he was trained. Then he left behind evidence, incontrovertible evidence, that proved he was on the scene. After that he was found to have the stolen property, and then, believe it or not, he bragged about having committed the crime.

"He may not be a master criminal, but he is a deadly one.

"This is not the time for me to go over the evidence with you; trust me that you will see and hear all of it. And then you will make your decision. And as surely as you would have known that it had snowed in my example, you will know that Donald Carrigan committed the crime for which he is charged.

"So again, I thank you for your service, because what you are doing is very important. You have an opportunity to take a killer off the street, to see to it that he never again claims another victim. There are few jobs more crucial than that.

"I know and rely on the fact that you will do your job."

I'm going to give my opening statement after the lunch break, so I use the break to call Pete. He answers the phone with, "Hey, I was just going to call you. Your boy has been arrested."

Since I have no idea what he is talking about, I ask, "What are you talking about?"

"We got one print off the glass, sent it to NYPD, and they were supposed to make the arrest when he showed up for work this morning."

"Who? Work where?" This is not successfully computing.

"The waiter from that restaurant. He was wanted on a breaking and entering charge."

"I didn't want the damn waiter, Pete."

"Then why did you give me his print?"

This is not going anywhere productive. "That was the only print on the glass?"

"Yeah. The others were smudged. It was a water glass; they have a tendency to get wet," he says.

"Thanks for sharing that news. What about the photograph?"

"I didn't do anything with it because we got the print. I can ask around if anyone recognizes the guy."

"You arrested the waiter." I say it out loud, because I can't really believe it.

"Yeah. Good work, Sherlock."

I get off the phone and call Laurie. I tell her about the fiasco with Pete and ask her to call Cindy Spodek, something I should have done in the first place. Cindy is a good friend of mine and a better friend of Laurie's; she also happens to be the number two person at the Boston FBI headquarters.

She's helped us in the past, and we've helped her. But she complains that I only call her for favors, never to chat about friend stuff. She's right, but I never call anyone about friend stuff.

In fact, I have no idea why anyone would call anyone about friend stuff; that's why they have emails and texts. Phone calls can go on forever, and they have empty pauses, and you have to figure out a way to end them. With emails you hit send and you're done with it.

"Ask Cindy to run it through their facial recognition software," I say.

Laurie doesn't like to take advantage of Cindy, but doesn't push back this time. She knows it's important.

"Okay . . . I'll call her now."

I hang up and reflect on what just happened. The bad news is that our case is in deep shit. The good news is we just took a waiter off the street.

Just before court is about to start, Laurie calls me back. "Cindy says she'll do it; I'm emailing her the photo now."

"Did she send me her best?" I ask.

"No."

"Oh."

L ike Mr. Tasker, I would also like to sincerely thank you for your service."

That's how I begin my opening statement, and now that the horseshit is out of the way, I can get to the important stuff.

"I would also like to point out that our gratefulness for your service will be the last thing you hear Mr. Tasker and I agree on for the duration of this trial.

"Just to be clear, while circumstantial evidence can be compelling and persuasive, it can also be contrived and fabricated and misleading. And that describes the prosecution's case quite well."

Out of the corner of my eye I see Tasker start to get up to object, but then decide against it. It's considered bad form to interrupt opposing counsel's opening or closing argument.

He is upset that I said the prosecution will be presenting fabricated evidence, and since I will be doing exactly that and can prove it, I wish he would object.

So time to goad him again. "Yes, you heard me right. You will be asked to listen to fabricated evidence . . . intentionally made up out of whole cloth."

"Objection, Your Honor. That is an outrageous charge."

"Overruled. But you'd better be prepared to back it up, Mr. Carpenter. Continue."

"Thank you, Your Honor. The prosecution did not discuss their evidence in any detail, or tell you what you would hear from their side. So there is nothing for me to respond to; I'll let the trial speak for itself.

"But I would just like to tell you a little about Donald Carrigan. He not only served this country admirably as a Green Beret, but he is a war hero. Highly decorated at that. We owe him our admiration, not our accusations.

"But his post-military life deteriorated, wholly as a result of his service. I won't go into it now, because it isn't relevant, and it's private. Some of it will come out in the course of the trial, which is unfair but unfortunately necessary.

"But for now I will tell you this; there is no way, no possible way, that he committed this crime. The very idea of it is ludicrous.

"Thank you."

I sit down and Carrigan thanks me for what I've said. Tomorrow the prosecution will start presenting its witnesses. I will tell him to gear up for tomorrow and the days to follow; during the prosecution's case, Tasker will be the puncher, and Carrigan will be the bag.

I'm still annoyed with myself for waiting to ask Cindy Spodek to run the photograph through the FBI's facial recognition system. The days are going by; before we know it the jury will be deliberating, and we need a hell of a lot of help.

When I get home, Sam Willis is there, but Laurie and Ricky aren't. I certainly wasn't expecting him, so I'm glad I didn't yell out "Honey, I'm home." I wouldn't want to give him the wrong impression.

"Laurie and Ricky went to the market," he says. "She forgot to get something for dinner. We're having pasta."

I nod. "That explains why they aren't here, but it doesn't quite cover why you are."

"I have news for you."

"I hope the news is not that you're renting the room above the garage."

"Nope, even better than that. Way better than that."

I like the turn this conversation just took. "You know who our cell phone guy is?"

"No, but I know where he's been."

"Where?"

"You know where that body was found the other day? In that warehouse near Market Street?"

"He was there?" I ask.

"Not only was he there, he was there the night before the body was found. He got there at ten fifty, and left at eleven fifteen."

"You're sure about this?"

He nods. "GPS doesn't lie."

I pick up the phone and call Pete and am told he left for the day. I know he'll be at Charlie's; there's a Knicks game on tonight. "Tell Laurie I've got to go to Charlie's to talk to Pete."

"Should I tell her why?"

"Have you told her about our boy being at that warehouse?" I ask.

"Yes."

"Then she'll know why."

I head down to Charlie's and sure enough, Pete and Vince are in their seats. They're here so often, I think there's a chance they're even nailed to those seats.

"Well look who's here," Pete says. "You want me to identify your prom pictures next?"

"There is no reason to talk to our meal ticket, I mean close friend, like that," Vince says.

I ignore him and talk to Pete. "Just tell me one thing: The guy whose body was found in that warehouse . . . was he killed the night before he was found?"

"Why?"

"Just tell me. And if the answer is yes, I am going to make you the happiest incompetent detective in America."

"Yes," he says.

"Time of death around eleven P.M.?"

He can't hide the fact that he's interested; for all his complaining, he knows that I have never given him bad information.

"They can't narrow it down that much, but that is definitely within the range."

"Was his neck broken? The cause of death wasn't mentioned in media reports."

Now I really have his attention. "Yes."

"Last question. Who was he? I haven't seen that in the media."

Vince interjects. "Then you haven't been reading my newspaper. His name was Charlie Keller. Paramilitary guy, served as a mercenary in various places around the world. No criminal record here."

I turn to Pete. "Is that right?"

Vince gets annoyed. "Is that right? You think we write bullshit? Of course it's right."

Pete nods his agreement.

I'm still talking to Pete. "Okay. Listen carefully. I am going to tell you what I know, but I am not going to tell you how I know it. The guy in that photograph that I gave you? I don't know his name yet, but I know where he lives. And I know that he is your killer."

Tasker's first witness is Sergeant Tom Quaranto.

I'm not familiar with him, just like I won't be familiar with many of the witnesses Tasker calls. They are Essex County people, and I've never tried a case there.

Tasker gets Sergeant Quaranto to confirm that he and his partner were the first ones to arrive at the Steven McMaster murder scene.

"What made you go there?"

"We received a phone call from a neighbor, a Mr. Walter Zimmer. He had discovered the body."

"What did you do when you arrived?"

"Mr. Zimmer was outside the garage waiting for us. He brought us in and showed us where Mr. McMaster was. We determined that he was deceased, then called in Homicide and the coroner."

"Did you have an idea as to the cause of death? Was it obvious to you?" he asks.

"That's up to the coroner to determine, but Mr. McMaster's head was twisted at a grotesque angle, and there was no blood."

"Did you see anything else at the scene that interested you?"

Quaranto nods. "A woolen cap, lying on the floor of the garage. We left it there for forensics, and Sergeant Frierson took control of it."

Tasker asks him a few more essentially meaningless questions, merely to further describe the terrible scene Quaranto had come in on. Tasker introduces photos of the body into evidence, and I can see the jury recoil at the twisted head and neck. Then he turns the witness over to me.

"Sergeant Quaranto, did Mr. Zimmer tell you why he happened to be in Mr. McMaster's house?"

"Yes, he said that Mr. McMaster's wife called him and asked him to check on the place, that she couldn't reach her husband and she was worried."

"What time was this?"

"I don't know what time she called him, but I arrived on the scene at ten forty-one."

I'm trying to plant a seed that it was mighty early for her to be so worried that she called a neighbor. It won't register with the jury now, but might later as I start to paint a target on Karen McMaster.

"You said you were interested by the presence of a hat in the garage. Was it cold that night?"

"Pretty cold, yes."

"Mr. McMaster was likely accosted in the garage. Isn't it possible that it was his hat?"

"Possible."

There is no sense in me badgering Quaranto, trying to score points, because they would be meaningless. His testimony is accurate and unbiased; he came to the scene and he found a body. We have no interest in claiming otherwise. "No further questions."

Next up is poor Mr. Zimmer himself. If I'm right, not only did he discover a murder, but he was sent to the house for the express purpose of discovering a murder. It was not a terribly neighborly act on Karen McMaster's part.

Tasker wastes a bunch of time establishing a relationship between the Zimmers and the McMasters. It turns out there wasn't much of one; they didn't exactly play charades or bridge once a week. The best thing that Zimmer can come up with is that they were apparently the only neighbor that the McMasters had anything to do with.

"I think they stayed at their New York apartment quite a lot," Zimmer says.

"But Karen McMaster felt close enough to you to call you to check on her husband?"

Zimmer nods. "Apparently so, though she actually spoke to my wife."

Zimmer describes walking to the house and seeing it mostly dark. The garage was open, which was apparently an unusual occurrence. He walked to it, then saw that the door to the house was also open. He called out and got no answer, then nervously entered the house, and saw the body.

"What did you do?"

"I went to him. My thought was that he had fainted, or even had a heart attack. I went to feel for his pulse; I have some CPR training. But then I saw the way his head was bent . . . it was horrible. And I knew he hadn't fainted."

"What did you do next?"

"I backed away and walked down the block a short ways;

I walked backwards, because I was afraid whoever did it could still be around. While I was walking I called the police and then waited for them to arrive. They were there very quickly."

Tasker turns him over to me. "Mr. Zimmer, how old was Steven McMaster, if you know?"

"I think I read that he was thirty-eight."

"What night of the week was this?"

"A Friday."

"Did you wonder why Mrs. McMaster would be so worried about her husband being out at ten thirty on a Friday night?"

"No, I didn't think about it."

"Did she ever call you and ask you to do something like this before?"

"No. First time."

"No more questions. Thank you."

His original name was Yuri Ganady. He was a captain in the Serbian military back in the Milosevic days," Laurie says.

She's reading from the notes that she jotted down during her conversation with Cindy Spodek. Apparently the cell phone owner formerly known as Carl Betters has a face that is well-known to the FBI's facial recognition system.

"That already doesn't sound good," I say. "What do they know about him?"

"Surprisingly little. He seems to show up in various places around the world, basically and literally as a hired gun. He's been here at times, they know that, but they have never been able to connect him to anything. Having said that, they don't think he falls into the 'tourist' category."

"Has he done anything that they can take him into custody for?" I ask.

"Apparently not anything they are aware of. Cindy must have repeated five times how careful we should be with this guy."

"Message heard."

I'm not sure what to do with this information. We know

that he called Karen McMaster the night of her husband's murder. With the description that Cindy just provided, there simply cannot have been a benign reason for that call. There is little doubt in my mind that the purpose of it was to tell her that the murder had taken place, and she could call her neighbor.

I can't throw Sam under the bus and tell anyone how we know about that call, but I might be able to finesse it. The problem is that the existence of a phone call is not probable cause to make an arrest, and I don't want Betters, or Ganady, or whatever the hell his name is, to know that we're onto him.

Hanging over all of this is what has to be my first priority, which is getting this in front of a jury. Yes, I want to put Karen McMaster and Ganady and anyone else involved in the murder into prison, but it's much more important to me to get Carrigan out. That's how the system works.

I decide to call Pete, which proves to be unnecessary, since Pete calls me first. "I know his name," Pete says.

"Let me take a wild stab at it. Yuri Ganady."

"How did you know that?" he asks.

"I grew up with his cousin, Shirley Ganady. I met Yuri at her bat mitzvah. Small world."

"Are you ever going to stop being a pain in the ass?"

"Apparently not. If I was going to make that radical a transformation, I think it would have happened already."

"So we need to talk," he says.

"Isn't that what we're doing?"

"We haven't even begun. What can you tell me about this guy, and how do you know he committed the murder in the warehouse?"

"I can't tell you that, and it wouldn't matter if I could. You should just take my word for the fact that I know he was there at the time of the murder. I didn't see him actually perform the act, but I think we can assume he did."

"Keller, the guy that was killed, was a paid mercenary around the world. A connection with Ganady makes sense," he says.

"It certainly does."

"You must have evidence that I can use to demonstrate that he was there," Pete says.

"Actually I don't, definitely nothing that you could take to a judge." I'm telling the truth, the fact that a cell phone in the name of Carl Betters was in that warehouse is nowhere near what Pete would need to get a warrant.

"What else do you know?" he asks.

"Okay, I'm going to tell you something, as long as you promise not to repeat it."

"I can only promise that if not repeating it does not prevent me from doing my job."

"It has nothing to do with your job. It's not one of your cases."

"Okay, then I promise."

"Our boy Yuri either killed Steven McMaster or had him killed. Probably the former."

I expect Pete to ridicule what I am saying as the rantings of a criminal defense attorney, but he doesn't.

All he says is, "We need to put this guy away."

The key part of the trial is today, and the jury won't hear a word of it.

Tasker is going to attempt to bring in testimony about Carrigan's assault history to portray him as a violent person, his so-called prior bad acts. He also wants testimony about Carrigan's military training, basically to show his proficiency in "neck-breaking."

We have filed a motion to keep all of it out. Hatchet could have handled this in the pretrial stage, but he chose not to. I would have argued with him about the timing, but the last lawyer who argued with Hatchet about timing was found floating in the East River with a gavel up his ass.

So we are meeting in open court, but with no jury or gallery present. "Let's hear it," Hatchet says to me.

"Thank you, Your Honor. The previous assaults for which my client was arrested bear no resemblance whatsoever to the crime alleged in this case. The so-called 'prior bad acts' must be of a kind with the current charge, and these are not. And they would be far more prejudicial than probative, which is the standard.

"To make the admission of such testimony even less

consistent with the very clear rulings of numerous appeals courts, these prior bad acts are not even bad acts. After law enforcement examined each case, those entities chose not to file charges. This court should not reverse their considered and informed opinions by punishing my client after they chose not to.

"Regarding his army training, that is even further from relevance to these proceedings. Just because Mr. Carrigan once had an ability does not mean he has used it for nefarious means. Are we really going to take his outstanding service and use it against him?"

Hatchet's expression gives away nothing; I have no idea if he found my arguments compelling or ludicrous. All he says is, "Mr. Tasker?"

"Your Honor, taking this in reverse order, the military training is absolutely relevant in that the broken neck was administered in the exact manner in which Mr. Carrigan was trained.

"Suppose the sniper shooter, Chuck Simmons, were captured and brought to be tried in this courtroom. Would his training as a sharpshooter not be relevant? How many people could do what he has done, with that accuracy? How many people could do what we contend Mr. Carrigan has done? Not enough to reduce its probative value.

"In terms of the prior bad acts, they speak to Mr. Carrigan's violent outbursts. He is prone to physical violence, and physical violence is what we are alleging in this case. His hands are his weapons; that remains consistent through all of these acts, and for the murder of Steven McMaster. The fact that a robbery was committed at the same time does not make that violence less relevant in any way.

"Further, we have a witness prepared to testify that in one of those incidents, he grabbed a victim from behind by the neck in the exact manner we are alleging, and he was pulled away by bystanders. Had they not intervened, Mr. McMaster might be alive today, because Mr. Carrigan might well have been convicted of a different murder."

We bat this around for a few more minutes. Hatchet is known for quick, decisive action, and that's what he does in this case. He rules the army training testimony in and rules out the prior bad acts. We came out fairly well, but I disagree with the first part of the ruling. Because I have a well-developed self-preservation instinct, I'll keep that disagreement to myself.

We head back into court, the jury is called in, and Colonel Jonathon Casey is called to the stand. He's wearing his dress uniform, which seems to me to be a little much. But he's an intimidating presence, and he commands the courtroom. I feel like asking him if he ordered the Code Red.

"Colonel Casey, what was your relationship to Mr. Carrigan?" Tasker asks.

"I was a captain back then, and I was his training officer at Fort Polk."

"Did you train him in hand-to-hand combat?"

"I did."

"Was he a good student?" Tasker asks.

"Excellent."

"He became proficient at such combat?"

"Very," Casey says.

"Did you see a photograph of the victim in this case, Steven McMaster, taken where he was found in his house?"

"I did."

"The violence that was inflicted on him, is that consistent with what Mr. Carrigan was trained to do and, as you say, he was very proficient at?"

"He was not trained to murder; he was trained to combat our nation's enemies."

"I understand. I am talking about his physical talents. Would he physically have been capable and competent at this kind of violence?"

"He is very capable of it, but that doesn't mean he did it."

Score a point for army guys sticking together. Casey does not want to be responsible for one of his men going down.

"Thank you, Colonel. The jury will hear other evidence addressing that. I am simply asking about his training and his capabilities. So, just to recap, he was trained to do things like this, and he was good at it?"

"Yes," Casey says, with some obvious reluctance.

I start the cross examination with, "First of all, Colonel Casey, thank you for your service." I figure if it works with juries, it should work just as well with colonels. And colonels are doing what they do voluntarily, which is not the case with a lot of jurors. In any event, no harm no foul.

I continue. "Colonel, what kind of a soldier was Donald Carrigan?"

"In what sense?"

"Was he a problem for you to handle?"

"Never."

"Did he question authority?"

"Not to my knowledge."

"Did he execute the assignments he was given?"

"Always."

"Did you consider him a credit to his uniform and his country?"

"Absolutely."

"Ever charged with a crime?"

"Never."

"Thank you. No further questions."

For Judge Eric Yount, the pressure hadn't let up.

The trial that he inherited from the deceased Judge Alexander was over. He had ruled for Baxter Optics in the patent case. He had known all along which way the case would go but even delayed the ruling a few extra days to give the appearance of serious contemplation. Otherwise the parties might think the pressure of all the sniper shootings had affected his concentration.

As long as the shooter was not yet captured, the security around him was still airtight. He didn't want them around, didn't believe he needed them, but couldn't send them away. The Younts were even staying at a friend's apartment in Manhattan; the friend was out of town, and being in the city made it easier on the security detail.

As bad as the pressure was on Eric, his wife, Nancy, felt it even more. She knew, on a very deep level, that her life and their marriage would never be the same.

But on this particular evening, he said to his wife, "I've got to go out."

"Eric, don't go. Stay home, please. This has got to end."

"I agree. Which is why I am going now, without being followed."

"Eric, please listen to me. This is dangerous. After all that has gone on, don't do anything that will get you killed."

"I'll wait until it gets dark, and I'll sneak out the back. Just a few hours, and I'll be back."

Once again she couldn't stop him, but that was no surprise; she had been powerless since the nightmare began. So at eight thirty he snuck out on the service elevator, went out the back door of the apartment building, and got to his car unnoticed.

So Eric drove upstate, from the Henry Hudson Parkway to the Taconic. He knew how worried Nancy was, so once this was over, he'd call her and reassure her he was fine.

After almost two hours of driving, he pulled into a rest stop, parked, and used the bathroom. When he came out, there was someone else there.

"Hello, Judge," the man said.

"Couldn't you have found a closer place?" Eric asked. It was dark, so he couldn't see the gun.

The man shook his head. "No, this is perfect." And then he fired two bullets into Judge Eric Yount's chest.

Tasker's next witness is Sergeant Mike Frierson.

Frierson works in the Essex County forensics lab, and an earlier witness testified that he took control of the woolen hat to do testing on it. Frierson is there to say that the hairs in the hat matched Carrigan's. Carrigan's had been in the database because of his military service.

Tasker goes on to take him through a long, drawn-out process of describing how definitive the match is, how the chance it isn't a match is one in many billions. That's all fascinating but ultimately unnecessary, since I have no intention of challenging it.

When it's my turn, I ask, "Sergeant Frierson, when did the hairs arrive at that hat?"

"What do you mean?"

"How long were they there?"

He shrugs. "I have no way of knowing that."

"Could it have been months?"

"That's possible, I suppose, but—"

"Thank you. Now on the night of the murder, who was wearing that hat?"

"I imagine the defendant."

"Thanks for that. But we're not here to test your imagination. Your role is to present facts, and if you aren't sure of something, it's okay for you to admit it."

Tasker objects that I'm badgering the witness, but Hatchet overrules him.

I continue, "So, do you know for sure who was wearing the hat that night?"

"No."

"Do you know if anyone was wearing it?"

"No."

"Do you know how it got onto the floor of that garage?"

"No."

"Thank you. No further questions."

Next up is Sergeant Richard Fusina. Tasker introduces the ring that was allegedly found in Carrigan's locker at the Welcome Home shelter. He gets him to say that Karen McMaster identified it, and that they confirmed the purchase three years earlier at a local jeweler.

I ask a couple of perfunctory questions to demonstrate that Fusina has no way of knowing who put the ring in the locker, and then let him off the stand. I'll be challenging his testimony, just at another time.

The next name on Tasker's hit parade is Jaime Tomasino. Jaime has dressed down for the occasion; even though he has taken to eating at nice restaurants, it hasn't translated into a sense of fashion. Most likely Tasker wanted him to dress shabbily to burnish his image as a poor homeless guy who sat next to Carrigan at shelter meals and hung on his every word.

"Mr. Tomasino, were you a patron at the Welcome Home shelter at mealtimes?"

"You mean did I eat there? Yeah, when I was hungry."

"Did you have occasion to meet the defendant when you were there?"

'Yeah, we talked a lot."

"Did he ever mention Steven McMaster?"

Tomasino nods. "Yeah. He told me he killed him. That he broke the guy's neck and robbed his house."

"Why did he confide in you about this?"

"We were friends; we talked about a lot of stuff. And he was bragging about it, like he was proud of what he had done."

It feels like it takes forever for Tasker to finish with Tomasino, so he can turn him over to me. It's all I can do to avoid salivating at the prospect.

"Mr. Tomasino, would you describe yourself and the defendant as buddies?"

"Yeah, sure, I guess so. I mean, we hung out."

"You shared personal stories?"

"Some, yeah. He talked more than me."

"But you're a good listener?" I ask.

"Yeah, I'm a pretty good listener."

"Can you share with the jury any other personal things that the defendant told you? Other than the fact that he murdered Steven McMaster?"

I can see the worry come into his face as clearly as if he had a neon sign on his forehead that said "WORRY."

"I can't remember any of it now; it's been a while."

"Do you remember when I recently came to talk to you at the restaurant you were eating in?" I ask.

"Yeah."

"Do you remember what we talked about?"

"Yeah."

"You're a better man than me; I forget everything. But I wanted to make sure that I didn't forget a conversation that I knew would be memorable, so I recorded it."

I introduce the recording as evidence, subject to confirmation by the witness or a voice identification expert that I was prepared to call. Tasker objects, but gets nowhere.

"You didn't tell me you were taping it."

"I would think that based on your vast experience as a lying informant, you would have known that New Jersey was a one-party consent state."

Tasker objects and Hatchet warns me to be respectful to the witness.

I start the recording.

"Hey, aren't you Jaime Tomasino?"

"Yeah. Who are you?"

I stop the recording. "Just to be clear, this is you and I talking, correct? Just a reminder, you're under oath."

He sneers at me, but admits that it's him, so I resume the recording.

"Andy. Andy Carpenter! Don't you remember me? We went to different schools together."

"What the hell are you talking about?"

"Hey, not a bad menu. You going to have the filet? I thought you were more into soup? Anyway, I hear you know Don Carrigan."

"Who's that?"

"You don't know Don Carrigan?"

"Oh, yeah. Carrigan. The guy who did that murder. Who are you?"

"I'm his friend. I'm trying to help him, but not if he's guilty."

"They told me not to talk to anybody."

"Who? The prosecutors?"

"*I don't want to say. You should take off.*"

"*I just have a couple of questions, then I'm out of here. Carrigan told you he killed that guy?*"

"*Yeah. He bragged about it.*"

"*You sure it was the same Carrigan? Short black guy?*"

"*Yeah, that's him.*"

Out of the corner of my eye I think I see Tasker actually wince. "Mr. Carrigan, would you please stand up?"

Carrigan stands, all six foot three of him, white to the point of being pale.

"Mr. Tomasino, is this your short black buddy?"

Hatchet calls for a meeting in his chambers, lead counsel only, which is fine with me.

He leaves the bench and Tasker and I follow him. Tasker looks like he's heading for the electric chair; he should be so lucky.

Once Hatchet is seated behind his desk and Tasker and I are seated across from him, Hatchet says, "Mr. Tasker, I'm not sure how you work things in Essex County, but here in Passaic County, we generally prefer witnesses who tell the truth. It's one of our idiosyncrasies."

Tasker looks pained, as well he should. "Your Honor, surely you don't think that I had any idea that the witness would not be forthcoming."

"Not be forthcoming? Is that what you call it? The guy lied through his teeth. He thought the defendant was a 'short black guy.' If I said I think Mr. Carpenter is Miss New Jersey, would you call that 'not forthcoming' as well?"

I chime in with, "Your Honor, in all fairness to Mr. Tasker, I was first runner up. The swimsuit competition was my downfall. It's all politics."

"Can it, Mr. Carpenter," Hatchet says. "The worst part of this entire incident is how happy you look about it."

"Sorry, Your Honor."

"Now, Mr. Tasker, how will we deal with this? Mr. Carpenter told the jury in his opening statement that they would be hearing fabricated evidence and then you go ahead and call Mr. Tomasino to prove him right."

"I don't think there is anything to be done, Your Honor. The jury saw it all, and they will reserve the right to hold it against us. Rehashing it in front of them would seem unnecessary and prejudicial. Mr. Carpenter will no doubt refer to it in his closing statement as well."

"Heck, that's a good idea," I say.

Hatchet turns to me. "Do you have anything to add that isn't snide and sarcastic?"

"Yes, Your Honor. Tomasino is a slime ball and he lied, but I would suggest that we look at the bigger picture here."

"You will enlighten us on what that is?" Hatchet asks.

I nod. "Right now. The real question is why did he lie? This is not an inmate looking to get a reduced sentence. I can't imagine that Mr. Tasker offered him money for fabricated testimony. But somebody with a motive got him to lie.

"That recording was done in a fairly expensive restaurant. This guy was testifying about conversations that he alleged took place in a homeless shelter kitchen. There is something wrong with that picture.

"He was clearly paid to lie. So I don't care if you remind the jury that he lied; they already know that. What I want the jury to know are the implications of that. I want the jury to know that someone was willing to spend money, and break the law in the process, to get Mr. Carrigan convicted."

Tasker says, "I suggest we have the police interrogate and investigate Mr. Tomasino to find out who put him up to this."

"That's all well and good," I say, "but if I'm right, and I can't remember the last time I wasn't, then it won't accomplish anything. Because Tomasino is going to be a hell of a lot more afraid of the person who paid him than he will be of the police. And that will be the first intelligent assessment he's made in a very long time."

Hatchet asks, "You think you know who paid him to commit perjury?"

"I believe so, Your Honor, but I'm not yet ready to come forward with it. Hopefully during the defense case."

Hatchet nods. "Very well. For the time being, here's what we'll do. I will refer Mr. Tomasino to the police for investigation, with a recommendation of a charge for perjury. Mr. Carpenter, you can refer to the obvious lies in your closing statement, and you may also discuss your theory of Mr. Tomasino being paid. You also obviously retain the right to bring forth evidence of that at any point during the defense case. I will give limited instructions to the jury.

"Mr. Tasker, I very strongly advise you to more carefully vet your remaining witnesses. Because you are one lying witness away from a directed verdict of acquittal."

"Yes, Your Honor."

Hatchet calls the bailiff and tells him to take Tomasino into custody. But when we go back in, Tomasino is already nowhere to be found, and Hatchet tells the jury that obviously Mr. Tomasino was not telling the truth. They can assign whatever weight to that they wish, understanding that they may hear more about it as the trial progresses.

I'm quite pleased with how the court day went; it isn't

often that defense attorneys get to experience a "Perry Mason" moment, where the witness is actually proven to have committed perjury while on the stand. Unlike in Perry's many triumphs, in this case the victim didn't break down in a tearful or angry admission of guilt, but this was close enough.

By the time I get home it's fairly late. Laurie has held dinner so we could eat together, and Ricky has already finished his homework. I've looked over his shoulder at it a few times, and I dread the day that I will be called on to help. It's upsetting to know I don't have the smarts or knowledge to make it out of fourth grade.

Ricky is upstairs watching television when I get home, but Laurie calls him down to eat. "Hey, Dad," he says. "What's a town drunk?"

I turn to Laurie. "What kind of environment are you providing for this young, impressionable lad?"

"Ricky, where did you hear that expression?"

"On that Mayberry show, the one with Opie."

"Opie's old enough to be your grandfather," I say, but nobody pays any attention to me.

Ricky continues. "They said this guy Otis is the town drunk, and then everybody laughs. What does that mean?"

I turn to Laurie. "You want to take this?"

She nods, sort of wearily. "Ricky, that show was made a long time ago. That person drank too much alcohol, which is a very bad thing to do. Today we know better than they did back then, and we know it's not really funny."

"Same thing with the movie *Arthur*," I say.

"Thanks, Andy, that's helpful," Laurie says, and then turns back to Ricky. "Do you understand?"

"Why is too much of that alcohol stuff bad?"

"Because it takes away your ability to think and it hurts your body."

Ricky nods. "Otis looked like he was going to fall down."

"Yes, Rick, and that's bad," I say. What I don't say is that he gave me an interesting idea. It isn't directly connected to our case, so I put it back in the future idea bank, but I'll be retrieving it soon.

I take the dogs for a walk and Laurie is on the porch to greet me when we return.

This could be good or bad, but it's going to be something. I don't see her holding my pipe and slippers, so that can't be it. Behind her I can hear Bing Crosby singing "Silver bells, it's Christmas time in the city." Laurie needs a holiday intervention.

"Marcus called," she says. "I've had him watching the Montana, to follow Ganady if he left the building, just to see where he goes."

"Why did you do that?"

"Because we need to shake things up. If we learn nothing from it, then we learn nothing. It's called 'investigating.' Marcus and I are 'investigators.'"

She seems annoyed that I might be questioning her tactics; I may not have handled that little conversational maneuver correctly. Time to reboot. "Good idea, honey."

"That's better. And it turned out to be a great idea. You want to know where Marcus followed him to?"

"I definitely do."

"Karen McMaster's apartment building. He spent forty-five minutes in there, and then went back to the Montana."

This is huge. We have an incontrovertible connection between Karen McMaster and such bad guys as the late Ernie Vinson and now Yuri Ganady. And the connection goes back to the days up to and including the one on which her husband was killed.

We can't get it to a jury yet, but I'll figure out a way. Whatever it is has got to include rattling Karen McMaster into making a mistake.

I find Craig Kimble's cell phone number. He answers with, "Carpenter, you're becoming as annoying as every other lawyer in my life."

"Stop, you're making me blush."

"What do you want?"

"Nothing that will make you happy. I'm informing you that I'll be calling you as a witness in our trial."

"Bullshit."

"I'm afraid it's true."

"What the hell do you need me for?"

"To testify to Steven and Karen's marital troubles, their infidelities. Just like you told me."

"I don't know what you are talking about."

"I'm talking about the affair that you and she had. About your telling me that they had an open marriage."

"I never said any such thing. Karen and I are still friends, so you are wasting your time."

He's lying. He knows it, I know it, and he knows I know it.

"I assume one of your many lawyers has explained the subpoena process to you?"

"I testify every twenty minutes; I've been in courtrooms

more than you. I'm testifying tomorrow in a trial a lot more important than yours. So you don't need to lecture me on the legal system. Let me say this very clearly: I have nothing to say that will help your case."

I'm not going to get anywhere with him, especially if he's prepared to lie on the stand. For now, I'll back off, because I want a favor. "Okay, you win. Then do me one favor and I'll leave you alone."

"You're a pain in the ass."

"I am aware of that. I want you to look at two photos and tell me if you can connect Karen to either of them, from back at the time before, or even after, her husband was killed."

"You think Karen killed Steven? Is that what this is about? You're out of your mind."

I'm not surprised that Kimble thinks Karen is innocent. They're still friends, and it's pretty disconcerting to think of your ex-girlfriend as a cold-blooded killer, especially when the apparent victim is the lover she had just before you.

"Just please look at the photos."

"So you're going to come to my office again? Maybe I should get you your own cubicle."

"No, I'm still paying off the parking loan I took out last time. I'll email them to you. What's your email address?"

"Is this important?" he asks.

"Life and death."

He sighs. "Okay. Send them to me." He gives me his email address, and I say I'll send them within ten minutes, which I then do. Or at least Laurie does; uploading photos and emailing them does not fall directly within my technological skill set.

We've sent him photos of Vinson and Ganady. He told me

in his office that he had never heard of Vinson, but perhaps he'll recognize his face. Can't hurt to try.

Less than five minutes later I get back the answer.

"I've never seen either of them before. Since I assume they are not upstanding citizens, I am pleased to say that I certainly can't connect them to Karen. Please remove my phone number from your contact list . . . even though I don't know how the hell you got it in the first place."

I'm not surprised by the answer. I doubted that Karen would have met with either of them with anyone else around. My hope and belief is that Kimble, still friends with Karen, will call her and tell her about his interaction with me.

I want Kimble to warn Karen McMaster that I am after her.

I want her to panic. Especially now, because she will be on the stand very soon.

J ason Morris has been a jeweler for twenty-seven years.

One of the first things he conveys to Tasker when he gets on the stand is that a jeweler is different from someone who sells jewelry. Morris, by his own estimation, is an artist.

And the truth is, he's correct. Tasker gets him to project slides featuring some of his work. They consist of rings, necklaces, and bracelets that he has made for his clients. They are beautiful, even to my jewelry-unappreciating eye.

"Did you ever make jewelry for Steven or Karen McMaster?" Tasker asks.

"Oh, yes. They were among my favorite clients. Not because they bought so many pieces, but because they appreciated them. They both had a fine eye and excellent taste."

Tasker introduces the ring found in Carrigan's locker as evidence, and then hands it to Morris. "Does this look familiar to you?"

"It certainly should; I created it. Mrs. McMaster purchased it three years ago for her husband."

"You take photographs of all your pieces when you make them?"

"Yes."

"Did you bring a photograph of this ring?"

"Yes."

Tasker projects a slide photo of the ring, which he says was taken three years ago. The jury then gets to see the actual ring, which is obviously identical.

Tasker then gets him to wax semi eloquently about the uniqueness of the ring, and how there can't possibly be another one like it.

I have little to gain by going after Morris. "When was the last time you saw this ring?" I ask. "Before today."

"I'm not sure, probably about a year ago. Steven bought something then, and I think he was wearing it."

"But you're not sure?" I ask.

"Not completely."

"So it could have been on eBay, it could have been stolen, it could have been regifted, it could have been lost, and you might not know it?"

"Anything is possible, but I would be surprised if any of that was true."

"You don't think it was stolen?"

He's confused, since the entire premise of Tasker's case is that it was stolen. "Well, maybe stolen."

"Who put this ring into the locker at Welcome Home?"

"I don't know," he says.

"You couldn't know, unless you saw it take place, correct?"

"Yes, that's correct."

"No one could know, unless they saw it take place, correct?"

Morris says "Correct" before Tasker can jump to his feet to

object. Hatchet sustains the objection, obviously meaningless since the jury heard the answer.

Next up is Sean Aimonetti, the director of Welcome Home. Here with him is James Lasky, the guy who seems to do most of the "hands-on" work there. Both of them had been on the witness list, but I suspect Lasky was on there to vouch for Tomasino. Since vouching for Tomasino is no longer within the realm of possibility, he's probably going to be called if Tasker can't get what he wants out of Aimonetti.

Tasker gets Aimonetti to run through his history and qualifications. This is a guy who has spent his life helping people, not just to get them off alcohol and drugs, but to survive. I give money; he gives everything.

Aimonetti is there to talk about the ring that was found in Carrigan's locker. He describes how each person that wants one has a locker which they can keep belongings in, even when they're not there. He says that it gives them a sense of permanence and belonging and helps ensure that they will be back. Aimonetti wants them back because he wants them sheltered and fed.

The important point that Aimonetti makes, at least as far as Tasker is concerned, is that the lockers are locked and that the users possess the only key.

When I get up to cross-examine, I trot out the old "thank you for your service" line. Then I introduce as evidence the photograph that I took of the locker room when I was there.

"Is that the locker area at Welcome Home?"

He nods. "It is."

"And were you with me when I took the photo?"

"Yes."

"Was there any planning or setting up anything special before I took it?"

"No. I showed you the room, and you asked if you could take the photographs. I gave you permission."

"Some of the lockers in this photograph are open, yet the people who use them aren't there. Is that correct?"

"Yes."

"And you can see that some of the open lockers have possessions in them, correct?"

"Yes."

"So someone could come into this room and place something inside one of the open lockers, even if it wasn't their locker?"

"Yes. We encourage people to make sure their lockers are closed and locked, but obviously not everyone listens."

"Could someone place a ring inside one of the open lockers?"

"Yes."

"Thank you. To your knowledge, has Donald Carrigan ever caused a problem at Welcome Home?"

"No."

"No violence of any kind?"

"No."

"Thank you, no further questions."

Tasker redirects and gets Aimonetti to say that he was there when the search warrant was executed on Carrigan's locker, and that it was locked when they arrived and had to be broken into.

The court session is adjourned and I head home. Late night tonight because I'm pretty sure that tomorrow is the day Karen McMaster will testify.

I'm going to go easy on Karen McMaster.

That doesn't mean I'm going to treat her with kid gloves; I'm just not going to unload everything on her. I am planning to call her back during the defense case and much of what I'll be doing will be more effective then.

Another way to put it is that although I'm not going to destroy her, I'm damn well not going to thank her for her service.

Tasker, on the other hand, makes it clear from his first words that he's going to treat her as the poor, grieving widow. "Let me first say that I am sorry for your loss."

"Thank you," she says, sounding very sad. Any minute she's going to ask for a tissue so she can dab away the fake tears.

He takes her through how she and Steven met and married and what a happy life they shared. I could object on grounds of relevance, but since I want to go after this on cross, I let it go.

"Please tell us what happened on the night your husband lost his life," Tasker finally says.

"I was in New York at our apartment working on details for a charity event, and Steven was in Short Hills. He told me he was going out for dinner with a business associate. Steven always liked to eat early because he was at his desk at work by seven o'clock every morning." She smiled. "He was a self-described workaholic.

"He was ordinarily home by eight thirty and I called him at nine. I got no answer, so I kept trying. By ten fifteen or so I was frantic, so I called a neighbor, Walter Zimmer, to see if he was home and just not answering the phone for some reason."

There is a slight bit of truth in what she is saying. The records show she did call Steven repeatedly without getting an answer; I believe she made those calls knowing he wouldn't answer, but also knowing that doing so would enhance her credibility in a situation just like this.

Her voice drops down some. "I was expecting Walter, or maybe Steven, to call me back. Instead it was the police."

Next Tasker brings up the ring. She identifies it again, which is really not necessary after the jeweler's testimony. But she does say that she knows Steven had it until the night he died, that she had seen it just a couple of days before. It is designed to leave no doubt in the jury's mind that the ring was taken off his finger at the time he was murdered.

I am limited in what questions I can ask on cross-examination; I can cover only those areas that Tasker brought up on direct. That's not a big hindrance, since I want to save a lot of it for our defense case.

"Mrs. McMaster, you said that by nine o'clock you were starting to worry about your husband being out so late."

"Yes," she says. "Not terribly worried at that point, but it was unusual."

"Was he a really fast eater?"

"No." She smiles. "Just an early starter."

"Was Cimino's a restaurant he patronized often?"

"Yes. Mostly for business dinners. It was near his office, and he loved their pasta."

"Would it surprise you to know that in the two years before his death, he ate at Cimino's a hundred and fifty-one times? That averages close to one and a half times per week."

"That wouldn't surprise me," she says.

"Let's try this one. Would it surprise you to know that in ninety-seven of those times, his reservation for dinner was at eight P.M. or later? And that the majority of those times it was for eight thirty or later?"

"I couldn't say."

I introduce Steven McMaster's credit card records, which we had subpoenaed, into evidence. Laurie did a great job investigating all of this.

"These records show that your husband paid the check more than ninety percent of the times he ate at Cimino's. The average time he left the restaurant was ten fifteen P.M. Are you surprised yet?"

"That doesn't seem right," she says.

"You can check the records if you want," I say.

"My understanding was that he was eating early that night."

I wish I had the credit card payment record for the restaurant that night, but he apparently did not pay for the dinner. The police report did confirm that he ate at Cimino's.

"Nine minutes before you called Mr. Zimmer, you received a phone call. Do you remember who that was calling you?" We have also subpoenaed her phone records. We knew what was in them through Sam's efforts, but to bring it up in court, we needed to have obtained the information legally.

She looks puzzled. "I don't remember."

I nod, as if that settles the issue. "You testified that you and Steven had a wonderful life together."

She nods. "We did."

"Did that wonderful life include infidelity and adultery?"

Tasker objects that it is outside the scope, but it clearly is not, and Hatchet tells him so in overruling the objection.

"We didn't have a perfect marriage," she says, hesitantly.

"Mrs. McMaster, that would be an acceptable answer if my question was 'What didn't you have?' But that wasn't my question, so let me restate it. Did your wonderful life with Steven include infidelity and adultery?"

A pause, and then, "Steven made some mistakes."

"Did you make similar mistakes?"

"No," she says, in the process committing perjury.

I tell Hatchet I am letting her off the stand, pending recall during the defense case. He so advises her and then asks Tasker to call his next witness.

"Your Honor, the prosecution rests."

I have no doubt that Karen McMaster was behind her husband's death, as surely as if she had broken his neck.

I don't know who the actual neck-breaker was. It was either Yuri Ganady or Ernie Vinson, or a combination of both. If I were forced to give my best guess, which I'm not, it would be Ganady, since I think he demonstrated his ability to break a neck with that murder in the warehouse. I don't know what that was about, but it doesn't seem to relate to the Carrigan case. Ganady obviously operated in a dark and complex world.

It's the Carrigan case that is my focus and I really don't have a choice of strategies. There is no way I can prove that Carrigan is innocent, so I have to demonstrate the very real possibility that Karen McMaster is guilty.

Tasker will argue that tales of Ernie Vinson and Serbian killers like Yuri Ganady are not relevant and represent a fishing expedition. I am confident, however, that Hatchet will let it in.

I take Tara and Sebastian for a walk; it's always a time when I can do my clearest thinking. By the time I get back I've decided that when it comes to the admissibility issue, I am going to raise it myself, on my terms, and not wait for Tasker to set the agenda.

But the one thing I am wrestling with, and have been all along, is the question of where Carrigan fits in. I get that Vinson stole his hat and someone planted the ring for the purpose of framing him. He may well have been chosen at random . . . an easy patsy because he was homeless. But once that was accomplished, why did Vinson come back? Where was he trying to take him that night?

When I get back, before I do my witness preparation, I tuck Ricky into bed. It's a ritual I try never to miss. We talk for maybe five minutes each time and it's invariably my favorite five minutes of the day.

This time he asks, "Will you take me fishing?"

"Sure," I lie. I'm not the fishing type in that I don't want to touch worms or fish. I also hate the idea of tricking fish to bite on a hook; it seems cruel and disreputable. And I would be in favor of throwing them back, but that would mean touching them. In case you weren't aware by now, I have mental issues.

"Good. Opie's father takes him fishing."

So Ricky has learned about town drunks and fishing from *The Andy Griffith Show* reruns. "You shouldn't be watching that show. Can't you find something with foul language and gratuitous violence?"

"What is gratuitous violence?" he asks.

"It's a phrase you shouldn't tell your mother I said."

"Okay. Hey, Dad? The kids in school say Christmas is over. But Mom says it's still going."

"Who do you want to be right?"

"Mom," he says, without hesitation.

"Then it's still going. And those kids don't know what they're missing."

After Ricky and I are finished chatting, Laurie updates me on the information she has collected on Karen McMaster. I'm not calling her tomorrow, but when I do, this information will come in very handy.

I get to court early, and Carrigan seems more upbeat than usual, because we're starting our case. "Our turn," he says, though it's more of a question than a statement.

"Our turn," I say.

Before the jury is brought in, I ask Hatchet for a meeting with him and Tasker in chambers. Once we're in there, I say, "Your Honor, I don't believe in surprises, so I think it's best to lay out the defense theory of the case, prior to calling our witnesses."

"This is, I believe, a first for you, Mr. Carpenter?"

I nod. "I'm turning over a new legal leaf. So if I may . . . the defense will demonstrate the strong likelihood that it was Karen McMaster that arranged the murder of her husband, and that Donald Carrigan was framed by her and her associates."

Tasker fakes trying to stifle a fake laugh. Then, "Your Honor, this is not close to being supported by the facts. Mr. Carpenter is simply trying to confuse the jury by creating a fantasy out of whole cloth."

"I agree that it is not supported by the facts that you presented in your case," I say, "but I am going to supply the true facts. Your Honor, this is not a fishing expedition. We have a suspect, just as Mr. Tasker does, and we are going to prove that our theory is correct, just as Mr. Tasker attempted to do. If I was a betting man, and I am, I would wager that at the end of this trial, if the jury were to be asked to pick between Karen McMaster and Donald Carrigan as to which is the guilty party, McMaster would win in a landslide. But at the very least, they will be neck deep in reasonable doubt."

There is no way Hatchet can refuse us the opportunity to present our case, and he doesn't. He rules in our favor, but adds in his ominous voice, "I'll be watching you."

We open the defense case with Dr. Lucia Alvarez.

She was Carrigan's VA hospital shrink who filled me in on the PTSD issues he was dealing with. She had agreed to testify when I asked her back then, and didn't hesitate when we called her now.

I take Dr. Alvarez through her credentials, which include an undergraduate degree at Cornell and two post-graduate degrees at Princeton. This is a woman who could be making a fortune talking to people trying to find their inner selves on Central Park West, but instead is making a fraction of that helping veterans back from the horrors of combat.

I would thank her for her service, but I'm afraid the jury would think I'm overdoing it.

"Dr. Alvarez, has Mr. Carrigan given you permission to reveal the details of his medical condition?"

"He has, yes."

"For how long was he your patient?" I ask.

"A little less than a year . . . eleven months."

"Can you describe his condition in terms that even I can understand? If I can understand it, then the jury will have no problem." After I say this I feel like cringing at my own pandering.

"The commonly accepted term is that Mr. Carrigan is suffering from PTSD, or post-traumatic stress disorder. It is as a result of his experiences in Iraq, which could very accurately be described as the horrors of war."

"Is there anything unique about his version of the disorder?"

"I wouldn't say unique, in that certainly others suffer from it, but Mr. Carrigan's symptoms include a rather severe form of claustrophobia."

"Is he under treatment for that now, if you know?"

"Yes, I was contacted by the prison psychologist, and we consulted on it."

"Dr. Alvarez, do you think Mr. Carrigan is capable of the crime for which he is accused?"

Tasker objects, but Hatchet overrules.

"I can't speak to his physical capabilities, but I do not think there is a chance he robbed and murdered someone. The possibility is close to zero."

"Thank you."

Tasker begins by getting her to talk a bit more about PTSD. Once she does, he asks, "Do you run into many cases of it in soldiers who have spent their entire army career stationed in New Jersey?"

"I don't know any such people," she says.

"Is it usually prevalent in soldiers who have seen combat?"

She nods. "Certainly."

"Where there is death and destruction? Where killing is most often the goal?"

"Yes."

"You're aware that Mr. Carrigan was trained in the art of killing?"

"I am aware of his training, yes," she says. "His was no different from many thousands of his comrades."

"Finding himself in the middle of all this violence in Iraq, did he ever kill in Iraq, as he was trained to do?"

"I don't know."

"But it's possible?" he asks, pressing her.

"I don't want to speculate on something I know nothing about."

"Is it fair to say that his experience there changed him?"

She nods. "Of course. It changes everyone."

"In unpredictable ways?"

"Sometimes."

"When you last spoke with Mr. Carrigan, was he homeless?" he asks.

"No."

"So at least in that way, his circumstances had changed?"

"Yes."

"If combat always changes a person, can living on the street, not knowing where your next meal is coming from, can that change a person as well?"

"It's possible."

"Thank you, Dr. Alvarez. And thank you for your service."

My next witness is slightly risky. I'm recalling Sean Aimonetti to the stand to make a point, but at the same time it will allow Tasker to make his own point, at least he will if he's done his homework.

"Mr. Aimonetti, at Welcome Home do you keep a record of who comes in and out for meals or shelter?"

"We do. All clients are asked to sign in. They don't always do so, but the sign-in books are at the door and we have a monitor there, so I think compliance is pretty good."

"Did Mr. Carrigan sign in frequently?" I ask.

"Oh, yes. From all accounts he was respectful of the process."

"Did I ask you to check the dates and times he logged in?"

"Yes, you did," he says.

"And did I ask you to compare the frequency of his visits to Welcome Home for meals before and after the date of the McMaster murder?"

"You did."

"Did you see any difference in the pattern or frequency?" I ask.

"No, I did not."

I introduce as evidence a chart that Aimonetti prepared tracking Carrigan's appearances, and showing what he just testified to.

"Would you find it surprising if someone came into a good amount of money, through whatever means, and then kept coming into the shelter for free meals?"

"It would be somewhat surprising, yes." He smiles. "Our food is nourishing and tasty enough, but there are better restaurants."

"Last question, we talked during the defense case about the lockers, and how sometimes they were left open rather than locked."

"Yes."

"Earlier in this trial, a man named Jaime Tomasino testified that he had spoken with Mr. Carrigan and that Mr. Carrigan confessed to him. Are you aware of that?"

"Yes."

"Are you aware that he was exposed as a liar?"

"Yes."

"Was he actually a client of yours? Did he in fact go to Welcome Home for meals?"

"On occasion, yes."

"Would he have had access to that locker room, with all those open lockers?"

"Yes."

"Could he have slipped a ring in one of them?"

"It's possible."

"Thank you."

Tasker gets Aimonetti to say that he had no knowledge of Tomasino doing anything untoward in the locker room, nor did he know that Carrigan kept his locker unlocked.

When the cross is finished, Hatchet adjourns for the day, and I notice that Aimonetti hasn't left the courtroom yet. I call out to him to wait a moment, then I say goodbye to Carrigan and walk over to him.

"Thanks for your help," I say.

"No problem; glad to do it."

"You said you're an expert on alcoholism, right?"

"I've certainly spent a lot of time trying to help people recover from it."

"Does it affect someone physically, their reactions, reflexes, et cetera?"

"Certainly."

"So if someone is a very serious alcoholic, drunk every day, would they be affected physically in those days even when they were temporarily sober?"

"They would still be affected, at least to a degree, yes. Hands might shake, less than perfect balance . . . that kind of thing. If you tell me why you're asking, maybe I can be more specific."

I decide to tell him, leaving out the "Ricky–Otis Campbell–Mayberry" connection. "Okay. The guy they are looking for in the sniper shooting case, Chuck Simmons, I am told he was a serious alcoholic. If that were true, could he have made those shots, with the apparent incredible accuracy they demanded?" I also don't mention having gotten the information from Carrigan.

Aimonetti thinks for a while. "Interesting. I have my doubts."

"Was he a client of yours?"

"Not that I recall, but I'll have it checked." Then, "Very interesting."

About an hour later, Aimonetti reaches me on my cell phone. "I looked into it," he says. "We have no record of Simmons ever coming here."

The defense calls Sergeant Nathan Robbins."

Robbins was the detective assigned to the incident the night that Ernie Vinson was bitten by Zoey. His investigation was casual and incomplete, possibly because Carrigan was not considered important, and there were no serious injuries suffered.

I establish that Robbins indeed handled the case that night and take him through what he knows of it. "Did you ever come up with a suspect?" I ask.

"Nothing that we felt confident of, no."

"Did the attacker leave any trace of himself behind?"

Robbins nods. "He was bitten by the dog and part of his sleeve was torn off. There was blood on it."

"Did you test it for DNA?"

"No."

"What did you do as a result of your investigation that night?"

"We placed the dog in the custody of animal control. He had bitten someone, so the protocol is to keep him under a watch in case he showed symptoms for rabies," he says.

"So just to be clear, Sergeant Robbins, Mr. Carrigan was attacked, and the net result of your investigation was that you took his dog from him?"

"I followed the correct procedure."

"Was your lack of follow-up due to the fact that the victim was homeless and thus somehow less important?"

"Absolutely not, and I resent that."

I establish that there was a video of the entire incident, and play it in the courtroom. "Did you make any effort to trace the SUV, or find the assailant's accomplice?"

"We had nothing to go on."

"You mean other than the assailant's blood, which would have contained his DNA? Is that a gun in the assailant's hand?"

"Very hard to tell."

I then show a blown-up version of the visual, which makes it clear. "What about now, Sergeant Robbins? Still very hard to tell?"

"It appears to be a gun."

"So this was an attempted armed robbery? You phoned in your investigation on an attempted armed robbery?"

Tasker objects and Hatchet sustains. I turn him over to Tasker's cross, but he actually makes very little effort to rehabilitate him. His last question reflects his approach. "Sergeant, in your investigation, did you find that this incident had any relation whatsoever to the Steven McMaster murder?"

"No," Robbins says.

My next witness is Sergeant Mike Frierson. I'm actually recalling him, since he was part of the prosecution's case. I gave him a bit of a hard time on cross-examination, so I'm not expecting him to be friendly now. Fortunately the facts are the facts, and that's all I want from him this time.

"Sergeant Frierson, regarding the bloody part of the sleeve that was left behind from the dog bite, did I ask for it to be tested for DNA?"

"Yes, and that was done." He goes on to identify Ernie Vinson as the person whose DNA matched that of the blood on the sleeve.

"Is every citizen's DNA available to be matched?" I ask. "Are we all in the system?"

"No."

"Why was Ernie Vinson's DNA in there?"

"Because he had been arrested and convicted of crimes in the past."

"What kind of crimes?"

"Assault, attempted murder, racketeering."

"Had he spent time in prison?" I ask.

He nods. "Almost six years, in two separate terms."

"To your knowledge, was he what is called a mob enforcer?"

"Yes."

"Now that you've learned who the assailant was and you've learned that he was carrying a gun, has the investigation been reopened?"

"No."

"Why not?"

"Vinson is dead."

I feign surprise. "Ernie Vinson? The man carrying the gun in that video is dead?"

"Yes."

"Boy, that really puts things into perspective. He died of natural causes, I assume?"

"No, he was shot and killed."

"Has his killer been captured?"

"No."

"Thank you. No further questions."

Tasker hasn't objected to this line of questioning since he knows that Hatchet would shoot him down because of the Tomasino fiasco. So once again he simply gets Frierson to say that he is not aware of any connection between Vinson and the McMaster murder.

Hatchet has something he has to attend to, so he adjourns the trial early for the day. My guess is the jury is pleased at this; I know I am.

For the first time in a very long time I am able to pick Ricky from school, and then we take Tara and Sebastian on a long walk. After that we head down to the foundation to see how things are going; I've been out of touch for too long. Zoey and the puppies are doing great. This is the second time Ricky has visited them; he loves laying on the floor and letting them walk over him.

The little ones, who define the word "adorable," are nearing the age when they can be adopted, and Willie and Sondra already have a waiting list of families ready to do just that. Puppies are the easiest to place, though that is a fact that doesn't necessarily please anyone in rescue.

Laurie is going to a friend's baby shower tonight, the first time she has been out in quite a while. When I'm on a case, even though she has a full plate as my investigator, most of the burdens in the house fall on her. When I'm not on a case, most of the burdens of the house fall on her.

She is concerned about what we might have for dinner, but I tell her not to worry, that we'll order in. What I don't tell her is that Ricky and I have designed a plan to order pizza and garlic bread, which is what we do.

By the time we're done stuffing ourselves, we have to be rolled out of the kitchen. I swear him to secrecy as to what we ate, but from past experience I know he'll cave under Laurie's pressure. That's okay, it was worth it.

Once I have him tucked into bed, I head to my upstairs office to work on the witnesses for tomorrow. We have only a few days left in the defense case, and we have to make the most of them.

And then will come the dreaded wait for the verdict.

At first I think the noise is Laurie coming home.

Then I realize it isn't her, unless she's decided to throw herself against the outside wall of the house before coming in.

It's coming from the backyard, and when I look through the window I see Marcus and someone else facing off against each other. One of them has just bounced off the wall, but I don't know which one.

I'm feeling panicked and not sure what to do. The first thing I do is run to Ricky's room and make sure he's sleeping. Then I lock his door from the outside; no matter what happens I don't want him coming out.

Next I go get Laurie's gun, which is at the top of the closet. She keeps it unloaded, so I have to get the ammunition, which is in another closet. Once I do that, I have to figure out how to load the damn thing, even though she has shown me on more than one occasion.

I do that while running down the stairs, and then I grab the phone, call 9-1-1, and report what is going on. I should have done that first. I run into the yard, which is not the brightest thing I've ever done, but I feel like I have to.

Now for the first time I can get a better sense of what is happening. Marcus is fighting with someone at least three inches taller and thirty pounds heavier than he is. And the guy does not look fat; my grandmother would say that he is "built like a brick shithouse."

They are smashing each other, but seeming to block most of the blows. I never thought I would say this of anyone, but the guy might be a match for Marcus.

"Marcus, take my gun!" I scream, mostly because it is worthless in my shaking hand. Not only could I not hit the intruder, I doubt that I could even hit the garage. Also, in the dim light I would be afraid I would hit Marcus. But having said that, I am going to do what I have to. Marcus is not going down.

Not surprisingly, they both ignore me; it's as if I didn't say anything. And maybe I didn't; maybe I'm so nervous that my voice didn't register a sound.

They're now grappling, with their arms around each other. Suddenly, the enemy seems to get the upper hand and throws Marcus against the garage. He moves incredibly quickly, and he grabs Marcus from behind, his hands in the head and neck area.

He's going to break Marcus's neck.

I don't know how to shoot without hitting Marcus, but I'm about to try when I see Marcus put both his hands on one of the guy's arms. Then he does something I would never have thought remotely possible, he snaps the arm.

Just breaks it. Like a twig. The sound that it makes is the most disgusting, beautiful, revolting, exhilarating sound I have ever heard.

The man screams and drops his other arm. Amazingly, he

uses that arm to throw another punch at Marcus, but it doesn't land. Marcus slips it, grabs the man, and pounds his head into the wall. Three times. I would yell at Marcus to stop, but I don't want him to, and it wouldn't matter anyway.

The man finally slips to the ground, just as the area erupts in light and noise.

In seconds cops are everywhere, guns drawn. Two of them train their weapons on Marcus and me, and two others go to the bad guy with the crushed head.

One of the cops says, "He's dead."

"Good," I say.

I introduce myself and Marcus to the cops and explain that I live here, and that I called 9-1-1. Two of the other cops recognize me, so they lower their weapons.

I'm squeamish about stuff like this, but I summon the courage to walk over to take a look at the dead guy. I am not surprised that he looks just like Yuri Ganady, except for the crushed head part.

Laurie pulls up in front of the house; she can't get into the driveway because of all the police cars. She comes running up the driveway in a panic, and I try to quickly assure her as soon as I can that everyone is all right.

The police have set up camp by the back door, which is where the coroner is retrieving the body as well. So Laurie and I go around the front to enter the house.

I point to the Christmas wreath on the front door and ask, "Any chance we can take that down? The neighbors must think we're nuts."

She shakes her head. "If they don't have the holiday spirit, that's their problem."

We go upstairs to make sure Ricky is okay, and somehow

he has slept through the entire thing. On the way back outside I tell Laurie what has gone on. I've got a hunch that she's going to think this was not a great night for the baby shower.

My other hunch is that she won't think to ask what Ricky and I had for dinner.

Pete shows up and takes charge of the investigation.

His first question to me is, "Have you noticed how many times people have tried to kill you?"

"Actually, I have."

"It could be a personality thing," he says. "Now suppose you tell me what happened."

"I'm afraid you're going to have to question Marcus; there's not that much that I know."

"Damn, we're going to have to bring in a translator. I can't understand half the things he says, on the rare occasions he says anything."

"I think Laurie can help with that," I say. "All I know is that we've had Marcus tailing Ganady, and . . ."

"Why?"

"Two reasons. He murdered Steven McMaster and your warehouse guy, so we're trying to catch him in something incriminating. And the other reason is that Laurie thought it was a good idea, which is why I am currently still living."

"Okay, so Marcus was following Ganady . . ." He gestures for me to continue.

"Yes, and he apparently followed him here and prevented him from entering the house. Ganady attacked him, and believe it or not, it was a fairly even fight for a while. Then Ganady got behind him and tried to break his neck, and Marcus didn't react well to that. But Marcus was totally acting to save my life, and in self-defense as well."

"Don't worry, nobody's going after Marcus for this," he says.

"Good. And do me a favor?"

"What's that?"

"If Ganady is carrying his cell phone, can you give me the number? I need to subpoena his phone records."

He looks like he's going to argue, but then says, "Okay." He calls over one of his officers and sends him off to find out the number.

Pete then goes off to question Marcus, and enlists Laurie for help. I go back in the house to make sure Ricky still hasn't woken up. With all the noise and lights it's amazing that he hasn't.

I actually shudder at the prospect of Ganady having gotten into the house with Ricky, and I give him a small kiss on the head. He doesn't wake up from that either, but I think I see him smile. I could be wrong about that, but I choose to believe it.

I'm not really sure what the effect of tonight's events will be on the case, but it probably cuts positively. If we can tie Ganady to Karen McMaster, then that connection will be made much more ominous by what Ganady did tonight.

The only negative is that the police will never have the opportunity to question Ganady, but if Cindy Spodek's report was correct, he wasn't the type that would be likely to break down and spill everything under interrogation anyway.

The excitement, such as it is, doesn't end until almost two thirty in the morning, at which point the only sign that anything happened is police tape and two officers guarding the scene. Our neighbors, all of whom came out to see what the hell was going on, have retreated to their houses and beds. If they're smart, they'll organize a meeting to figure out a way to throw us out of the neighborhood.

Laurie and I are still a bit wired, and we calm down by sitting in the den with a glass of wine.

"You probably saved my life by having Marcus follow him," I say.

I instantly regret having said that, because she starts to cry. I don't deal well with women in general, but with crying women I am a complete loser.

"Was it something I said?"

"Let's go to bed," she says.

"When you say, 'go to bed,' what exactly do you mean by that?"

"I mean you should hold me until I fall asleep."

"Okay, just checking."

As I stand up, I realize that I still have Laurie's gun in my pocket. "Whoa," I say. "You might want to unload this." I put the gun on the table.

"You loaded the gun and took it outside? Would you have shot the guy if you had the chance?"

"Absolutely. Actually, I would have shot at the guy. What I would have hit is anybody's guess."

So we go up to bed and I hold Laurie until she goes to sleep. Not bad.

wake up at six o'clock, which means I'm going on three hours' sleep.

For some reason I'm not tired; maybe it will hit me later.

I shower, grab a cup of coffee, and take Tara and Sebastian for an early walk. The dogs are clearly surprised at the timing, and are slow to spring into action. Sebastian looks at me as if to say, "How about if I just stay here and piss in the house later?"

Once I'm back I call Sam Willis. It's still early but I know he'll be awake. Sam is always awake. He answers, as per usual, on the first ring. "Talk to me," he says.

I tell him that I want him to go into the GPS phone records of Ganady in much more depth, not just since we have been made aware of him, but for at least two months before that. I want to know where he has been every moment of every day.

"I'm on it," he says.

My next call is to Hike, telling him to subpoena the phone records for Ganady, on a rush basis. I want a legal record of who he called, but I don't need the GPS records for now. One major positive result of last night's violence at my house is that we now have Ganady's number from Pete. This way we can legitimately request the records, and included in there will be his call to Karen McMaster the night of her husband's murder.

When I arrive at court, Hatchet calls Tasker and me into chambers. This is getting to be a regular occurrence. I'm tempted to say, "We've got to stop meeting like this," but I think I may have used up my allotted sarcastic comments with Hatchet.

"Well, Mr. Carpenter, there appears to have been some excitement at your house last night."

I was so busy I forgot to check and see if the media had the story, but it appears they have. "Yes, Your Honor, I was heroic as always."

"I trust your family is unharmed?"

This represents an uncharacteristic outpouring of humanity from Hatchet. "Yes, thank you, Your Honor."

"What effect do you gentlemen see it having on our trial? Since the news doesn't relate it to what we are doing here, it's possible that jurors have been exposed to it."

"Unless Mr. Carpenter informs us otherwise, I don't see a connection to our case," Tasker says. "I am not aware of Yuri Ganady having any relationship to what we are doing."

"Then let me take this opportunity to inform you otherwise," I say. "Ganady is directly involved, and will be a key part of the defense presentation."

"How is he involved?"

"He either murdered Steven McMaster, or had it done. More likely the former."

Tasker laughs at the idea. "I thought Ernie Vinson was the killer? It's getting hard to keep track."

"You need to concentrate more," I say.

"Enough of that," Hatchet says, which shuts us right up. "If you intend on bringing Ganady into this case, Mr. Carpenter, then we need to consider the effect on the jury if they've seen the news coverage this morning."

"I respectfully disagree, Your Honor, and I'd like to place an emphasis on the word 'respectfully.' I assume the news coverage presented it straightforwardly, and as you said, they did not tie it into our trial. My intention would simply be to re-present it to the jury, exactly as it happened, and exactly as reported. Then, of course, I will tie it into the McMaster murder. But the question of whether they are already aware of the events last night shouldn't prejudice them one way or the other, since they'll be hearing about it from me anyway."

Tasker really has to go along, mainly because he has no real alternative. I'm quite sure he doesn't want a mistrial, since he correctly considers his side to be leading. So questioning the jurors as to what they've heard about last night would serve no real purpose. Suppose they said they saw the coverage? Then what?

Hatchet agrees that there is nothing to be accomplished by questioning the jury, and no real harm if they have been exposed to the news reports. He says that he will reinstruct the jury not to watch media coverage of anything relating to this trial, but will not mention last night.

What is bugging me about last night, other than the fact that a Serbian paramilitary killer tried to end my life, is the question of why he would do it. The obvious answer, I suppose, is that he was in a conspiracy with Karen McMaster, and it has become clear that she is my target. But they should know that getting me out of the way wouldn't let her off the hook. Hike or another lawyer would simply pick up where I left off.

If they thought they would save themselves from exposure by killing me, they aren't as smart as I thought.

It must be something else.

There was one unusual aspect to the prosecution's case.

Tasker never called Lieutenant Anthony Reiner, who was the lead detective on the McMaster murder investigation. He basically didn't need him because his evidence was just factual, the DNA hat was at the scene and the ring was in the locker, and he could bring them in through other witnesses.

It's rare that the defense would be the only side to call the lead detective, but that's what I'm doing now. I could ask Hatchet to let me treat him as a hostile witness, but I don't think that will be necessary. I can always do it if Reiner's answers and attitude merit it.

"Lieutenant, you were the lead detective on the McMaster murder case?"

He nods. "I was."

"Once you got the DNA results on the hat and found the ring in Mr. Carrigan's locker, were you confident that you had identified the killer?"

"Yes."

"So you stopped investigating?" I ask.

"I wouldn't say stopped, but we just covered a few final

bases. Once we have enough to confidently charge someone, we tend to move on. We don't recommend charges lightly."

"I've often heard that the first person police always consider in murder cases is the spouse. Is that true?"

"Every case is different, but certainly we attempt to rule the spouse out," he says.

"Did you rule the spouse, meaning Karen McMaster, out in this case?"

"We had no evidence to tie her to the crime. But I would say it was more a case of ruling this defendant in, than ruling her out."

I nod as if now I understand. "I see. So you had this compelling evidence that Mr. Carrigan committed the crime. Did you ever discover how he got out to Short Hills?"

"No."

"Did you ever discover what he did with the money and jewels that were stolen?"

"No, it was a long time until Mr. Carrigan was found and arrested. It seemed as if he had disappeared . . . successfully gone into hiding."

"And in fact he had, correct? He was homeless, with no address, no driver's license, no car, correct?"

"Yes. As it turned out, apparently so."

I feign surprise. "Apparently so? You didn't restart, or really continue, your investigation after he was found?"

"No."

"So you never sought to learn how he got out to Short Hills?"

"No."

"You never checked rental car records for that time?"

"No."

"Did you think he hired a limo?"

Tasker objects and Hatchet sustains and admonishes me.

I move on. "Did you ever finally seek to learn what he did with the money and jewels?"

"No. It wasn't necessary."

"Did you ever learn that he has been a semi-regular patron of a soup kitchen before and since that night?"

"No."

"Now that you know it, does it give you pause, and cause you to question your investigation?"

"No."

"Because you got your man, no matter what."

"We got our man because of evidence."

"Mr. Tasker has implied that perhaps Mr. Carrigan had someone to drive him out to Short Hills, and maybe even took off with all the loot. Is that a possibility?"

"I would say it's possible."

"Now that you see how difficult it would be for Mr. Carrigan to have gotten out there on his own, have you investigated who that accomplice might be?"

"No."

"Lieutenant, do you still work on the police force? Have you retired, and I should be talking to someone else?"

Tasker objects, and Hatchet tells me that he's warning me, and will not warn me again.

"Lieutenant, are you aware that Karen McMaster inherited a fortune worth two hundred and fifty million dollars from her husband?"

"I knew he was quite wealthy."

"In your experience, is that kind of money ever a possible motive for murder?"

"It certainly can be."

I nod. "Certainly can. Might even be worth investigating."

T homas Ogden and his son Chris never missed a chance to go snowmobiling.

They were among that rare group of people who watched the calendar and dreaded the arrival of spring, because that would mean the end of these outings together.

They often went into the woods north of Parsippany and snowmobiled along the well-defined trails. It was always incredibly peaceful out there, especially early in the mornings. And right after a snow, when the trails were pristine, it was nothing short of perfect.

So on this day the Ogdens left their house in Wayne at 6:00 A.M., so as to be there when the sun came up. They'd then spend the next three hours lost in this unblemished white world and be back at home in time for lunch.

This particular idyllic morning lasted three minutes from the time they boarded the snowmobiles. Chris was the first to see it, and therefore the first to scream. Thomas did the same moments later.

What they saw was a human body, hung by a rope from a tree.

They didn't know it at the time, but the dead man was Chuck Simmons. The sniper had been found.

They raced back and as soon as they reached an area where they could get cell service, they called 9-1-1. Then they waited for the police to arrive, so they could lead them to the body.

They led the police on foot to the place where they found it. It took twelve minutes, and once they got there, the police asked them to stay back. So they never got to see the note nailed to the tree.

It simply said, "My work is done."

I have to say that my hunch about the sniper shootings was way off.

The media is reporting that the hanging death has been ruled a suicide, and that there was a note essentially admitting guilt. I hadn't thought that a person with such a drinking problem could do that kind of shooting, but maybe he had the incentive to sober up at the prospect of killing those that he wanted to take revenge on.

Now that Judge Eric Yount, the son of the judge that Simmons believed wronged him, was dead, Simmons apparently decided it was time to check out of this world himself.

Today's court session is starting after lunch because a juror has a doctor's appointment. I've decided to hold off on calling Karen McMaster to the stand, and instead will call witnesses that are less important, but that help me paint an overall picture.

The first one is a forensic cyber investigator named Paul Ness who uses subpoenas to legally do what Sam Willis does illegally. Of course, he's a lot slower and much more expensive, but he gets the job done and comes off as a very credible witness.

I take Ness through the work he has done on this case. First, he confirms that no car rental company within five hundred miles has any record of Don Carrigan renting a car the week of the murder, and that in fact Carrigan has no current license that he could have used.

Then he describes how he has searched for any financial accounts, checking or otherwise, that Carrigan could have used to store any of the money or jewelry taken in the robbery. There is also no record of any pawn shop activity that could be tied to Carrigan or to the jewelry taken.

Ness also found no large purchases Carrigan might have made, no hotel rooms booked, no apartments rented. Ness concedes it's impossible to completely research all of that, but expresses doubts, based on his professional opinion, that any such purchases existed.

Tasker on cross again alludes to the possibility of an accomplice, who drove Carrigan to the murder/robbery scene and then took all the proceeds for himself.

Ness admits that he cannot speak to that and makes my day when he tells Tasker that if he has the name of such a person, he'd be happy to research it. It exposes the flaw in Tasker's case; he needs such a person to exist, but has no idea who it might be, and has apparently made little effort to find out.

As I'm leaving court, I see that there is a message from Sam Willis to call him, so I do so. "Andy," he says, "I've been checking the GPS records on Ganady's phone for the past couple of months, like you asked."

"And?"

"And I found something."

Sam has a habit of drawing out his revelations, but they

usually are significant. "I need to show you; it will help me make sure I'm right."

"So bring the records to the house."

"No, I really need to show you. I need to take you to the places."

"Is this important, Sam? I have to get ready for court to-morrow."

"It couldn't be more important, Andy."

"Okay. I'll meet you at the house and we'll go from there."

When I get home, both Laurie and Sam are waiting for me.

Ricky is having a sleepover tonight at his friend Will Rubenstein's house, and Laurie says she is going to go with us.

"Did he tell you what's going on?" I ask, referring to Sam. She nods. "He did."

"Does someone want to fill me in?"

She shakes her head. "Better you should see it fresh. Just bear with us."

So we get in Sam's car and drive to downtown Passaic. Twenty minutes later, Sam pulls into a five-story parking lot. It's one owned by the city and is free, to encourage people to patronize nearby stores and restaurants. Passaic is a bit different from Manhattan.

"We're parking here?" I ask.

"No," Sam says.

"Yet here we are in a parking lot."

Sam wends his way up to the fifth and top floor, which represents the rooftop of the building. The floor is empty except for three cars, which have so much soot on them they could be abandoned. He drives to the far left of the lot and parks.

"Time to get out," Laurie says.

"This is fun," I say.

We walk to the edge of the roof, which has a four-foot wall preventing us from falling down to the street. "Take a look," Laurie says, pointing.

"I'm looking," I say, but I still don't know what they're talking about.

"Follow my finger," she says, and puts it in front of my face, pointing slightly to the left.

"Holy shit," I say, as the truth hits me. About three short blocks from the end of her finger is the restaurant that Ronald Lester, the lawyer who represented Chuck Simmons's wife, walked out of when he was shot.

"You can say that again," Laurie says.

But I don't. Instead I say, "Ganady was here? At the time of the shooting?"

"No, two days before," Sam says. "But we're not finished with our field trip yet."

"Let's cut it short, Sam. Tell me what we're going to find."

He nods. "Okay. Ganady, or at least his cell phone, was present where every sniper shooting took place. But never at the time of the shooting; it was anywhere from two to four days beforehand."

"He had to be scouting out the locations," Laurie says. "Most likely for someone else to execute the kills."

I turn to Sam. "You're sure of this? You've been to the other locations?"

He nods. "I can show you if you want. But I've checked them out, just like here."

I believe Sam, as does Laurie, and neither of us thinks it's necessary to visit each scene. Instead we have him drive us home, so we can talk it over and figure out what the hell this means.

On the way I call Hike and tell him to get a subpoena for the cell phone GPS records of Ganady's phone, so we can get legally what Sam has already gotten illegally. I don't know if I'll have any use for it, never mind need it, but it just instinctively feels like something we should have.

Sam drops us off and Laurie and I go into the den. "Glass of wine?" she asks.

I nod. "Better make it a double."

We sit down and Laurie says, "Let's start with what we know. We know that Ganady and Vinson called Karen McMaster, we know that Ganady killed the guy in the warehouse, and we know that Ganady was at the locations where the sniper shootings took place. And we know that Carrigan is innocent."

"Agreed," I say. "Too bad the list of things we don't know is longer. Is it possible that the McMaster murder and the sniper shootings are connected?"

"Only if Simmons killed McMaster. Maybe Ganady hired him to do it, and he used the money he got from it to finance his revenge killing spree," she says.

"But why would Ganady have scouted shooting locations for him?" I ask. "What would he gain from Simmons killing those people?"

Laurie doesn't have an answer for that, so instead she asks another question. "And what would Karen McMaster gain from it? I get that she wants to get rid of her husband; I can certainly identify with that feeling."

"I beg your pardon?"

She ignores the question. "But how could she fit in with Simmons?"

"And while we can't figure out these new events, we shouldn't forget the old standbys that we haven't cracked," I say. "Namely, what the hell does Carrigan have to do with this, and why was Ernie Vinson trying to kidnap him?"

"I say we have more wine," Laurie says.

"I'll drink to that."

We call Sergeant Luther Hendricks."

Luther Hendricks is a Passaic County cop who arrested Jaime Tomasino on suspicion of perjury when Hatchet ordered that he be taken into custody.

"Sergeant Hendricks, you're familiar with Jaime Tomasino?"

He nods. "I am."

"And you are also aware that he gave obviously untrue testimony in this courtroom when he said the defendant had confessed to him?"

"Yes, I arrested him for that perjured testimony."

"Have you interrogated him about that testimony?"

"Yes."

"What is his explanation?"

"He denies having perjured himself. He claims that he was simply mistaken."

"Just to refresh the jury's recollection, his mistake was in thinking that his good buddy Donald Carrigan was a short black guy?"

Hendricks smiles at the ridiculousness of it. "That's correct."

"In your experience, Sergeant, what is the reason that witnesses generally lie in this fashion? By this fashion, I mean when they claim that a defendant confessed a crime to them?"

"Usually it is to get law enforcement to go easy on them. If they are in prison, they're hoping for parole or a shortened sentence. If they have recently been convicted themselves, then they are hoping for the prosecution to recommend favorable treatment to the judge."

"Can any of that be the case here?"

"No. Tomasino was not on law enforcement's radar at all. He was not in prison, nor was he charged with a crime."

"So in your experience, why might he have lied?"

Tasker objects, saying that conjecture is not evidence, and is not called for here. I counter by saying I am asking his expert opinion based on his experience, and the jury can assign whatever weight to it that they wish. Hatchet lets him answer.

"I certainly believe that Tomasino was being paid to lie. His lifestyle improved immeasurably in recent weeks. He went from being homeless and eating in a soup kitchen to dining in nice restaurants and buying fairly expensive clothes. He also was able to rent a house at fourteen hundred per month."

"If he was being paid to lie, would you then say he was being paid to incriminate Mr. Carrigan?"

"Yes. Absolutely."

Tasker's first question is, "Sergeant Hendricks, you have no personal knowledge of why Mr. Tomasino was being untruthful, is that correct?"

"That's correct."

"And other explanations, besides being paid by a third party, are possible?"

"Anything's possible."

"Thank you. For example, is it possible that Tomasino just craves being in the spotlight and that he thought this would draw attention to himself?"

"It's possible."

"Is it possible he is just a compulsive liar, and does so for the sake of lying, without a sinister motive?"

"It's possible."

"Is it possible that he had another reason we could not right now even guess at?"

"It's possible, but whatever that reason is, it allowed him to live an expensive lifestyle." I couldn't have scripted a better answer for Hendricks to give. It is so perfect that it removes any need for me to question him on re-direct; I'd rather just leave it there.

My other witness this morning is Pete Stanton. I only want him to do one thing: to talk about Yuri Ganady. I start by placing into evidence the photograph of Ganady and ask Pete if he knows who he is.

"Yes, his name is Yuri Ganady. He is Serbian paramilitary. Basically travels the world performing missions for hire."

"What is your source of this information?"

"The FBI."

"Do you have any idea what he was doing here?"

"I believe he committed a murder. I don't have any proof of that, but it was under investigation. I also do not know his motive. He was a suspect, that's all."

"Who was murdered?"

"A man named Charlie Keller. Also paramilitary, but American. He was killed in a warehouse here in Paterson."

I nod, as if I'm learning something as we go along. "Okay, back to Yuri Ganady. Do you know where he is now?"

"Physically? No. But that's not really terribly important, since he's dead."

"How did he die?"

"He was killed the other night attempting to break into your home."

"Thank you. No further questions."

Tasker asks Pete the question he's been asking everyone. "Captain Stanton, are you aware of any connection between Mr. Ganady and this case?"

"You mean other than he tried to break into the house of one of the lawyers?"

"Did he do so because of this case?"

"I don't know."

"Thank you. No further questions."

I'm going to call Karen McMaster after lunch. She'll be the most important witness of the trial, at least from our point of view. It's the last chance we have to create enough reasonable doubt for the jurors to consider a vote for acquittal.

I still don't have the slightest idea how Ganady's apparent involvement with Simmons in the sniper shooting relates to Karen or this case. The good news is that doesn't matter, at least for this trial. I won't bring it up and therefore won't have to advance a theory.

But I sure as hell would like to know.

Karen McMaster looks nervous as she takes the stand.

I've made it clear throughout the trial that I am going to be pointing at her as a possible alternative to Carrigan as the killer, and the word has obviously gotten back to her. She's right to be nervous.

"Mrs. McMaster, you testified during the prosecution's case that you and your husband did not have the perfect marriage. You said that 'Steven made some mistakes.' Do you recall saying that?"

"Yes."

"What did you mean by mistakes?"

"There were other women."

"He had affairs? Is that what you're saying?"

"Yes. But we were past that at the time . . . when he died."

"But you did not make similar mistakes?"

"No."

She's keeping up that lie. Laurie dug up enough information that I could challenge her even without Kimble testifying, but I'm not going there. If I'm going to accuse her of murdering her husband, then I'd rather she was a woman wronged, rather than someone in an open marriage.

"Did you resent him for it?"

"At first, but we got by it," she says.

"Did you have a prenuptial agreement?"

"Yes."

"Based on that agreement, how much money would you have gotten if you had divorced?" I ask.

"It's complicated."

"Then simplify it for us and give us a ballpark figure as to how much you would have received."

"Five million dollars and our Manhattan apartment."

"But upon his death you inherited his entire estate, correct?"

"Yes."

"Do you know how much that is worth?" I ask.

"Not precisely."

"Public filings say in excess of two hundred and fifty million dollars. Does that sound about right?"

"I suppose so."

"You testified earlier that on the night of your husband's death, you had reason to believe he was having an early dinner. What was your reason?"

"He had dinner with Craig Kimble, a mutual friend of ours. I think Craig mentioned it to me."

"On the telephone?"

"Yes."

"There is no record of his having called you that night, or you having called him."

"Maybe it was earlier that day, or maybe the day before. I

don't remember. Steven might even have been the one to tell me. At the time it wasn't very important."

"We have heard testimony about two men, one named Ernie Vinson and the other Yuri Ganady. Each has been recently killed. One was murdered in a Connecticut hotel, and the other was killed in the process of trying to enter my home. Have you ever met either of these men?"

"No. Never."

"Ever spoken to them?"

"No. Never."

I introduce her phone records into evidence. Then I say, "According to these records, Mr. Vinson phoned you two days before your husband's death, and Mr. Ganady phoned you the night of his death."

"I swear I never spoke to either of them."

I let her off the stand, reasonably pleased with how things went. I established money as a motive, raised questions about her actions that night, and connected her to two dangerous criminals, both of whom have recently been killed themselves.

That will put reasonable doubt in the minds of the jurors.

Or it won't.

I've been doing this for a while, ladies and gentlemen," Tasker says.

"Longer than I care to admit. I've spent my professional life trying to make criminals pay for their crimes.

"A lot has changed over the years in the way police conduct their investigations. As technology has advanced, so have the tools law enforcement has been able to utilize. But believe me when I say that the absolute best advancement, far and away, is the advent of DNA.

"DNA simply does not lie. Even eyewitness testimony can be shaky, because it involves humans, and humans can be wrong. DNA cannot be wrong. It seems that every week we hear that a cold case, often decades old, is solved because of a DNA match. I've prosecuted some myself, and it has given me great pleasure.

"Mr. Carrigan's DNA was found at the scene. He dropped his hat in the darkened garage when he accosted Steven McMaster, minutes before he brutally broke his neck. But he had other things on his mind; he was there to rob everything of value that he could find. So he forgot to retrieve the hat.

"And he kept one of the stolen items with him. He locked

it in his locker so no one could get to it. But someone did get to it, the police got to it, and it is one of the pieces of evidence that has brought him to justice.

"It took a while to find Mr. Carrigan; he was living off the grid, so conventional investigative techniques took time to work. But he turned up, ironically because of a robbery attempt on him, and here we are.

"And what about a murder weapon? That's easy, ladies and gentlemen." He points to Carrigan. "There's the weapon right there, his hands. He was taught to kill by our government, as a member of the Special Forces.

"But he was taught to kill, not to murder. There's a big difference. You and I can make the distinction, but apparently Mr. Carrigan cannot. Or chooses not to.

"I would like to apologize for something. Jaime Tomasino sat before you and lied about his alleged conversations with Mr. Carrigan. He came to us with this story, and we confirmed he had access to Mr. Carrigan, that they ate at the same homeless shelter.

"We had no way of knowing that his story was not true, and we have absolutely no way of knowing why he lied. But he did, and for that I do apologize. Sometimes we hit, and once in a while, very rarely I hope, we miss. We're human . . . we missed once.

"The last thing I want to talk to you about is Mr. Carrigan's capacity to have pulled off this crime. You've heard about the lack of rental car contract, the lack of apparent spending of the proceeds of the robbery, and so on.

"We have never said, and never will say, that Mr. Carrigan did not have an accomplice. It is likely that he did. That accomplice could have brought him to the scene and made off with the profits. He or she may well have used Carrigan for his deadly skills.

"Mr. Carpenter has implied that perhaps Mrs. McMaster arranged for and directed the murder of her husband. I have no evidence of that; if I did, she would be on trial. But could she be the accomplice? There is that possibility.

"But the fact that we haven't brought the accomplice before you does not exempt Mr. Carrigan from punishment. The evidence against him is compelling and establishes proof beyond a reasonable doubt.

"I know you will do your job. Thank you."

Hatchet calls on me to give my summation, but I'm actually finding it hard to catch my breath. I think that Tasker's closing argument, particularly two phrases that he used, may well have told me everything I need to know.

He meant them in a different context, but they jumped out at me, and suddenly everything makes sense.

"Off the grid."

"We're human . . . we missed once."

Thank you, Mr. Tasker.

It's going to be hard to concentrate on my summation.

The thoughts going through my mind have very little to do with what I am going to say. In fact, I am going to make an argument I do not believe in. I am going to point the finger for this crime at Karen McMaster, but I now think it's unlikely that she deserves it.

I'm maybe crossing some ethical lines in the process; I've never been in a situation like this before, so I really don't know. But I'm going to do it simply because it is the only chance I have to get my innocent client to not be convicted.

So basically I am going to have to focus like I have never focused before. Because all I can think about are those phrases that Tasker used.

"Ladies and gentlemen, thank you for your service." I start by saying this because it puts me one "service thank" ahead of Tasker. Since the trial is over, I have won that particular competition.

"off the grid"

"I'm going to cut straight to the chase; the evidence against my client has been planted. He didn't leave that hat at the murder scene, and he didn't place that ring in his locker.

"Now that is easy for me to say, but I have to give you some evidence to support my belief. It's not enough for me to tell you that I have come to know Don Carrigan and understand that he could not do such a thing.

"We're human . . . we missed once."

"Which brings me to Jaime Tomasino. He lied in an attempt to get you to convict Mr. Carrigan. That in itself is enough to prove beyond a shadow of a doubt that someone would break the law in order to get you to vote guilty. And if you believe that Mr. Tomasino acted on his own, I would like to play poker with you, any time, anywhere.

"The only plausible explanation for his testimony is that he was paid to lie. His entire lifestyle changed around the time he was on that witness stand, so to think otherwise defies credibility. But what if he wasn't paid? What if somehow there was some other motivation, and at the same time he happened to cash a lottery ticket? The point is that there were forces out to get Donald Carrigan.

"off the grid"

"For a while I thought Mr. Carrigan was picked at random to be the patsy, but I don't think so anymore. I think he was chosen because he was hidden from society, as homeless people are. And I think the real killers knew his military background, and performed their killing in a manner that would point at him, because of his Green Beret training. It was a horrible, cynical way to take advantage of a veteran who had served us all so well.

"So with all that in mind, is it not reasonable to think that someone stole his hat while he slept, and placed a ring in his open locker? Might Mr. Tomasino have even placed the ring? He had access; if he was willing to commit perjury, ring-placing would be a piece of cake.

"We're human . . . we missed once."

"So I think we have done enough to make you reasonably doubt Mr. Carrigan's guilt. But then we went one step further; we told you about someone else who might in fact have been the killer, or at least ordered it to be done.

"Karen McMaster spoke on the phone with two criminals, two murderers. One two days before her husband died, and one that night. She denied that, but we showed you the records. What were they talking about? The upcoming charity ball? The new opera at the Met?

"off the grid"

"She had a husband that she admitted cheated on her, while she claimed to be faithful. Maybe he was planning to leave her; we will never know if that is true. But we do know that his death left her with a two-hundred-and-fifty-million-dollar fortune.

"And maybe Karen McMaster was not involved, despite all this evidence, in her husband's death. Hopefully the police will conduct the full and complete investigation they should have conducted back then, and then the truth can be known.

"Judge Henderson will instruct you as to your procedures and responsibilities. He will tell you that in order to find Mr. Carrigan guilty, you must do so beyond a reasonable doubt.

"I think you will find that you are swimming in reasonable doubt.

"Thank you."

When I get back to the defense table, Hike gives me a

thumbs-up. I never even knew he had thumbs. I must have an intense look on my face, because Carrigan leans over to me and says, "You were great. You okay?"

I nod, but he doesn't seem convinced.

"Take it easy, Andy. You did your best, and your best was outstanding. Don't view the verdict as all or nothing because the truth is that to me, it's nothing or nothing."

T hey say that stress can take years off of someone's life.

Based on that, with the stress I feel while waiting for a verdict, and the number of verdicts I've waited for, I'm pretty sure I'm not going to live past Wednesday.

At least this time I have things to do . . . a lot of things to do. My first stop is the Welcome Home shelter to see Sean Aimonetti. I've called ahead and asked for a few minutes' time, just him and me alone in his office.

I've already asked Sam to do some quick research on recent court cases, and gotten back the answer I expected. I've also asked him to get a list of the tenants in Karen McMaster's apartment building, and again we hit a bingo. All of this makes me surer than ever that I am right.

"Has there been a verdict yet?" Aimonetti asks as soon as I arrive.

"Is there a place we can talk in private?"

He leads me into his office, and I close the door behind me. "No. Verdicts are like sudden death overtime. No time limit and it all could end, good or bad, in the blink of an eye."

"Doesn't sound like you like it," he says.

"I hate it, but I didn't come here to complain."

"Why did you come here?"

"To ask you where your other shelters are."

"Garfield, Elizabeth, and Newark. But you could have found that out in ten seconds on Google. So what's your other reason?"

"Do you have one employee that's involved in all of those shelters? That would have occasion to talk to patrons in all of them, and most specifically here and Garfield?"

He thinks for a few moments. "I mean, our accounting people cross over, but for what you're asking, just James Lasky. You met him when you were here."

"I called you recently and asked you to check if Chuck Simmons had ever come to your shelter."

"Right," he says, "and I found out that he hadn't."

"Who did you find out from? Who checked into it for you?"

"James Lasky."

"Did you tell him about my questioning whether a heavy drinker like Simmons could be capable of perfect marksmanship?"

"Yes."

When I leave I extract a promise from him that he will keep our conversation a secret, mentioning it to no one. He promises to do so; I hope he keeps his word. I think he will.

My next stop is a risky one and is going to take special handling and sensitivity. So I stop at the house to pick up Laurie, who happens to be my Vice President in charge of Special Handling and Sensitivity.

We drive out to Pomona, which is at Exit 11 off the Palisades Parkway. It is in New York State, though on the New

Jersey side of the Hudson River. Our GPS takes us to a modest redwood home in a development of similar homes.

There is a car in the driveway, which is a good sign. We hadn't called ahead, due to the strong likelihood that we would not be invited to come up. We needed, and need, a face-to-face meeting.

Laurie rings the bell and about twenty seconds later a pleasant-looking woman, maybe forty years old, opens the door. She has a sadness to her face and the reddened eyes of someone who is grieving. I doubt we're going to make her feel better.

"Mrs. Yount?" Laurie says, but we both know that's who she is.

She looks at Laurie with some surprise, not knowing what this is about. Then she looks at me and must recognize me, because after a split second, her face gets even sadder, and she sags in resignation. I don't mention that women have been having that reaction to me for most of my life.

"We know about your husband. And we know about Craig Kimble."

She pauses for a moment and then says, "Come in." We do just that, and she closes the door behind us.

I knew that eventually I would have to tell someone," Nancy Yount says. "I think on some level Eric felt the same way. Or at least that's what I choose to believe."

"Tell us about it, please," Laurie says. "In your own way, however you are most comfortable."

She smiles. "I'm afraid there is no comfortable way. Kimble came to Eric maybe a year and a half ago. He gave him money, with the promise of much more. He said that at some point he might need a favor, and that point might never come.

"Eric was a sick man; his cancer was diagnosed four years ago. It went into remission, but no one was confident that it would stay that way. They were right; it came back about a month before Kimble approached him. It was eventually going to kill him.

"Kimble knew about his illness; Eric thought it was because he owned a health services company that had computer access to the details.

"Eric wanted to provide for me; that was his motivation. He convinced himself that what he was doing was tolerable. He even thought that maybe the ruling he might be called upon to make could be consistent with what his ruling would have been anyway.

"But then it started to fall apart, and Eric realized what was happening. And so Kimble threatened Eric—really, he threatened to hurt me—and he brought that horrible man to see him, to scare him." She looks at me. "The one that died at your house.

"I didn't know all of this for a long time, but I'm not blind, and I finally confronted Eric. He broke down and told me. And then when poor Lawrence Alexander was killed, pretending they were shooting at Eric . . . it was all to make sure Eric presided over that case."

She starts to cry.

"We are going to need you to testify to this," Laurie says. "To save other people from going through what you have gone through. And worse."

"It will destroy Eric's legacy."

"I'm afraid Eric destroyed Eric's legacy," I say. "One way or another this has to end, and you have the power to end it. Eventually the truth will come out, but it is important that it come out now."

We're back in the car and approaching the George Washington Bridge when I get the call from the court clerk. "Andy, you need to get down here. There's a verdict."

We head west on Route 80 toward downtown Paterson and the courthouse. I call Hike on the way, but he already knows about it. He feels that the fact the jury came to a verdict so quickly is bad news. Had they taken a year and a half to deliberate, Hike would have interpreted that as bad news.

No matter what happens, Hike remains Hike.

Carrigan is brought in looking a hell of a lot more calm

than I am. "I'm more nervous than I thought I'd be," he says. "You have any idea what is going to happen?"

"None whatsoever," I say. Usually in these situations I am positive we are going to lose. This time I'm more confident, which probably means we don't have a prayer. Either way, I'm going to keep my mouth shut and let the jury do the talking.

Tasker and his team are across the way at the prosecution table. Our eyes meet and he gives me a slight nod, which I return. It's either a sign of mutual respect, or just a couple of guys nodding.

Hatchet comes in, and we all rise on command. He tells us to be seated. He looks pissed off; I think it's because in a few moments one lawyer will be declared the winner, and he hates when a lawyer, any lawyer, is happy.

He calls the jury in and asks if they have reached a verdict. They say that they have, and my stress level elevates to the point where there is a significant chance my head will explode.

I think I can ultimately prove Carrigan's innocence, but if Carrigan is convicted, he is going to spend a long time in jail, no matter what. We need the jury to set him free.

Today.

The foreman gives the verdict sheet to the clerk, who gives it to Hatchet to look at. Hatchet hands it back to the clerk to read aloud, and Carrigan, Hike, and I stand.

The clerk reads it without emotion, an amazing trick, since there is nothing more emotional than the moment a verdict is read. She drones on about the various counts, and New Jersey, and statutes.

But finally she gets to the key words:

"Not guilty."

Carrigan turns to me and takes my hand. "I know I said it didn't matter," he says, "but, turns out, it matters."

I signal to Laurie, who is in the front row and has given me a thumbs-up about the verdict. Then she does even better than that, as she comes over and gives both me and Carrigan a hug. I think she's crying, not big sobs, just teary stuff.

I tell Carrigan that he'll need to do some paperwork, but that then Laurie will take over.

I start walking over toward Tasker and it turns out that he is coming toward me. We meet halfway and shake hands. He graciously compliments me on a job well done. I praise the job he did as well, but refrain from thanking him for his service.

Then I say, "Can we go in the anteroom for a couple of minutes? We need to talk."

"What about?" he asks.

"You won't believe it."

Tasker's office is in Newark, which is the county seat in Essex.

I'm sitting in that office; it's just he and I. Other people are going to have to be involved, but this is not yet the time.

It's a little awkward, since we've been adversaries throughout the entire case. But he's a smart guy and seems to be one of those public servants who really want to get to the truth and see justice done. Hopefully we're about to.

His intercom buzzes and he picks it up, listens, and then puts it down. "She's here," he says.

Moments later the door opens, and one of his assistants shows in Karen McMaster. She sees Tasker first and then reacts in surprise when she realizes that I am here as well. "Why is he here?" she asks, referring to me with obvious disdain.

"Mr. Carpenter is here at my request," Tasker says. "He's a part of this, and his involvement right now is to everyone's benefit, including yours."

"He publicly accused me of murdering my husband," she says. Then, "Maybe I should have my own lawyer with me."

"That is your right, but I think after hearing what we have to say, you won't consider it necessary. Please sit down."

She does so, albeit a bit warily. Tasker turns to me and says, "Andy?" It's the first time he's called me that; I think we're becoming buddies.

"We have reason to believe that Craig Kimble is responsible for your husband's death."

"Oh, come on . . ." she says.

"It's true. He set up Don Carrigan to take the fall. But he had a plan B in case that didn't work out. That plan B was you."

"What does that mean?" she asks.

"As I am sure you know, he has an apartment in your building, purchased in the name of one of his companies. You and he were in a romantic relationship—"

She interrupts. "That's not true." She's still clinging to that lie.

I nod. "Okay, you were really good friends. But he was in your apartment a lot; I suspect he even had a key. He received calls from Ernie Vinson and Yuri Ganady in your apartment on your phone; if there was ever any scrutiny, he wanted it to appear that the calls went to you."

She's not interrupting anymore.

"And as you testified, he did tell you that he had an early dinner with Steven that night, and got you worried enough to call your neighbor. But the reason that there was no phone call proving your claim is that he was in your apartment when he told you. You just didn't want to admit it on the stand."

Tasker hands her a photograph from the building security camera, showing Ganady going into her apartment building the day that Marcus followed him. "He even had Ganady come to the apartment, knowing he'd be seen by the security camera," I say. "If Carrigan was convicted, then it wouldn't matter. If he wasn't, then you were the backup."

"Why?"

"I'm just guessing now," I say. "He might have been doing it to get Steven out of the way, because you were such . . . good friends. Or, believe it or not, he might have been doing it to test out a system."

"What does that mean?"

Tasker interjects, "We can't talk about that right now, but it doesn't involve you."

"Is Kimble a large investor, even a silent partner, in your husband's company?" The company is privately owned, so there is no way to tell ownership.

She looks surprised at the question and then nods. "Yes."

"So he may have some legal arrangement where if you went to jail he could buy your share. It's an added bonus for him; he had all the angles covered."

"That son of a bitch," she says, her voice lower in volume but higher in intensity.

The way she says that reassures me. Until now I thought there was a chance that she conspired with Kimble on all of this; now I no longer think so.

"He's even worse than you think," Tasker says. "But what we know and what we can prove are two different things."

"So what do we do?"

"That's why you're here," I say.

need to see you; it's urgent," Karen McMaster says into the phone.

She's speaking to Craig Kimble, who is in his own apartment, just three floors below her. "Please come up here, Craig." She hangs up the phone and says to me, "He'll be right up."

Three minutes later the door opens; Kimble obviously has a key. "What is . . ." he starts to say, and then sees me. "Well, this is a surprise."

"Mr. Carpenter has been telling me a story," she says. "I want you to hear it and tell him he's crazy."

I stand and say, "Actually, I don't need to be here for this. Karen can fill you in."

"No, I think you do need to be here," Kimble says. "I have a strong feeling you need to be here. So sit down."

He talks in a tone that says that he is in charge and not to be challenged. So I do as he says and I sit down. Once I do, he adds, "Go ahead, Karen."

"Mr. Carpenter says that you arranged for Steven to be killed and that you framed Mr. Carrigan. He also says that you were planning to frame me if that became necessary."

"That's crazy. Karen, you can't believe that."

"He says he has proof."

I nod. "I know about James Lasky, and Ernie Vinson, and Yuri Ganady . . . and Judge Eric Yount."

The last name gets his attention, and he pauses before he responds. When he finally does, that response is as much physical as verbal. He takes out a gun and holds it on us. It's a small gun, but I suspect it can do a lot of damage. "That changes the calculation."

"Craig, what are you doing?" Karen says, fear evident in her voice.

"Don't do this," I say. "I'm going to leave now."

He points the gun at me. "No, you're not."

"You can't keep me here against my will," I say. "This is kidnapping."

He smiles. "It's worse than that. I sense a murder suicide is coming. You came here to confront Karen and she panicked and shot you, then killed herself. All very tragic."

He keeps the gun trained on us and walks toward the door to the bedroom. "In here," he says. "It'll add a sordid touch to it."

Just then there is a knock on the door, and he turns slightly to look toward it. The next thing he does is drop the gun and scream, probably because Marcus has chopped down on his arm. Based on the cracking sound his arm made, I suspect it will be in a cast until next Christmas.

Marcus tosses Kimble into the wall with less difficulty than I would throw a tennis ball. When Kimble crashes to the floor, Marcus leans on him with one knee on his back.

Karen goes to open the door, and when she does, a bunch of New York cops enter, guns drawn. They take custody of

Kimble as Marcus lets him up. Tasker comes in behind them, just as I would have. We lawyers tend to lead from behind.

Tasker comes over to me, and referring to Marcus, says, "I can see why you insisted on him."

I nod. "We are the two toughest guys you will ever want to meet."

The cops take Kimble away; he is still yelling in pain from his arm.

I go over to Karen McMaster and say, "I'm sorry for what I put you through during the trial. I was wrong, and I will do my best to fix it."

She nods. "Thank you. You've already fixed a lot of it. Seeing Steven's real killer caught helps a lot."

For the first time, our victory party is not at Charlie's.

It's at the house that Don Carrigan is renting, with an option to buy. It's got a lot of open space, a lot of glass, and a lot of windows to open.

I am footing the bill for this, but I will get paid back once we successfully win our civil case against Craig Kimble. It's a slam dunk; Carrigan will be a rich man. He will then pay me back, including my fee for handling the case. It's a win-win.

The other guests at the party, not surprisingly, are Laurie, Hike, Edna, and Sam. Laurie tells me that Willie and Sondra will be a little late, but that they are on their way. I've also invited Pete and Vince, since they would have been at Charlie's if we had it there. They will also happily consume free food and beer wherever it's served.

I've brought Tara and Sebastian to reconnect with their old friend Zoey. Zoey seems quite at home here; she has her own bed and a treasure trove of chew toys. She shows Tara and Sebastian around as if she is hoping they might make an offer on the house.

The media has obviously covered Kimble's arrest extensively, but they haven't had nearly all the facts. Vince wants to do a follow-up piece for his newspaper, so he comes armed with a bunch of questions for me. In two days I am going to do a TV interview exonerating Karen McMaster, and Vince wants to get his story out before then.

I explain to him that what the McMaster case and sniper shooting case had in common is that Lasky identified for Kimble two homeless people who would make perfect people to frame. Kimble would then take advantage of their being off the grid, to use Tasker's phrase. They were as close to being invisible as is possible in this day and age.

But Vinson was supposed to have captured Carrigan the first time, when he took the hat. He would then have killed him, preventing him from ever being found and brought to trial. I assume he told Ganady and Kimble that he had killed Carrigan, assuming they would never find out otherwise.

When Lasky told Vinson that Carrigan was back, he tried to finish the job, but Carrigan again fought him off, and Zoey bit him. Once Carrigan's name was in the paper, Ganady found out that Vinson had lied, and killed him.

Simmons's case was a bit different. They held him prisoner while they killed one person after another, making it look like Simmons was getting revenge on those who wronged him.

They made the shooting of Judge Alexander appear as if Eric Yount had been the target, but the shooter had missed. To quote Tasker again, "We're human . . . we missed once." It was all to get Eric assigned to the Baxter Optics case; Kimble owned a majority stake in that company, and the verdict meant three hundred million dollars to him.

Once that was done, they then killed Simmons and made it look like a suicide.

Lasky has been arrested and is cooperating; it turns out that he also planted the ring.

"When did you know it was Kimble?" Vince asks.

"Oh, yes, Sherlock, please tell us." Pete has the gall to sneer at me while eating my food and drinking my beer.

"Basically, Vince, what I try to do is approach it the way Pete would, and then go the opposite way. He would have arrested Karen McMaster, so I knew she couldn't be guilty."

"You want me to quote you on that?" Vince asks.

"If you do, they'll be identifying both your bodies tomorrow morning," Pete says.

"Okay, the truth is, Vince, that there was no 'aha' moment. I knew that the sniper shootings and our case were connected, but I couldn't for the life of me see how Karen McMaster would have benefitted from those other killings. If she was guilty of killing her husband, the motives would have been money or sex or love, or any combination of the three. That didn't fit with the sniper case."

"What about Kimble?"

"I went toward him one step at a time. When I had told him he was going to testify in our case, he mentioned he was about to testify in a more important one. He had the money to pull all of this off, and he had the international business connections to possibly get access to these mercenary types.

"So I slowly built the case against him in my mind. First Sam found out that in fact he lived in Karen's building, registered in the name of the same company that was before Judge Yount in a very important patent case. And I knew that Kimble had dinner with Steven McMaster the night of his murder. Karen said that he told her they had an early dinner, and since he hadn't called, he must have been in her apartment when he told her. It was an easy jump to his having been in the apartment when Vinson and Ganady called as well.

"But it wasn't until Nancy Yount confirmed it all that I was positive."

"You may not be as dumb as you look," Vince says, which is pretty much the nicest thing he has ever said to me, or anybody.

The party starts to thin out, and Laurie and I are having a glass of wine on the couch when Carrigan comes over to us. He tells us that he has arranged to see a therapist to help him deal with his PTSD. "It's going to be a slow process," he says, "but I'll get there."

"I know you will," Laurie says.

"You've given me my freedom and my life back," he says to us. "Even my dog. I can never thank you enough."

"Make that 'dogs,'" Laurie says.

"What do you mean?"

Laurie signals with her hand, and Willie and Sondra come into the room holding the cutest puppy that has existed on the planet, except, of course, for Tara.

"She was the runt of the litter," Sondra says. "We thought you might want her."

Carrigan doesn't say anything for a few moments; I think he is holding back tears. I know I am. Laurie, for her part, is not interested in holding them back, she is openly crying.

Finally, Carrigan says, "You have no idea how much I want her."

"And if you want to hang out at the foundation once in a while, we can use the help."

Carrigan smiles. "I'll be there every day."

It's left to Laurie to sum it up. "Merry Christmas."

Carrigan smiles again. "Still?"

I nod. "It's getting hard to tell when one Christmas ends and another begins."